Indulge

A Fatfur Anthology

Edited by

Buddy Goodboy, Esq

Indulge

Production copyright FurPlanet Productions © 2025

Text Copyright © Robert D. Scully 2025

Layout and Typography by Ajax B. Coriander 2025

Cover Artwork @ Bravo Woof 2025

Published by FurPlanet Productions
Dallas, Texas
www.FurPlanet.com

Print ISBN 978-1-61450-688-1
eBook ISBN 978-1-61450-689-8

Table of Contents

Introduction

November 1, 2025.

"Everything in excess! To enjoy the flavor of life, take big bites. Moderation is for monks."

— Robert A. Heinlein, TIME ENOUGH FOR LOVE (1973).

Fat furs, this book is for you. Whether you're a fat fur yourself, a gainer, encourager, admirer, feedee, feeder, or if you just can't get enough of that extra fluff, we see you and cheer your good taste. Ajax B. Coriander and Zia Mac Marten of FurPlanet and I realized that such a big group within furry didn't have many books just for them. Underserving fat furs just wouldn't do.

I pitched this anthology as a way to give back to the furry community what it gave me: a sense of abundance. A lot of us, me included, come to furry from a sense of scarcity. The world makes us think we can never be sure of having enough: money, love, security, understanding, friends, peace of mind, kindness, humor, joy. Furry stories like the ones in this book showed me unequivocally that the people and things that make life worth living are truly abundant, if we're brave, patient, and persistent enough to find each other. And when we're sure enough that we'll have enough, we can let go of worry and truly indulge our deepest desires.

That's what we have on offer here: eleven stories of queer animal people chasing satisfaction and fulfillment. Hot, spicy, saucy, sweet, and in serving sizes that'll feed the biggest appetites. Don't be afraid to desire, and let that desire run free. Take big bites.

Your editor and maître d',

Buddy Goodboy

The Gentleman Of The Bedchamber

Ajax B. Coriander

Quin's eyes danced over the ashen colored stonework of the castle as he was guided down the hallway. The tail of the older dalmatian bobbed before him. He could see a few graying wisps of fur in the black spots, and he especially noticed how the portly steward's backside filled out the black suit he wore. The curves and contours of the fabric made the young golden lab's imagination run away in a way that made the insides of his ears turn red.

"Just to confirm, you know exactly what this position entails, right? You read over the contracts, NDAs, and other instructions we emailed you very carefully before signing them, correct?" the older dog said as he glanced over his shoulder.

Quin brought his full attention back to the other dog and nodded his head fervently. "Yes, Mr. Inkwell."

"I would like to hear a summary of it in your own words, just to put my own mind at ease. I don't want any scandals to get out about my dear king, saying you were tricked into this role."

Quin blushed a bit, a slight bit of pink showing on his cheeks under his yellow fur.

"I am to be the Gentleman of the Bedchamber," the lab gulped, the uncomfortable tightness growing in his pants getting harder to ignore as the assigned royal chastity cage squeezed against his sheath. "I am to work closely with him. Intimately. I am to take care of his every need and do whatever he requires of me without question." The dog's tail curled between his legs, and he looked down. "And I was selected because of the few videos I had posted on my OnlyFetch account, which seemed to match with the king's desires. It's why my immigration papers were sped up, and I am now a legal resident of his kingdom."

"Brilliant!" Mr. Inkwell said with a wag of his tail as they turned a corner and started to walk down a lengthy red carpet. The massive hallway had suits of armor lining the walls, various coats of arms, and paintings which all led to a large set of wooden doors. The doors were carved with kings of yore fighting battles, beasts, and other tales from the wolf kingdom's history. A large ram's skull took up the center, two golden eyes acting as the knobs to open it.

Mr. Inkwell stopped, and he turned towards the young golden lab. His bulk filled out his black suit, his curves perfectly framed as if the tailor had designed it to show off his wonderfully plump body. The four hundred pounds of older dog made Quin's muzzle water, but he bit his tongue to keep it from lolling from his muzzle. The dalmatian raised an eyebrow, and he gestured with a gloved paw at the lab. "I take it you're wearing your uniform underneath your street clothes, yes? Or did you have them packed away in the bag I made you check at the entrance?"

"Yes, sir, I have them on. Is there somewhere you would like me to change?" Quin nervously asked as his tail tucked a little tighter between his legs.

"That won't be necessary. You may strip here. It is your uniform, after all; you should get used to wearing it around the castle. The king has made it very clear that you're to wear it unless instructed otherwise."

"Yes sir, but, um…" the lab squirmed a bit, "what about the cage? I was given a key for emergencies… but like, do I keep it on even when I'm off duty, or is it supposed to stay on 24/7?"

The dalmatian grinned toothily and slid in close to the golden-furred dog. Mr. Inkwell pressed his bulk into the younger dog, and a soft lustful whimper escaped the lad's throat, before the dalmatian's paw squeezed Quin's caged jewels.

"That's up to you, lad. Technically, what you do on your off days is up to you, but if you want to be a needy horny puppy who has to beg for his king to give him a release, who am I to stop you?" The steward leaned in, and whispered, "I know if you were my puppy, I'd make you beg for it every time." Mr. Inkwell started to rub Quin's balls through the fabric of his pants. The golden lab squirmed in the touch, the tip of his cock drooling inside of his cage, and the salty liquid pooling into his sheath. "Honestly, I would only let you cum while my dick was splitting you open and your chastity cage was pressed into the underside of my fat gut, and a magic wand gave you the buzzies you need to cum into the underside of the paunch I allowed your little chew toy touch," the steward breathed heavily, squeezing the younger dog tight, before he relaxed his grip and shrugged. "But, that's just me."

The golden lab humped into the man's stomach, their clothes separating them, and dulling the feeling. But the sensation of the older man's softness against his thrust almost made him cum then and there. He felt dizzy, and he let out a needy whimper as the older dog slid away from him.

Mr. Inkwell licked his lips, teasingly, and then he did a slight readjustment of his jacket; before he easily slid back into his steward persona as if nothing had happened. The same confident air radiated from him as before, and he brushed away a miniscule speck of dust. He returned to his professional posture and cleared his throat.

"Anyway, I do have other duties to attend to, so if you would kindly don your uniform, I'll take your overclothes and put them with the rest of your things."

The golden lab nodded, and he took a breath before he began to strip off his hoodie. Underneath was a simple white tank top that was obviously chosen to be too small for him. Quin wasn't as large as the older dalmatian, but he was heavy enough to have a bit of a belly that poked out from under the tight form fitting garment. It clung to his flabby chest, and he felt his blush grow brighter as he kicked off his sandals on his bare hindpaws. He undid his pants next, snapping the clasp above his tail, and letting the fabric pool around his ankles. He stepped out of them and bent down to gather his clothing.

Mr. Inkwell took the outer layers the young lab had shed, and he then gave an appraising eye over the golden-furred dog. The tight, black, very, very form-fitting shorts clung to his ample hips, and the shiny fabric was tight enough to show the outline of the chastity cage inside. Two little black elastic bands peeked out from just under the boy's shorts' waistline, showing the black straps that helped keep the cage in place.

Indulge

"Good, good," the dalmatian said with a nod of his head. "Alright, follow me, pup." The dalmatian pushed open the large oak doors, and Quin got his first real look at his new king.

The German shepherd sat on a large ornate wooden chair. He was a few years older than Quin, 32, according to his Snootbook and the research Quin had done beforepaw. He had a few specks of gray in his black fur, and that just made the younger dog's muzzle water as he looked over his new king. He was Expansive. His love handles spilled over the arm rests of the wooden chair, and his belly pressed firmly into the table he was sitting at. But it was hard to make out the shape of him with the voluminous purple robe he had wrapped around him. His only other defining feature was a small golden crown that rested jauntily on his head. It was small enough to fit between his pointed ears, but he had lowered it over one of his instead. It made the ear droop to the side a bit, but the gold paired so well with his tan fur.

An absolute feast was laid out before the king. It had every type of meat and side dish the Quin could imagine. A mound of mashed potatoes sat next to a casserole of sweet potatoes, a roast suckling pig was squeezed between a roast turkey and some kind of roasted leg of a gigantic animal. Sausages sprawled over the edges of silver trays, boats of gravy were so large they seemed like they needed life rafts, and desserts that sparkled with enough sugar to make a dentist weep.

The king lifted the gigantic roast leg up into his paws and ripped a chunk out of the thigh with his teeth. The meat steamed as he broke the finely seasoned surface, and grease dribbled over his chin and onto his expensive purple robe. He took another bite, before dropping it, and reaching for the turkey. His claws tore off a hunk of the breast, and he stuffed that moist, juicy, meat into his muzzle, and before he was done chewing, his paws were already scrambling for the next thing.

The German shepherd seemed like he hadn't noticed them, and he didn't look up from his feast until Mr. Inkwell cleared his throat. "King Gunther Hawkins the Third, may I present to you your new Gentleman of the Bedchamber, Quin Butcher."

The hefty German shepherd finished chewing on a piece of pork loin and he straightened to look Quin over. His eyes stared hungrily at the younger dog, and he licked his chops—to get grease off or in lust, the young golden lab wasn't sure, but it made him shudder with desire either way.

"Thank you, Mr. Inkwell," the shepherd said in a confident voice. "I would like to get to know my new…"—the dog paused as he airily waved his paw through the air, trying to think of a word for his new chewtoy, playmate, fleshlight, cumdump, or… many other possibilities, before settling on— "…friend, so please, leave us for now." The steward bowed, and he left, letting the door close behind him.

Quin was alone with the king for the first time. They'd talked on the phone a few times, and over emails, but nothing more than the basic stuff. Now he was here. Standing before an actual king. It sounded like a fairy tale. Something he had pawed himself to sleep thinking of. One that would make his puppyhood fantasies explode with envy. He knew it had to be real, because how much his cock throbbed in its cage and how blue his overfull balls felt. . His tail curled between his legs, and his floppy ears folded back a bit. He worried that one wrong word would burst the bubble of whatever dimension he was in, and everything would fade like a dream.

"Do not be scared. I know meeting a king can be intimidating, but I do not bite," the king said, before taking a thoughtful pause and adding, "Well, not yet, anyway."

The lab felt his cock strain against the inside of his cage at that. The thought of being under that massive older canine, teeth buried in his scruff, and knot locked in his ass just made him want to beg to be bred right then and there.

"I'm not scared, your majesty," the lab admitted as he got closer. "Excited. Maybe nervous, but not scared. Everything happened so fast, between Mr. Inkwell messaging me and getting here, it's only been two weeks. It's a little overwhelming, I guess."

"Fair enough," King Gunther said. "Now let me get a good look at you. Come stand next to my throne."

"Isn't a throne supposed to be in a throne room?" Quin asked as he walked forward.

"This place was one once, but after I took over, I decided to put the room to better use. I had Inkwell bring in the heavy duty stone feasting table, and it has been one of my favorite spots ever since. It makes a much better banquet hall, even though it is mainly just for me these days. The other nobles never seem to be able keep up, not matter how hard they try. I think they are often intimidated by how much I could put away."

Quin walked closer, and then he spied what was next to the king's chair. It was a very wide stool that was set up to match the height of the king's seat and was pressed right against the king's throne. The cushions pressed together, and the king's stomach overflowed the boundaries of the armrest and shadowed the edge of the other piece of furniture. It had a red cushion with golden tassels and a golden seam that went around it. Both seats had their wood covered with gold leaf or paint, and up close Quin could see the ornate woodwork, and the spots on the throne's legs where it had once been clearly bolted to the floor somewhere. A quick glance, and the young dog could see the raised platform that the chair had clearly once sat, before being moved to the grand feasting gray polished stone table. The stool looked newer, as if it'd been commissioned to match the existing throne.

As he took in the sight of the room, the king took in the sight of him. A hunger flickered in his eyes, one that had matched his burning desire for the food. He licked his chops as he took in the sight of the golden lab's protruding belly. Quin felt his heart flutter a bit as he felt himself inside of the king's gaze.

"I, uh," the young lab said, squirming, "have to ask one last question before we start this…"

The king looked up, tilting his head to the opposite side the one his crown hung from, and he looked curiously at Quin. "And what is that?"

"This isn't some sort of… arranged marriage, is it? Like, I'm not in some Beauty and the Beast situation and I didn't read the fine print, right? You don't need me for some grand scheme or something?" the lab asked.

"Oh, no, nothing of the sort," King Gunther chuckled and shook his head. "You are merely my Gentleman of the Bedchamber, which basically means you are to tend to me. Help me dress, do basic tasks, serve me when I eat, guard me, and…" His hungry eyes did another once over of the younger lad. "…provide companionship." The German shepherd leaned back in his chair and ran his paws over his belly. "As a king, I cannot just go to clubs or use Knotted's app for random hookups. But even as I king, I am still mortal, and I have needs. Which means I need some help with my more lustful urges. I need an outlet that will nor create heirs out of wedlock. Mr. Inkwell does his best, but he is so busy and cannot give me the level of attention I desire. If I am to marry someday and make someone into a queen—or prince consort—one day, I would make sure they were well and truly aware what they were getting into. Not to say it might never happen," the shepherd said with a sly smile, "but we have not even had a meal together. You may not ever think of me in that way, nor I you, but this should be fun at least, no?"

"Yes, Your Majesty!" Quin said with a wag to his tail. "So, where do I begin?"

"A good question," the king mused, "let us start with you serving me, but I should get more comfortable. I only put this on for guests, and you are my royal Gentleman; you should get used to seeing all of my royal rolls." The German shepherd said as he stood and grabbed the golden sash that held his robe closed. He unfastened it and slid it from his shoulders.

Quin's caged cock pulsed painfully against the bars as he saw the king before him. Those chubby arms, that soft chest highlighted by his shiny chestnut fur and outlined by seas of inky black splotches. His gut hung down just over his crotch, and his belly spilled forth with no pride or shame. His tree-trunk thick legs squeezed together, and his pillowy ass, which was a thing of dreams itself, rested before his finely groomed tail. He passed the robe to the panting young lab.

"Hang this up on the backs of one of the chairs, and then you can start serving me by paw."

"Yes, Your Majesty!" Quin said eagerly. The king sat back in his throne, provoking protesting noises from the wood.

Quin glanced at the head of the table where King Gunther sat, after he'd leaned back, his large pecs had shifted to the side, as his belly jiggled a bit before it came to a rest after everything else. Quin looked for the best place to stand and attend to his king, but he soon realized the one place, and really the only place which would work, was upon the stool next to His Majesty. He kneeled on the seat, and he turned to face the table.

"Where do I start?"

"Whatever you desire. I will speak up, but I just want to relax and not have to think about my meal. When I host dinners, I always feel like I need to put on a show, but here, I want to be able to just not worry about what my next bite might say politically. Plus, this frees up my paws for anything else I might desire," King Gunther said as his fingers traced down the smaller dog's spine to his rump, his fingers gently stroking at one of those pudgy glutes. A hungry rumble came from his stomach, and he grinned. "Better not waste time, I am a very hungry king."

"Yes, Your Majesty!" The golden lab looked over the banquet table and realized a lot of the food that had been prepared could be easily grabbed by paw, or at least he wouldn't have to grab a spoon or fork for most of it. He eyed a plate of meatballs that were stacked two high and had a stick pretzel shoved through the top. He grabbed one and held his paw under it as he moved it towards the king's muzzle. The royal lips parted, and Quin was able to see the pearly white sharp teeth and canines inside. He could feel the king's hot breath over his paw as he slid those two thick meaty balls into the older dog's muzzle, the man's tongue almost seductively drawing them in, before his muzzle gingerly shut around them, and he began to chew.

Quin hadn't been so hard for so long in years. Everything this shepherd had done kept the throbbing trapped erection between his legs going. Pre surely soaked through the outside of his shorts, and it seemed like he'd never be soft again. It made the tightness of the ring of the cage even more pronounced as his sheathed cock twitched again and again, making him feel every tug caused by his own arousal. Every move he made reminded him of his place in life now, and it made him shudder with desire.

He panted once to clear his head, before he turned back and grabbed a pizza bagel while the man chewed. When he came back the king's lips were already parted and waiting for the treat. He brought it to the king's muzzle, and the shepherd leaned forward and took it with his teeth from the pup's paw. He made eye contact with his royal gentleman as he used his tongue to rotate the pizza bagel, so the cheesy side rested in his maw, but it stood vertical between his teeth.

King Gunther kept eye contact as he licked off the sauce and cheese, before his wide canine tongue pushed through the tight golden hole and slowly slide in and out of it, before he deliberately closed his muzzle and began to chew.

The golden lab watched in amazement of the skilled tongue as it poked and prodded every crevice of that toasted golden ring. The dexterity of the tongue slathering it, before the king finally demolished that doughy stretched hole. Quin panted—strangely feeling jealous of the hors d'oeuvre.

The Gentleman Of The Bedchamber

The very flustered Quin looked back to the table and grabbed a very thick and long sausage. The skin was firm under his fingertips, it was still warm, and little rivulets of melted fat oozed from the end as he grasped it between his pudgy fingers. He turned back and went to bring it to the king's muzzle. However, he let out a startled yip as a thick arm wrapped around him and he was pulled in close to the king's side. Quin saw a gold necklace with a small key around it, before he looked up and saw the king's smirking muzzle.

"You know, one other thing you will need to do is be my food tester. You are going to have to eat what I eat, and drink what I drink, to make sure nothing is poisoned. I trust my staff full-heartedly and I am well liked abroad, but it's tradition. So you are going to have to share with your king every few bites. Let us start with this sausage. I will take one half, and you take the other, and we will meet in the middle."

Quin nodded, and he squirmed a bit in nervous anticipation. He could feel a blush start to run across his cheeks and the insides of his ears almost felt like they'd burst into flames. The golden lab held that thick sausage between his fingers, and the king leaned forward and took just the oozing tip between his lips. The royal tongue slipped past his teeth, and the shepherd slowly licked along the underside of that juicy meat, while his green eyes looked at the young lab, expectantly.

Quin had to lean into the other dog's bulk to keep himself from falling over dreamily from the sight. He could feel the shepherd's doughy body and curves against his, that fat softer than any mattress he'd ever felt. His caged cock pressed into the man's side, the fabric of his small tight shorts the only thing between it and the royal belly. He was sure the pre from his constantly leaking cock was matting His Royal Majesty's fur, but he couldn't care less at the moment. He had better things to worry about. Like, for example, how good it felt when his paws came to rest on the older male's stomach. The slight give between his fingers caused him to squeeze, which enticed a happy little growl from the king. Quin leaned forward, looking as the cocky dog held the sausage expertly between his lips, a soft smirk on his royal muzzle as his teeth just gingerly teased the meaty tip.

Quin's breath quickened and he leaned in, taking the other end into his mouth. He felt his head gently pulled forward as the king began to slowly suck that thick warm meat down. Quin began to suck to keep up, their muzzles moving closer. His jaw strained around the hefty tube inside of him. His heart beat faster as they got closer still. The king gently cocked his head

9

to the side as he reached up a free paw and cupped Quin's face. The golden-furred dog whined, and he thrusted forward in need against the soft belly that taunted his trapped cock, and their muzzles met. Teeth clamped down slowly, teasing his lower lip, before taking that half of the sausage and starting to chew. Quin did the same, the two of them kissing as that salty fatty flavor burst across their tongues and their lips met in passion. The king's arm around the dog's waist slid down, and a paw cupped his soft puppy butt and squeezed as the two got lost in the flavor and their lust.

The king slunk one paw down along Quin's hip to the hem of his shorts, and, sliding his pudgy fingers inside of that stretchy black fabric, he snuck his paw up the inside back of the lab's golden fluffy thigh and to just behind his balls. A pudgy finger traced around the black plastic ring that held the pup's bits in place, and he traced a digit along it teasingly. He gingerly traced over those straining full orbs in their golden coin purse, before sliding his finger up along his taint, and sliding along the edge of the ring that helped trap Quin's jewels. He pulled the younger dog in closer and let his bulk feel the straining trapped dog cock through the fabric between them. A few moments went by before the shepherd broke the kiss and rubbed his nose against the lab's.

"And that is how it is done. You just need to taste my meat every once in a while. Not too hard, is it?"

"N-no, Your Majesty," the younger dog panted as he humped against the older man's paunch instinctually. "I think I will like tasting your sausage."

The king chuckled and his paws slid over the younger dog's belly. He nuzzled at the lab's neck, and the king let his teeth gingerly slide through the soft golden fur. The shepherd inhaled deeply, breathing in the scent of horny young dog resting against him as he idly decided what to do next.

Quin couldn't help but hump against that gut as he felt those sharp teeth poke against his flesh. The wandering paws of the king poked and prodded him like someone checking a Sunday roast to see if it's done. It made Quin's tail wag, and a proud feeling run through him. Not everyone would be good enough to help fill out the lap of a king, and he felt so worthy of the honor in that moment. He felt desired. Or maybe...

Hungered for.

King Gunther growled lustfully and he swept his arm out and knocked back a few of the plates and dishes off the table. He guided the younger dog onto the spot he just cleared, and he urged him to scoot back , so the king would have enough space to join him. The heavy stone table was made for this. Its sturdy legs supported the ton of combined dog upon it without so much as a groan of protest.

The golden lab couldn't help but start to pant as he watched the king stand. Quin felt the title *"His Majesty"* was so fitting in that moment, because the way those rolls and mounds of lard moved with the shepherd could only be described as: *Majestic.* It more than justified the capital *M*, because nothing about *His Majesty* could ever be considered lower case. The older dog grabbed the unnoticed royal scepter beside the throne. It was made of an ivory-colored wooden handle, with two rounded knobs at the end, and a large golden lumpy hunk.

Quin nearly laughed as he realized it was in the shape of a piece of fried chicken. But, the humor turned to astonishment as the shepherd twisted off the golden knob at the end, and revealed a compartment inside. A silicone head poked from where it'd been sealed inside the golden fried chicken fallacy, and the king grabbed it. He yanked the rest of the device free of the royal scepter, and a modern cordless vibrating wand was now held between his pudgy kingly fingers.

King Gunther twirled it in his fingers as an evil smirk grew across his features. Quin gulped, and he swore those pointed ears curled like devil horns and the shadows in the room grew a bit darker. The shepherd gave it a testing buzz that shook his whole arm, and made the fat of his upper arms jiggle. He slashed it through the air like a practice sword, before turning to give a playful wink at Quin, and with some effort, pulled himself up onto the table. He kneeled between the younger dog's golden legs, before he grabbed the golden pup's shorts and peeled them off.

Quin's trapped bits sprang into view, the black plastic of the cage glistening with the pre that had coated it. King Gunther lifted up the shorts, and licked over the damp spot that had formed there, looking hungrily into the golden lab's eyes.

"Tasty," His Majesty growled.

The lab's cage was one that had a ring that circled around his balls and then had a lock and shaft that inserted itself inside of his sheath. Where his tip would normally poke out, just a bit of black plastic with a hallow tube did so.

Indulge

Pre still oozed from it, and his sheath was plump from the backed-up and straining cock that was kept inside of his sheath. His knot was even visible as it puffed out the sides of its fuzzy home. The larger dog reached down and ran a finger teasingly over that sheath, his eyes staying locked with Quins, as he brought that slick covered finger to his muzzle, and slowly, sensually sucked it clean. He then moved his paws up, and started to gently rub at Quin's belly, his fingers kneading and feeling his girth as he began to work off the lab's shirt.

"You know, pup, if you are sharing meals with me, I wonder how long it'll be until you are as big as me," the shepherd mused. "Hopefully, I can stay just a little ahead of you, my golden trophy pup. I think as the only one of us with a real bone in this game, I should be the bigger male, do you not agree?" Gunther leaned down and started to kiss along the younger dog's belly, and Quin shuddered. He'd done this to other men in the past, but no one had ever done the same to him. It was almost breathtaking. The king slid his secret scepter between his gentleman's legs and pressed the silicone head against the boy's golden balls. King Gunther gave the pup's trapped bits a few pulses of vibrating pleasure, the lad's balls jostled as his cock flexed with need in his cage. Quin yelped in pain and pleasure from the vibrations and the tugging of the ring against his nuggets, and his claws tried to dig into the stone below him. Quin whined with frustration as the king finally pushed the constructive shirt off, and then kissed the younger dog deeply once more. His Majesty held the vibrating wand to Quin's bits, and Quin could only take it as he instinctively sucked on the older man's tongue, which got an approving growl from the larger dog teasing him. .

The king flipped the vibrator off again, and he broke the kiss to tease the smaller dog's neck with his lips and teeth again, suckling on the lab's fur and flesh.

"Well, regardless of how much either of us indulge ourselves, I know we are going to have so much fun at this table. Today is just the start, Quin, my oh-so-handsome Gentlemen of the Bedchamber," the shepherd said in a singsong tone near the end. "I am going to take you to heights of debauchery and pleasure only a king can give. I am going to make you howl with pleasure, squirm with anticipation, and beg to be stuffed by my paw. You are going to whine as I have you hump my paunch and feed me like the good little pup you are." King Gunther nuzzled at one of the dog's floppy ears, and whispered, "and that is just here at the table. My little gentleman is going to have all kinds of fun in my bedchamber..." The shepherd shifted, sliding a paw under the lab's leg, and pulling it up, while he straddled the other leg.

Quin wanted to have a witty comeback, but as he felt the dog's shaft rub against his straining sheath, his voice turned into a mixture of needy whines and whimpers. He could feel the king's balls against his own. Those massive spheres filled with royal potency and a line stretching back centuries round against his smaller golden ones, making them feel so small in comparison. The golden dog humped forward, and he could feel them churning. Brewing a hot and heavy load just for him.

King Gunther lifted his belly and let it fall on the other dog with a soft pat. The softness of their bellies intertwined, those fat mounds rolling together and forming new tantalizing hills of buttery lard. Quin felt the king's cock shift down, and slide across his balls, which were currently straining against the ring that held them in place. Pre oozed from the tip of his sheath, and down over the king's shaft, the heat of their bodies making the space between their bits feel like a sauna ready to burst forth with steam.

Quin felt the king thrust a few times, churning his royal pre with that of his gentleman's. Soon his fat sword was resting against that tight swollen sheath, letting Quin feel just how much bigger the king would be even if he was allowed out of his cage. He felt the king's weight settle on him, pressing him firmly against the table. The wand pushed its way between them with a grunt from the king, and its head ground the king's shaft and the young lad's caged bits together. Quin bit his lip in anticipation, and then...

King Gunther flipped the switch.

Quin howled out in ecstasy as the buzzing traveled through his shaft. The pent-up need in him made him squirm under the larger dog's bulk, unable to escape the pleasure as the older shepherd growled with approval above him. He tried to hump against King Gunther, but the weight of the larger dog kept him firmly in place, left only to squirm and whine as the bigger dog humped against his trapped cock. The pre from their shaft mixed and sprayed across their chubby fluffy crotches as the vibrations from the wand's head sent it cascading off in every direction.

"I have so many ideas for my golden gentleman," King Gunther said in a lustful growl. "For example, I could have you on your paws and knees,

Indulge

sucking my cock as I eat. I could just slide my paw down to feed you treats alongside my shaft. I could even have my dessert served off your caged cock, the vibrator teasing your shaft until you burst and I get a shot of cream between bites of whatever sweet treat you've had drizzled on you."

"Oh, yes, please, Your Majesty!" Quin cried in ecstasy.

The golden lab was in heaven. The flesh under his fur and the insides of his floppy ears turned bright red as he listened to the king's words. His ears flopped along the table, and he tried his best to thrust into the older dog's fat pad with his caged cock. The vibrations teased him while the shepherd's heavy belly pushed him back into the stone table.

The shepherd's body shook and jiggled as he thrust against the pent-up pup. The king's girth caused parts of him to take thier time to catch up as they moved along his heavy body.

"I want to see you swell, pup. I want to watch that golden body of yours fill like a treasure chest ready to burst. I want you as big as a prized hog." The shepherd panted, saliva dripping off his tongue on the dog below him, like a hungry wolf standing over his prey. "Your cock shrinking further and further into your soft crotch until I have to struggle to get the key in your cage's lock. And then I'll have you tied up like a hog at a party," the shepherd said with a deep resonating hungry growl that shook his chest and vibrated against the dog below him, "Pineapples along your back in neat little rows, your caged cock pulled back on display, a carrot in your rump, and a juicy red apple in your muzzle. Inkwell and I jacking off above you, glazing you, and then descending to lick you clean. Our muzzles meeting around your trapped cock, kissing around that little caged nub. The vibrating wand against your trapped bits, just like it is now, but with so much more jiggling, until you shoot your fat lardy load into our muzzles, and give us our feast." The shepherd said as his face twisted into a snarl, his eyes closing for a moment, like he was holding back. "Then I'll yank out the carrot and give you the proper stuffing a fat, happy puppy-hog should have."

Quin whimpered below him, imagining it all, and wanting nothing more in the world. The future puppy-hog's balls pulled up just as the king's did. That caged cock straining as the free hard powerful royal one did the same against his chubby crotch. Quin reached up, and held onto the king's lovehandles, squeezing them to hold on as he finally shot, the king joining him in shared ecstasy. The two of them howled as they shot a thick creamy mess between them, powerful kingly cum mixing with his gentleman's. The wand kept going, vibrating it into a slurry that mixed together and oozed into each other's crotch fur.

The two exhausted dogs panted, and they held each other tight. Quin felt his body wrapped in the king's softness, that heavy weight pinning him down, but wanting to be nowhere else in the world. Their cocks still twitched between them as the last bits of cum they had to offer oozed from them.

"I think," the king panted, "I need a bath." His Majesty gave a little thrust and felt the stickiness of their fur, before he added, "Well, we both do. I guess it is time for you to start on some of your other duties," the king said with a wiggle of his eyebrows. He pushed himself up a bit to take his weight off of Quin, and his flabby chest hung down, his fat pecs just gingerly resting on the younger man's smaller chest.

"Yes, my King," the lab panted. He looked to the side and spied one of the trays of forgotten food. He saw a pig in a blanket and thought about how much it must have looked like his trapped cock. A little red nub trapped in a golden sheath of softness. He picked it up, and he smirked. "But first, I think my king must have worked up an appetite, and what kind of gentleman would I be if I let His Majesty go hungry?" He held the little pastry between his lips, and looked playfully up at the king. The royal German shepherd smiled, leaned down, took the other half of the golden nub in his muzzle. They kissed around that warm soft stuffed pastry as ideas of their days to come danced through their heads.

And the two fat dogs, the king and his gentleman, lived happily ever after…

What's Good for the Goose

Oswald Beese

Running made Evan's body gross. It could be the dead of summer or the middle of winter, and regardless, Evan would trudge home a sweaty mess. As a slender greyhound, his thin fur would mat along his toned calves and firm thighs, glistening with perspiration despite its dark hue. His short dick stuck to his itchy stones. At his middle, his svelte waist expanded and contracted with huffing breaths, pushing his shallow six-pack in and out. The greyhound's form widened at his chest, with broad shoulders arcing over stale, smelly armpits. His long muzzle drooped with exhaustion.

But it was worth it. A quick, cool shower wiped away his odorous sweat, and it left him with the taut, limber form of a graceful greyhound. In his bathroom, standing on a fuzzy rug, he toweled himself dry. The process reminded him of what a hot piece of ass he was. He patted the towel to his firm legs, his round balls, his solid abs, and his lean arms. It was vain, but it was true: any man would go nuts for him.

Having prepared himself, he opened the door and entered his bedroom. Its air chilled the skin under his fur, still a bit wet from the shower. Plush carpet and lavender walls bathed in the warm, yellowed glow of a nightstand lamp. A fluffy, white comforter covered his king sized bed.

The evening's dessert, a beaver named Chuck, reclined on the bed. He had already disrobed. His webbed feet spread their toes, waving playfully at Evan, and his flat tail laid under his ankles. Chuck's calves splayed their modest pudge in bulges lined with brown fur. They were outdone by his thighs, though, which oozed in fluffy, rolling heaps out to his sides. The insides of his thighs kissed each other. They supported his meaty balls and his long, slack dick. His hips widened against the bed, hiding the two meteoric ass cheeks currently cratering the mattress.

That dick poked its head out from under a blanket of belly flab. Chuck's sizeable stomach tapered over his upper thighs in two puffy, grippable bulges. His hands folded over his paunch, but he parted them, showing off his round gut to Evan. Its surface curved inward, towards his deep navel. Laying down, his stomach spread relatively flat, although it still swelled to his sides like a big tub of blubber. Meaty breasts rounded over his chest.

A squishy roll of pudge padded his neck. On his fat face, his mouth, nose, and eyes looked tiny, giving him an aspect of sweetness. He leaned up on his elbows, scrunching his stomach into rolls, and looked to Evan. "Ready?" His tender eyes glimmered with a strange soulfulness.

After a few months in this relationship, Evan now recognized that Chuck's eyes, that complex expression he bore before sex, indicated something deeper than interest in an orgasm. What exactly that was still escaped Evan.Sappy eyes or not, Evan's cock didn't care. It lengthened to a chub because of Chuck's blubbery gut. He was no less enthralled with Chuck's body than the day they had met. "Hell yes."

It had been a long day. He'd worked late, which pushed his workout routine later, and he at least had to shower after that. He hadn't even eaten since breakfast. Taxing days like these always pushed Evan's libido.

On his white nightstand, a meatball sub and a cheesecake waited. They were the most potent sex toys Evan could possess. He would get to those soon, but not just yet.

He slinked to the bed, waving his wiry body in a show for Chuck.

Chuck watched with a hungry grin. This was a look Evan understood: lust.

Evan pulled his knees up onto the bed. He leaned down to Chuck's foot. With his his tight rump propped high in the air, he wagged his tail excitedly. He lapped at Chuck's lower paws.

The beaver's long digits and weary pads didn't interest Evan, but lately, he had begun experimenting with them. Chuck's weight bore hard on his feet, and Evan knew that he appreciated the care. It was odd, doing something just for Chuck, but it wasn't without reward. After a good licking, Chuck would be putty in Evan's paws.

Plus, from there, Evan could see between Chuck's rolling, dimpled thighs. His eyes traced up the fat beaver's body, soaking in his pudgy curves.

The beaver groaned. "Ooogh. You're ridiculously good."

Evan's tail wagged itself. How weird. He would have guessed he didn't care about Chuck's feedback, yet his own tail insisted otherwise.

Chuck took a deep breath, shifting his chunky pecs. His shoulders wriggled to get comfortable, subtly wobbling his succulent girth. His shifting weight ruffled the covers under him.

Evan moved up to Chuck's calves. He held himself steady on the bed with one hand. His other hand stroked Chuck's broad, leathery tail. Then, he craned his neck down and nipped at Chuck's calves. Evan appreciated every pound of fat on Chuck, even the relatively shallow portions of it on his lower legs. His teeth quickly teased in and out against the tender limbs.

But Evan soon tired of his appetizer. He inched up the bed and met Chuck's thighs next.

Fat swaddled Chuck's upper legs over and over, drooping around them in wide reserves.

Evan lowered his jaw, then closed it slowly on a portion of Chuck's thigh. Sensually, he drew his jaw up and down, gently squeezing its flab.

Chuck's thigh yielded only too easily to Evan's teeth. Evan restrained his teeth. He loved going to town, gnawing on the beaver's plump girth. But that hurt Chuck, and over time, he had softened his bites. Instead, he dug his long schnoz right into the seal where Chuck's fat thighs met. Chuck's flab hugged Evan's nose. His soft, pillowy thigh and plush, cushy fur set Evan's loins on fire.

As his nose nuzzled Chuck's thick, luscious thighs, Evan's cock lengthened. The greyhound felt his member extend to its full length, stiffening all the while. His dick wanted so badly to be where his nose was. He explored a ripe, delectable body. He wanted to take it right there and then, but he couldn't let himself do that without bringing Chuck along with him.

Evan twisted and turned his head, rooting his nose through the tight crack. Low and gruff, he yipped and yapped. Once he reached the bottom, he nudged his nose upward, as if to flip Chuck like a pancake. Instead, the bridge of his nose just fumbled against Chuck's mercurial legs.

The beaver received the message. "Alright! Down, boy. Down, boy." He caught Evan's eye with a smirk. "I gotta admit, though, I cherish the way you go feral during foreplay. Never thought somebody like me would ever experience something like that."

Evan backed away. He knelt at the foot of the bed. His tail swished in anticipation; his cock throbbed for the same reason. "Oh, daddy. 'Feral' is exactly what you do to me."

Chuck propped up on one arm, leaning onto his side. His belly spilled out before him, long across the bed. Laying on his side like this, Chuck's tummy looked positively huge. Part of the magic of fat was its infinite malleability. Gravity could shape and reshape it. Gravity, or a lover's groping paw.

Before Evan could ponder the nature of adipose any further, Chuck flopped onto his belly. The bed bounced under him, and his body sloshed from all its lard. Ready for Evan's next move, Chuck lifted his tail. He even flexed his glutes, wobbling their substantial fat. Flesh filled his rump in two perfectly round, bubbly domes. They filled out the backside of his hips and trailed halfway down his thighs. Chuck was a bottom-heavy boy. If his face was sweet, then his ass was decadent.

Evan launched forward, diving into Chuck's ass nose-first. The greyhound's chest landed in the mattress, and he jabbed his sniffer deep between the two cheeks.

As nice as Chuck's legs were, his ass fluffed like heavenly clouds.

Evan could scarcely imagine what it felt like to sit on cheeks of such gelatinous joy. He tossed his nose side to side, testing how many ripples he could cast through those mountains of fat. His long nose allowed him to plow deep through Chuck's ass cleavage while gawking at its dimpled underside.

While Evan's nose was busy excavating, his ears listened intently to Chuck's passion. Bassy moans flowed from Chuck, alongside deep, slow breaths. Evan found Chuck's thighs tensing against his shoulders, and the beaver's tail lowered gently onto Evan's back.

Evan burrowed his slender arms under Chuck's tubby thighs, then wrapped his forearms upward to grope at Chuck's immense rear. Evan took massive pawfuls, squishing its fat between his fingers. No matter how far he fanned his fingers, though, he could only grab a small portion of the beaver's bubbly backside. He pushed his arms inward, compressing all that precious pudge against his face. Then, he relaxed, letting Chuck's flab flow away. Evan hugged himself with Chuck's ass.

He quested further into Chuck's booty. As his eyes met Chuck's rump, forcing him to close his eyes, Evan's nose met the precious rim between Chuck's cheeks. At the heart of two chubby cheeks, Evan found a taut ring of warm flesh.

Chuck groaned, "Hrnnngh." His tail whacked Evan's back. Whenever Chuck felt frisky, Evan could tell by the passionate flick of his broad tail.

Evan gingerly brushed his nose along Chuck's tender rim while his long snout nudged the puffy walls of Chuck's deep ass canyon. The greyhound could live there forever, worshiping the beaver's heavy butt.

But his cock hungered. He pushed himself upright, out from under the beaver's tail. "Alright. Ready to indulge, big boy?" Just as he finished speaking, though, his stomach writhed in hunger. Its grumbles echoed loudly.

Chuck flopped onto his side, quaking the bed under him. He looked up to Evan with concerned brows. "You sound hungry there. Why don't we switch things up a little? You take the meatball sub tonight."

The greyhound scoffed. "No, no! I could never eat like…" Evan caught the word before it escaped. He was about to call Chuck a glutton.

Chuck flipped onto his back. "Eat like what? Like the way you always feed me?" The shift in enunciation from soft to sharp was subtle, nearly missing Evan.

Evan's breath shortened. He retaliated. "The food… I'm sure it's not just when you're with me." He couldn't bring himself to spit out the full accusation: Chuck probably engorged himself on junk food all the time, not just during sex.

The beaver abruptly pushed himself upright. His gut oozed into his lap, covering over his dick, and his poochy breasts clapped the top of his belly. "You know damn well I keep a strict diet and work out. The only reason I break my routine is to let loose with you. And I did that because you made me feel safe! But I've done everything I can to lose this weight." His claim radiated with absurdity.

So, Evan had to point it out to him. "And yet, here you are."

Chuck shrugged. "Yes. Here I am. A fat fucking beaver. I was just starting to feel a little okay about it, too. I just wanted somebody who thought of me as more than a fat fuck. I guess I was naive to think that could be you."

Conflict burbled in the pit of Evan's stomach. He couldn't fathom that Chuck was telling the truth. And yet, he liked Chuck. He trusted Chuck. A strange emotion quivered in Evan's chest. For a fleeting moment, he questioned whether that was love.

Evan didn't have time to sort out his thoughts, as Chuck rose from the bed. Evan gripped his hand. "Wait!!"

Chuck looked down to him with distant, detached eyes. "Yes?"

The greyhound had no choice. He had to stop dictating the truth to Chuck, and he had to honor Chuck's perspective. Evan gave it his best shot. "I didn't realize what you've been through. I mean, you told me, and I didn't listen. I even assumed things about you, hurtful things. Please, let me make it up to you."

Indulge

Chuck turned his head away with a wet choke. "I dunno. You'll never know what it's like. My body just wants to be fat, and yours doesn't. I just don't think we fit together."

Evan held fast onto Chuck's hand. "I can't lie. I won't know what it's like for you. But I want to be there for you the way you've been there for me. You've given me so much love, and you deserve at least a fraction of it back." He was sure that was the right sentence to meet the moment. Whether it was accurate or not, he couldn't say. He'd never really thought about what kind of love was between them.

Chuck leaned down. "No. I'm done. You know what I think?"

Evan held his breath. "…What?"

Chuck poked Evan's empty stomach. "I think you've got some kind of psychosexual hangup. I think you want to be the one eating all those things, and you imagine yourself putting on weight. Only, you can't let yourself, because then everyone would see a big, fat greyhound."

Evan's penis lengthened to a chub. He wanted to reel it back in. He couldn't grant any credence to Chuck's bizarre idea.

Instead, Chuck continued. He put his palm on Evan's flat, ironclad stomach and rubbed it. "Yeah. I think you wanna eat all that fatty food. You want to gorge on meat and stuff yourself with sweets. How about a two-pound steak? Think you could finish it? Wash it all down with a thick, caloric milkshake?"

Reflexively, Evan panted with a lolled tongue. His cock came to full mast, despite his best efforts.

Chuck's lips quivered, and his expression softened. "Right on the money, eh?"

Evan glared at his own dick in shock. "Yeah."

Chuck ripped his hand away and screwed his face into a grimace. "I can't do this. I'm not a toy for your vicarious whims. It's hard enough being fat otherwise. You need help, bucko."

Evan saw one obvious solution, but he could scarcely get himself to acknowledge it. "W… wait."

Chuck waited. Despite everything, he hadn't left yet. His calm breath mounted tension on Evan.

Evan gulped, trying to make room for the words in his throat. "Would you still love me if I was fat?"

The beaver chortled bitterly. "Yeah. It's not all about your body."

A pang struck Evan's chest. He got along with Chuck, sure, but his romantic interest hinged on Chuck's juicy ass. Perhaps Evan could still spend time with those bubbly cheeks if he just made one modification to his own body. "What if... what if..."

Chuck didn't offer any help. He only responded with silence, isolating Evan even as they shared the same room.

So, Evan had to say it himself. "I could get fat."

"You know how that makes me feel? Fat is just some mode that you opt into because you feel like it? That's my life. I'm stuck here, without a choice. People use food to mock me, and here you are, using it on me in the bedroom."

"I can't change what other people do. I can't change your body. But I can change how I treat you." Difficult as it was, Evan gazed deep into Chuck's eyes. "I'm disgusted by what I've done."

Chuck pointed derisively at Evan's hard-on. "That doesn't look like disgust."

"I get it. You don't want to be fed. But for me, that meatball sub is still a sex toy, and, well... I wish you knew how wonderful it feels to feed someone."

"You can feed yourself."

"You're totally justified to be pissed at me. But you've got forever to do that. Right here, right now, don't you at least want to see what's so great about feeding a lover?"

"I hate you. I need you to know that."

"Okay. Hate me." Evan choked on the word "hate." It was a simple, one-syllable word. Yet something was unfathomable about it. For Chuck to hate Evan was unbearable.

Chuck sat on the bed again, slowly creaking it under his bulk. "You're serious? You'd get fat to keep me? You're so proud of those abs." He traced a paw up Evan's flat stomach. "With a body like yours, I'm sure you could pick up any fatass you wanted in a heartbeat."

Evan grabbed Chuck's hand and held it close. "That's the trouble. The only person I want is you." The words escaped him thoughtlessly. He was shocked to find those words within him, but they weren't wrong. He nibbled at Chuck's hand. His lips stroked the beaver's paw affectionately.

The beaver bit his lip. He ripped his hand out of Evan's grip.

The greyhound watched powerlessly.

Chuck leaned over to the nightstand, bunching his waist as he bent. With both hands, he picked up the meatball sub. "Open wide."

Evan choked back tears. "Really?"

"Yeah, this sandwich is kind of big." His dry wit came out of nowhere.

Evan burst into laughter, disarmed by the joke. "No, you asshole! About feeding me."

Chuck's nose twitched, nursing his own wet tear ducts. "This hurts. A lot. I kind of want nothing to do with you ever again. But we've both put a lot of work into this relationship. You're not the same shallow dickweed I caught staring at my ass. I think… I don't want to lose what we've already built together."

Those words struck Evan with absurdity. "Chuck. I want this to work out. I'm ready to do work. I just don't know why you would say I'm not shallow. When I want to get off, you want to make love."

The beaver poked Evan with his big toe. "Sometimes, it's kind of cute how naive you are. You're vain as hell when it comes to your body, but when it comes to the way you take care of me, you're all sheepish and modest. You haven't noticed the gentle way you touch me, the kind way you talk to me, the warm way you look at me?"

Tears burst from Evan's eyes, beyond his control.— "No. That's impossible. Those kind, sweet things couldn't be things I've done. I, I…" His mouth hung open in shock.

Chuck shoved the meatball sub right into Evan's maw.

Evan held his breath in shock. He didn't blink.

The beaver grinned mischievously. "Ooh. This is already kind of nice."

Evan bit down, ripping off a fraction of the sandwich. He took a fluffy portion of sub roll, two meatballs, a heap of mozzarella, and a gush of marinara. It all packed his mouth from end to end with warm, dense, and wet food. Delightful bread wrapped around savory meat and tangy cheese. He moaned through flavors he hadn't tasted in years. His stomach clamored for food, and so, he quickly gulped it down. Once it met his gut, though, it stoked an ephemeral hunger south of his abs. Heat flushed his cheeks.

Chuck licked his lips. "Ooh. You always pin your ears down when you're in heat."

The greyhound's heart raced. "I—I do?!" He reached up to feel his ears, and he found them standing on end.

Chuck rolled his eyes. "They were pinned down, until I pointed it out." He curled one leg up on the bed, letting his other leg dangle as he faced the headboard. His chunky hip brushed Evan's bony side. Then, he took a pillow from the head of the bed and fluffed it up against the headboard. With that in place, he put his palm to Evan's chest and gently pushed him towards the pillow. "Just lay down, relax, and don't worry about it. All you have to do is enjoy this sub."

Evan's upper back and head slumped against the pillow.

Chuck leaned forward, pooling his underbelly onto his leg. With one hand, he cradled the back of Evan's head. His other hand lowered the sandwich into Evan's open mouth.

Evan received the sub, letting the gooey, greasy meal fill his mouth. While his tongue occupied itself with delectable meatballs, his impish hands pined for something to do. They raised up to Chuck's midsection. He clutched pawfuls of the beaver's furry, doughy gut. His fingers kneaded through Chuck's cushy belly, affectionately grasping at their silken warmth.

Where his butt was more flabby and bouncy, his belly was more dense.

Evan wrenched a huge mouthful of sandwich into his gullet and immediately bit off more. His teeth ripped through the luscious sub as his fingertips clenched through Chuck's luscious gut. More and more, he consumed both food and flesh. Not a thought entered Evan's head. His libido and hunger both drove him onward, controlling his motor functions without a moment's reflection. In return, he received pure, mindless pleasure.

Chuck looked down on him. The sweet, subdued lover morphed into an assertive feeder. His two front teeth pinched his lower lip, and he took deep, strong breaths, heaving his jiggly pecs. His blubbery arm held steady. Despite the passion in his fiery eyes, he waited for Evan to swallow before thrusting more sandwich into the greyhound.

As Evan scarfed down the footlong, he wasn't spared a moment for rest. No, as soon as he swallowed, another few inches of sub tunneled right into his maw. He was crammed from end to end, from his stomach, up through his esophagus, into his mouth, ending beyond his lips. Just as his mouth had no shortage of food, his hands possessed enough tummy blubber to satisfy him forever.

Chuck crammed the end of the sandwich past Evan's lips. His fingertips lingered at his boyfriend's mouth.

The greyhound gulped a heavy swallow, stretching his stomach. His hands dropped to his sides. He smooched lovingly on Chuck's fingers, caressing them with his lips. His heavy stomach burbled with more food than it knew what to do with. He felt an inner swell that reminded him of, well, of receiving his partner. His words stumbled out, breathy and horny. "I feel huge."

Chuck ran a paw along Evan's middle, soft and warm. "You look the same to me." His cautious stroke soothed Evan's stomach, bringing peace to its strain.

Indulge

Evan laid there and panted ruttishly. Aroused as he was, he wanted Chuck's hand to wander just a tiny bit lower, where his cock ached with need. Then again, his belly was nice and full, and the joy of a stuffed belly rub was novel to him. He was too entranced to ask otherwise.

Chuck's warm voice cooed. "Good boy." One paw stayed on the greyhound's belly, but his other reached over to the nightstand and opened up the cheesecake. He plucked a fork from the nightstand, scooped off a portion of the cheesecake, and brought it to Evan's gaping mouth. He slipped it between the greyhound's passive lips.

Evan bit down on the fork. Lips sealed and hands stationary, he only admired his lover's eyes.

Chuck withdrew the fork, letting the bite of cheesecake slide right onto Evan's tongue.

The cake hardly needed any chewing. Evan simply mashed it with his tongue. Following the loud, heady meatball sub, the creamy taste and smooth texture of the cheesecake relaxed him. After enjoying that piece, he opened his mouth again.

His lover returned with another forkful of tangy, saccharine dessert.

Evan sucked this one down, too. Its chill cooled his middle. His cold stomach felt sensitive against Chuck's warm palm. Not to mention, each passing bite pushed his stomach walls further, making his flesh all the more tender. With each passing bite, his cooling, bloating stomach drew new heights of satisfaction from Chuck's doting massage.

The greyhound wondered if this is how Chuck had felt when Evan massaged him. Maybe this was where he had gotten all those corny words about Evan being nice and gentle.

Slowly but steadily, Chuck continually dipped the fork into the cheesecake and then into his lover's mouth. The voracious smirk on his face melted into a subtle smile, more caring than craving.

Evan still admired Chuck's ample curves, but as Chuck fed and rubbed him, he found himself drawn more to the beaver's face.

Soft pudge filled out Chuck's chin, while bubbly cheeks widened his face. His snout came to a dull point with a little button nose, and his tiny eyes sparkled. Even his behavior exuded mellow geniality, from the slow way he turned his head to the cheesecake, to the calm stroke of his palm against the greyhound's middle.

It was that same middle that pulled Evan from his reverie. It groaned, and despite the world's best massage, it could take no more. Evan swallowed one last bite. He had to push out the words, "That's all I can handle." He blew a haggard breath.

Chuck set down the fork. "Okay. You tucked away a lot more than I thought you could." His eyes opened wide as he peered down. "You're off to a good start."

"Huh?" Evan tilted his head down and peered along his snout. A stiff but shallow bump raised from his middle, obscuring his abs. His heart thumped, and his cock twitched achingly.

The beaver stifled a chuckle. "You're really turned on by this, aren't you?"

The greyhound blinked in disbelief. "I am?"

Chuck softly petted Evan's distended penis. "Yeah. This fella extended without a single touch."

Chuck's own cock snaked out from under his belly folds. Stuffed to the gills, Evan only yearned that much more for his lover's hard virility. "That makes two of us who are turned on, looks like."

Like a prowling tiger, Chuck purred. "You bet your tiny little ass I'm turned on. Although, it won't be tiny for much longer."

"You gonna miss it?"

"Miss it? How could I miss something that's only going to get bigger, rounder…"

"Fuck, get the lube before you jizz the bed."

Chuck responded with a guttural guffaw. "Don't you worry. I know exactly where I want my juices to go." He yanked open the nightstand drawer, clattering its contents. He pawed through it, then retrieved a bottle of clear liquid. He stood up, opened the bottle with one hand, and opened his other hand. He was about to lube up his dick.

"Wait, wait!" Evan stifled a burp. "Allow me." As he leaned onto his side, his guts sloshed with a loud churn. He extended his paws with open palms.

The beaver squirted lube into one of Evan's paws, filling it with runny, chilly fluid. "Have at it."

Using his clean hand, Evan gripped Chuck's underbelly. He lifted it off of Chuck's penis.

Its soft heft weighed in his paw like warm, delicious pudding. Chuck's cock jutted far forward and arced upward slightly. A nice, fat cock for a nice, fat boy.

Evan reached his lubed hand under Chuck's penis. He wrapped his fingers around it. The fur on his paw stood on end as he fondled the beaver's full length.

Indulge

He could hold most of the cock at once, leaving an inch or two bare along with its broad, meaty head.

Chuck heaved a breathy moan. His body shuddered, rippling his supple lard.

Evan pulled his hand down along the rock-hard penis, passing every inch of it through his rapacious grip. Lastly, he cupped Chuck's head, rubbing both its beefy outcropping from his shaft and its soft point. His hand left it slippery and glistening. With his job complete, he flopped onto his back.

"Now, it's my turn." Chuck squirted some lube in his own hand, then set the tube aside. He leaned over Evan and steadied himself with one hand against the bed. His pudgy face lowered to Evan's, catching the greyhound's lips in a kiss. In the same moment that his tongue breached Evan's lips, his index finger slid into Evan's lower entrance.

Gentle ache throbbed in the greyhound's rump. He let it out through a chest-gripping groan, and he channeled his pain into his kiss. His tongue pushed forcefully up against Chuck's kind lick.

The beaver delicately swirled his finger through Evan, taking care to gradually loosen him.

As Evan's pain faded, it gave way to arousal. His lips groped at his lover's, while his tongue lapped Chuck's with blunt, clumsy strokes. With a full ass and a full belly, carnal passion drove Evan too hard.

Chuck withdrew both his finger and his tongue.

Suddenly empty, Evan whimpered.

The beaver looked at him with doting eyes. "Can you get on your hands and knees?"

Evan scoffed. "Of course I can." He shifted again onto his side, swishing his gut's overloaded contents. Its heavy volume pulled at his insides. He put both palms to the comforter, then started pulling his knees under him. His shifting legs disrupted his stomach, though, sending a dull ache through it. "Oogh." He put a paw to his gut to rub it. His palm caressed the round contour of his bloat and eased its pain.

Chuck got on the bed behind him. His weight slanted the mattress backwards, towards him. "Not so easy, is it?"

Evan put his hand back down to the bed. He could barely breathe against his jam-packed gut. "No kidding. Is it like this every time?"

Chuck gripped Evan's hips. His pudgy paws wrapped thick and firm on the greyhound's bony sides. "You bet."

Evan's gurgling, burbling middle felt like a huge balloon, swelled with meaty, greasy, fatty food and weighing him down. The dull discomfort was nothing compared to the pure rapture of feeling his own body blimp with unprocessed calories. "Good."

The beaver took his hands off of Evan. Then, his cock's head met Evan's anus. Chuck's soft head made a gentle entrance, passing into Evan with a pleasant squish. It made way for his shaft, thick and sturdy.

Evan whimpered, but his tail flapped excitedly against Chuck's gut. He could barely stand the size of Chuck's manhood, both for how far it stretched him and how good it felt.

Once Chuck's long wood filled Evan, he gently set his stomach atop Evan's back. His warm, cushy underbelly overran Evan's hips on both sides and flowed halfway along Evan's back, smothering the greyhound's tail.

Evan preferred the feeling of Chuck's belly during missionary, but he doubted he could manage that with his belly in its swollen, volatile state. Given the circumstances, he could settle for a sexy slab of fat draped on his lower back. It wasn't like Evan needed any help getting aroused anyway. His belly had gorged on junk food, and now his anus gorged on cock, leaving his libido on overdrive. He slowly panted, lolling his long, dripping tongue. The sheer volume of stimulation left him unable to react any other way.

Chuck's pudgy thighs padded Evan's backside. The beaver backed away, running his head in reverse through Evan's booty. His cock's cap rubbed, full and plush, against Evan's walls. Chuck's shaft mashed stiff against Evan's P-spot, followed by his head, which applied a touch more pressure. His retreating manhood uttered wet squelches, harmonizing with the meaty gurgles in Evan's crowded gut. As he backed away, his fleshy thighs parted from Evan, and his underbelly slid along Evan's back, rubbing him with cozy blubber.

Chuck slowly grinded back into Evan. His head prodded deep, stretching Evan wide for jamming his stiff staff through him. The pull of his cock challenged Evan, but it was worth it. His belly crawled back up Evan's back, probably pushed by his hips and legs. After a long, strenuous journey, his thighs met Evan with a gradual press. His big, hanging stones nuzzled Evan's thighs.

Evan gritted his teeth. Tingles of ecstasy wriggled from beneath him and spread, ephemeral yet overpowering, through his legs and cock. If he so much as tickled his erection, he would've climaxed right there. But no, much like the tension in his rump and the tension in his distended gut, the aching need in his cock felt amazing. Too amazing to cut short in such a crude gesture.

Chuck gripped Evan's hips firm—a telltale sign that the beaver was about to get down to business. His secure grip was controlling yet comforting, paralyzing Evan while soothing him. No longer gentle, he backed through Evan at a moderate pace. He plunged forward, ramming his cock into the greyhound decisively. His thigh pudge plapped Evan, while his underbelly lurched over Evan. Again, he swept outward, emptying Evan's anus for a fraction of a second, before diving inward and packing him once more. Chuck's bopping rhythm clapped his fat into Evan and pounded the greyhound's skinny frame.

Without Chuck's grip, Evan would have fallen right over. Delirious pleasure burst from Chuck's thrusts. Evan's guts sloshed languidly, carrying the vibrations from Chuck's hammering. Bloated as he was, the stuffing in his ass and the rocking in his stomach made him feel huge, stretched, taut, and expanded to a state of unyielding stiffness. His cock throbbed in kind. The greyhound wrangled inwardly with the glut of carnal gratification. He groaned and clutched the bedsheets, while his panting grew hoarse.

Chuck's breathy grunts gave away the beaver's own mounting passion. His fingers gripped Evan a little too hard, digging his chunky fingers into the greyhound's hips. He ripped backward, then launched forward. His thighs slapped Evan, whipping the greyhound with plush fat. Chuck jerked his hips forward so forcefully that he tossed his gut, which pounded Evan's back. He heaved back and forth, rocking the bed with shrill creaks, and he grunted louder and louder over his uneven pace. Every hasty, frenzied thrust came too soon and too fast, bludgeoning Evan before the greyhound could tell he had left. The crazed pace made his cock feel bigger, bigger, bigger.

Evan barely held on. He whimpered, and his voice wavered from the shock of Chuck's poundings. He lifted one paw to his chest with the intention of finding his cock. His fingers slinked down his body, but they stopped at his bulging belly. Its outward curve excited Evan even further. He felt every ounce of its pressure from inside, and his hand groped at its swell from outside. All he needed was a little more filling.

Chuck bellowed out with a gruff cry, "Graaagh!" His cock pulsed, thick and strong, and he loosed into Evan. His pumping cock thumped Evan's walls, stretching him further while shooting warm, sticky loads into the greyhound.

It was too much. Evan yelped, and, gripping his gut, his cock burst. A hot load of cum spurted from him, drawing untold pleasure through him in the process. His tight, tense balls seized, and his gratified cock launched another thick stream of semen, pooling on the bed beneath him.

Chuck pulled Evan's hips hard, ramming the greyhound's ass against his pelvis. His voice burst out brutish and rough, more animal than person. "Oh—yeah—! Cum—for—me—!" He could barely talk over the pressure of his own exploding cock.

Evan yelped and barked. His gut bloated and groaned, heavy with luscious meatballs. His backside stretched that good stretch as Chuck's cock pulled it to its carnal limits. All of it swelled within his loins as ecstasy. Thump after thump of electric passion coursed through his length and splashed onto the bedsheets. Insurmountable stores of volume and pressure filled Evan, and they found an outlet through his long, throbbing cock. His fingers clenched the sheets as his body surrendered itself to stuffed euphoria.

A weary laugh lumbered out of Chuck, rocking his gut over Evan's back. "You did good." He slid out of Evan, trailing his juice between the greyhound's legs.

Slowly, Evan lowered himself to the bed, avoiding the quickly-cooling pool of his own cum. Taxed and tired, he laid on his side and cradled his gut. "I didn't expect it to hurt this much."

Chuck laid behind him, playing the big spoon. His hand wandered up to Evan's and held it. "We've had sex before."

Evan chuckled. "No, dummy. I don't think I've ever seen you so hurt as you were earlier. Even thinking about it now, I want to crawl out of my fur. I owe you an apology."

"Well. You did really, genuinely injure me. So it means a lot that you understand the gravity of it." Chuck squeezed Evan's hand. "Funny thing is, sharing pain with you feels good, even if you're the one that caused it."

With a long, slow breath, Evan let the concept sink in. Chuck's pain was his pain. He stood on the precipice of a new phase in their relationship, a phase which he hadn't realized existed.

Chuck nuzzled Evan's neck. "Love you. You really serious about gaining weight?"

"Yeah. I haven't been honest with myself." Evan recognized a mental weight lifted from him as he shed a shroud of denial.

Chuck's warm body snuggled close to Evan. "You'll be handsome no matter what size you are. I'm looking forward to seeing my little Evan open up to his true self. Now, why don't I start an epsom bath for you?"

Evan's sore body relaxed just at the thought of it. "Oogh. That would be amazing."

Indulge

Perhaps Evan could drop cardio. After all, some good weight lifting wouldn't hurt his journey of bulking. Whatever happened, no matter what state his body was in, he would take that journey with Chuck.

Body of Work

William Steele

PING!

Farid's eyes shot open as he felt the office fan blow a cool breeze under his desk, brushing his now exposed belly between two buttons around his furry navel. The lion's long thick tail thumped behind him in his rolling chair, feeling boxed in as the arms pressed into his doughier sides.

Shit, he thought; this was his last summer office shirt that fit. *Well... at least Malone would be thrilled to find out.* The thought of his husband flustering at his climbing weight caused a smirk to creep up his greying muzzle. Careful not to exhale too sharply, the middle-aged lion slowly untucked the front of his shirt. It was slightly damp from his underbelly and a bit wrinkled, but he'd rather look slovenly than try a "Casual Friday" on a Tuesday. Sweat beaded on his brow despite the A/C cranked up to 11—his thick dark mane shaved down on the sides to alleviate some of the summer heat. As his elbow bent out he felt the seams of the shoulder warn of another malfunction, and he eased off. He pulled out a red handkerchief with the Enterprise logo on it (Malone liked to call him 'Captain' when he was being cute) and dabbed at the sweat on his head and a growing double chin. He placed it near a kitschy store-bought card on his desk that read "*40 seemed like light-years away!*", along with several polished paper plates.

He hadn't planned to make a big deal of the big 4-0 that coincided with ten years at the university administration office. He also hadn't planned to eat as much cake - he licked his lips at the leftover strawberry cream

Indulge

frosting that cloyed at his mouth. All the younger hires had been under his wing and pitched in on the surprise party despite him never mentioning his birthday. He suspected Malone's handiwork again, what with the art history professor's knack for dates and gatherings. A thick hairy paw reached into his tight slacks' pocket and slightly arched his back in his office chair to grab his phone, sliding to the right to get the camera app open. He angled it just right where his belly sat in his lap, with dark salt-and-pepper treasure trail contrasting the exposed cream colour of his underbelly. With a muffled click and a satisfied nod, he wrote a message to his husband.

A short walk - or waddle for some - from the admin office led to an old red brick building with open windows and a loudly humming external A/C block half-fitting in a lecture hall's window. At the head of the class, there stood a stout striped hyena man of middling height and a pear-shaped figure. His neck fluff poked out over his shirt collar and gave his chubby cheeks an always smiling look from behind his small round spectacles. While his sleeves were rolled up with the heat, he still wore a light tweed vest with suspenders holding up his corduroy slacks. Furs at varying points in their degrees watched with varying interest as the animated Professor Malone continued his lecture. "…So you see, the *Venus of Willendorf* was quite likely an emblem of idealised beauty and fertility, and one of the oldest pieces of sculpture we still have access to. But what is even more fascinating is the possibility of the work as a self-portrait!"

He gestured over his own body, hands making curves over his perky moobs and around his belly and love handles, "When looking at the proportions of the figure, one can see how it might be depicted based on how the artist looked down at their own body—"

He looked down and noted that he couldn't see much past the fluff and the sea of tweed that overshadowed his toes, along with his hips. He heard giggling throughout the classroom and cleared his throat with a tug of his suspenders.

"A-Ahem. That is to say! The ideal of beauty in this work was one reflected in their own bodily experience, and one that even celebrated body shapes of—"

VMM. VMM. The professor's phone vibrated on his desk, perking up his ear. A sweeping glance of his class told him all he that he needed to know of their interest, tired eyes barely kept open in the afternoon sun. He clapped his dark grey paws together - startling a few of the dozing students - and gave a gentle smile with his white-stubbled snoot, "Alright! I think that's enough for today. Be sure to read pages twenty through twenty-eight in your textbook to brush up for the discussion on Friday. And just to add a consideration for next class…"

The hyena plucked a marker and stretched on his tiptoes to begin writing on the whiteboard, "Consider the bodies of work you've seen, and where you see your own body."

As he capped the marker to hurriedly set it down, he heard the clattering of plastic onto the linoleum tile floor. The shuffling of chairs gave way to chatter as students began to file out into the halls. He looked around before finding it rolled under his desk, prompting him to huff and squat a knee as he heard a soft *rrrRRIP* and a surge of softness on his inner thigh. He had to be careful not to bump his head as he glanced to be sure all his students had left.

He grumbled and poked at the squishy, white-furred flesh pushing out. Maybe it won't be too noticeable, he thought, pulling up his phone. Maybe Farid has a jacket he could-

The academic's mind short-circuited at his husband's texts—more notably the attached works of art. He let out a nervous laugh as he felt his ears burn.

Depicted was a lion, over six feet and pushing four hundred fifty pounds. If you'd told Malone that Farid had been a soccer player in college, he wouldn't have believed it. Dark blue slacks framed a squished bulge under a desk corner, with cream-coloured fupa pressing down into a wide "W" with plenty of bushy fur. Then came the real belly, pushing out and over into the vanishing point of his deep belly button that peeked through strained fabric. Soft folds arched out and held in as much as it could. The top two buttons of his shirt had been undone with his tie loosened up, fatty pecs of former muscle squished with one flabby arm drooping down to hold the camera. At first he failed to notice a missing button and then his art teacher brain went into overdrive analyzing the work of art that was his husband: His curly salt-

and-pepper mane did nothing to hide his fatty neck bulging out of his shirt collar, nor did it hide his chubby cheeks pushing into his bearded muzzle. His cheeks creased the corner of his silver eyes in his typical smirk as he looked directly at Malone through the screen. The text simply read,

> < *Birthday cake was your doing, I take it?*

Malone's chest fluttered like a sophomore in a forty-something's body as his paws fumbled to type,

> > *Fhor some part, hyes. I... >///>*

He hesitated and looked around once more before reaching up and taking a selfie where he could show his inner lap. One part of his pink briefs poked through on one side, with a sheepish smile on his pudgy stubbled face and a small moustache.

> > *I may need you to come bring me a jacket to cover up, darling. ;v;'*

> *There was a click of ellipses before the short message,*

> < *We're ordering in tonight, and I'm tearing those the rest of the way off. >:)*

Malone let out a giggle and began packing up his briefcase as a cloud of texts began to form.

The mid-day sun gave way to heavy dark clouds over the city and a welcome breeze, even with the humidity. Farid tugged at his collar and attempted to air out his arms where small sweat stains had begun to form. Malone didn't mind, quite used to the lion's casual demeanour in public. The train home was unfortunately rather crowded as Farid had lent Malone a jacket to tie around his waist. Meanwhile, the lion's hairy gut hung out of the bottom of his shirt, wobbling with every thump onto the cabin. The hyena had made a concerted effort not to stare, asking about how each other's day went. The lion licked his teeth and stifled a small burp as he smirked down at his shortstack husband, "Cake wasn't as filling as I thought, even after four slices…"

Some smaller furs noted Farid's presence and made space where they could, the lion squeezing through and holding a way for Malone to follow. The hefty hyena punctuated each step with a "scuse me," "sorry," "pardon me" until they made it to the back of the car. There was only one two-seater available, and Farid snuck a glance down to his husband's gift from

God. Those squishy buns pushed out the jacket around his waist and tail, causing the roundness to be accentuated like a cloaked exhibition piece. In a gentlemanly fashion, he gestured to the seat and said, "You can sit, hun. I've already been sitting around all day—" with a casual push and pop of his back. If his button hadn't popped off before, it certainly would have now as the remaining strained with the fat flex toward Malone's face.

The hyena flushed and let out a small "thank you" as he sat down and modestly placed his briefcase over his lap. What hadn't occurred to him was that as his hips took up one-and-a-half seats, his face was now at belly-height with Farid as he stood holding the safety bar. The metallic clunk and chugging of the train began to jostle the car as the lion's heft jiggled all over. His moobs squished and shook on top of his belly as one button came undone from the sheer vibration. He placed a large paw on Malone's shoulder to steady the hyena.

Malone remembered the first time he and the lion went on the train together. He was still a pudgy grad student while Farid had been a brickhouse forward working as a teacher's aide and library assistant. That same paw that held his shoulder would give him a small squeeze, his thumb grazing his striped chubby neck as he looked through him with those silver eyes. He was big before but now… he was massive. Any evidence of muscle had been covered with hefty flab, the only inkling still in his thick biceps that stretched his short sleeves. Love handles that rode up his shirt with little furry triangles tucked in slacks that stretched over those powerful thighs. His shocks of grey in his mane curled and wisped like clouds, his lined eyes and grey muzzle just as beautiful as that cream it used to be - maybe even more.

Malone stole a glance to see who was watching the back of the car, between so many furs and feathers and scales on their phones. He pushed up his glasses and quickly turned his head to push his snout into that deep hairy navel and give it a kiss before turning back as though nothing happened. Farid's eyes widened as the big cat let out a deep "mrp!"

Malone's stubble had matted slightly from the sweat, his moustache askew. He licked his lip and could taste the salt and smell the woodsy deodorant Farid used this morning. His green eyes gleamed mischievously as he said, "That's for all the teasing today."

Farid looked down at him with a half-hearted scowl that looked more like a pout with his extra cheeks and chins, but then he returned into a mischievous grin as he turned around. The hyena didn't have a chance to remark as half-a-ton of lardy lion ass came crashing down on him, squishing his own pudgy features against the window.

Farid, for his part, let out a yawn that stretched his maw wide. Malone could hear him speaking through the vibrations of that bassy growl, saying, "That's all for standing around today. I think I found the best seat on the train."

Now the hyena was stuck between a glass window and a soft place until they reached their stop, surrounded by the scent of his husband and feeling his deep growling purrs resonate through his body. Malone desperately tried not to squirm and get an awkward presentation when he stood up, but his face was burning all the same: there was payback, and then there was just plain *unfair*.

The next few stops crawled by until finally there was the familiar lurch on the cobblestone platform. The cool air rushed in as the doors slid open, and the scent of petrichor filled the couple's noses. Next to the lion, Malone could feel the heavy thumps of his footsteps as they descended the steps, both of them jiggling and jostling. It was a quaint one-way street on a hill, regrettably with their condo at the higher point of the incline. Farid had joked the hill kept him strong enough to carry all the extra "love weight" as he liked to call it. Malone liked to call it all the more to love. A cold wet drop landed on the hyena's nose as he instinctively shook. The gentle pit-pat signalled the cascade as it would become a downpour, and the two began a quick power walk up the hill. When they finally made it to the front of the blanched pink condo, Malone was quick to scamper to the shelter of the front door's awning.

Farid however, lingered back in the rain. His thick dark curls had already gotten soaked and he ran a paw through his mane to push them back out of view and spread his arms wide. He could feel the bulk of his arms hanging down as his palms faced the sky, flabby biceps dripping with water that trailed down. He breathed it all in, and felt the cool rain after a scorching day, the droplets trickling on each curve and resting in every fold of his fat body. He loved this. He loved being this—regardless of the sore back or the ankles or the waddling... he loved feeling all this space.

Malone chuckled as he fished through Farid's jacket pockets and found the lion's keys. As the lock clicked and he half held the door, he called out, "Come on! Aren't you going to join me for a shower before dinner?"

Farid shook his head wildly as his locks whipped around with cascades flying every which way in the rain, pulling the remains of his buttoned shirt up and off as Malone witnessed his husband shirtless in the rain, tongue out to catch water like a child. The way his chest hair curled in intricate swirls as his fur was soaked mesmerised the hyena. He wanted to trace over every pattern, feel his paw sink into that fatty flesh and smell that closeness.

Malone shook his head flustered and stepped in the doorway, but left it just enough ajar as he said, "Wouldn't want you to catch cold while you helped me out of these, would we?"

Farid had thrown his head back to catch more rain before cracking an eye open to see a flash of something pink and round at the top of the stairs. Malone had done away with the ruined corduroys and was only in his peach-patterned briefs that showed his fuzzy dark grey stripes all along his thighs that rubbed and wobbled as he shifted his weight. And that ass...by God's great providence he saw those pink briefs cling to two fatty globes that shifted as Malone lifted a paw to take off his loafers. He knew this was just far enough inside that only Farid was likely to see, but the strip tease made him get warm all over again. He bounded up-up-up the steps with heavy thumps before landing inside with a boom and closing the door.

"Twenty years and you're still such a tease with those assets..." Farid rumbled as he cozied up behind Malone.

The hyena made sure to brush his wide hips against him as he turned around, "Twenty years and you still haven't stopped 'bulking for next season,' hm?"

He emphasised the point with a two-handed lift of that big proud ex-jock gut and letting it drop and wobble, eliciting a grunt from the lion.

A trail of sopping wet clothes led from the front door all the way to the bathroom where the warm water began to run.

Indulge

Droplets cascaded down peaks and valleys of fur and flab as the two stepped into the shower together, paws already lathering and caressing the folds and hard-to-reach places. Farid growled and pushed Malone up against the wall, pushing out a small "yip!" as he towered over the hyena and pressed his belly against him. Malone was in heaven, surrounded by flab and fur and curly mane, looking up at his husband's lopsided grin on that grey muzzle and dark curly beard.

He remembered years ago having a similar sort of escapade with a broad-shouldered trim lion pushing a not-as-pudgy hyena against the shower wall in the university fitness centre. He recalled that was one of the last times Farid had been working out regularly after moving on from the rugby team. Then they'd have more dinner date nights, and movie nights... and late-night snack runs, and early-morning breakfast runs...until the runs became walks became waddles.

Even now, Malone could hear a heavier breathing from his lardass lion lover as he held up all this weight and flexed on the hyena. He reached for the water to turn it down and placed his glasses aside. Then, he got to work. He started on his tiptoes, pulling Farid into a bristly kiss with chubby cheeks and chins, rubbing beard and moustache. The two nuzzled noses between breaths as Malone began a trail of kisses from Farid's thick neck and fluffy mane down to his chest with those hypnotic patterns of swirling hair, down the rounding out belly and squeezing the love handles for good measure. Down further still, Malone would kiss and lick in Farid's deep navel, jiggling and kneading the lion's doughy tank of a gut. This was all full of love. Love that they'd grown together over the past twenty years.

"I wonder how much more you'll grow on me, eh, Mal?"

Farid had read the hyena's mind without him saying a word, and he continued down a treasure trail to the treasure trove. Back in the day, Farid was second to none on the team in the locker room (of course they compared at some point). What was an impressive piston of pleasure had gradually been enveloped in a furry pad of fat and pushed his groin outward, with those fuzzy peaches hanging lower. When before his bulge was obvious in work slacks, now Farid couldn't hide his fatpad. Malone took a deep breath in as he buried his nose in the folds. It smelled salty, but well-kept, the light scent from a long day of sitting down having those thunder thighs touching each other. He'd be touching himself too with those kinds of hams, rubbing circles as he ministered to that buried treasure.

"*Mmi-mff-mmuu…*"

Farid's ear flicked as he couldn't see over his gut nowadays, moaning at the tonguing of his furry fupa, "Mmf… didn't quite catch that, hun…?"

Malone paused his digging for that buried dick and kissed that fatpad, eliciting another grunt from the big lion.

"I love you. I love every pound and every inch of you, for gaining or for losing."

The grey hyena felt the cascade of water dripping over Farid's belly and down his back, and the large lion had quite the view as the water continued down the soft folds creased down to Malone's tail and fat rump. The lion growled and leaned down to pick up his husband and kiss him against the shower wall, rubbing and lathering as their bellies pressed together. After a few seconds, the two muzzles parted panting and Farid said,

"Greedy yeen, snacking down there before dinner, eh? Naughty naughty…we'll have to make sure you're nice and stuffed tonight."

Malone grabbed a thick roll between Farid's pecs and love handles, smirking with soggy stubble on his face, "If you even leave anything for me, you mean? The quarterback is enjoying all his quarter-pounders without as many pesky quarter-miles…"

Malone yipped and giggled at the nibbling and kissing on his fat fluffy neck, Farid rumbling with a chuckle and a growl as the two played in the shower a bit longer. Eventually Farid's growling stomach ushered them out, leaving the big lion slightly bashful at the audible interruption.

Malone put on an old episode of *Star Trek: Next Gen* while laying on the couch with a towel underneath, opening up his phone to order in. Farid had given up on finding towels large enough to reach around his expanding waistline and thumped around the apartment while toweling off his mane. Every so often, he'd stand in front of the fridge looking for a snack or leftovers, and catch his husband sneaking a glance. He made sure to lean with his arm against the fridge, his empty stomach hanging down and jostling as he pondered. The refrigerator's light shone on the rim like a planet facing the sun, while the rainy grey light outside gave him a faint halo. Malone regarded him with the presence of a Renaissance portrait: "*Feast of Ex-Jock Bacchus*", or perhaps "*The First Supper (with another soon to come)*."

Indulge

"Looking for something, hun? I got SnackAttack open to order," the hyena offered. Typically Farid would rattle off a list of combos for the two of them to share, ask to see the order, then add another flurry of items before swapping or upsizing and finishing with dessert. Thankfully, Farid and Malone mostly cooked for themselves on most days. But today was special, with Malone's big blubber-hubber's birthday. Why not indulge a little?

Farid had grabbed four pudding cups from the fridge (three for him and one for Malone) before thumping over in front of the couch and causing the furniture to shake with each step. The Enterprise's Doctor Crusher was cut from view as Farid's fat thighs and butt blocked Malone's view.

Malone rolled his eyes and continued with the food order before reaching around and putting it on the coffee table. Meanwhile, the lazy ex-linebacker lion (Malone would constantly get Farid's old sports positions mixed up, setting up an easy lewd joke for Farid) wiggled his wide rump before crashing down on the couch as the reinforced furniture groaned. Malone couldn't make out a "wait!" before over four hundred pounds of fat feline landed on his lap, with an obnoxious chuffing purr. Farid *looooooved* to throw his weight around, and it was partly because of that he was so easily won over to the idea of gaining. Every month he'd find a new way to push and press and snuggle the hyena into a puddle, while Malone would conspire new ways to pack more pounds onto him.

Farid plucked the phone and did his usual review of the order before catching an order for ice cream cake with the note "Please write, 'Happy 20th anniversary, my Big Cat'."

Farid's heart warmed at the message and smirked, showing it to Malone. "Another cake today?" He asked, "If I didn't know any better, I'd say you're *trying* to get me stuck in my desk chair—"

Malone let out an indignant "*mmrmf*" as Farid just chuckled and confirmed the order. "Well, we got… forty-five minutes while they make everything. Why not start working up an appetite?"

The hyena couldn't see much without his glasses on the coffee table, but his squinted eyes soon widened with the sheer weight laying on top of him. While not nearly as endowed as Farid, the hyena wasn't quite as buried down under. This made for some awkward poking as his member pushed into the blubbery big cat blanket. The rain continued to fall outside as thunder rumbled. The TV droned on in the background as Malone saw the blending of Farid's cloudy mane with the dark skies in the distance…

He thought back to that fateful rainy day when the lion had said "I think I wanna take a break from sports and the gym."

Malone had been the one laying on top of the lion instead, snuggling in on a couch in his residency dorm. His ear perked up and took off his glasses, looking Farid in the eye. He'd been in his twenties and had a rich black mane, gorgeously muscular like sculpted marble - with some extra softness that hadn't left after his last bulking cut cycle. Those same silver eyes were looking off to somewhere else in thought.

"Well, what would you want to do instead?" The hyena asked. He'd always been pudgy, though back then he'd had more of a baby-faced muzzle with his grey and white striped fur, with the hint of a goatee fuzz on his small double chin. Farid always loved to kiss him along it—"his fuzzy peach" he'd call him…

Farid continued to stare off in thought, a paw running to his stomach as it growled slightly. He hadn't had too much after the last game of the year, and the two had skipped out on the after-party to hang out together. "Maybe I'll just keep eating," he said flatly, with no real pomp nor circumstance.

Malone chuckled, "I mean, I'd hope you would keep eating and breathing and sleeping! Those are pretty paramount components to survival."

Farid shook his head. He had felt his small squishy shortstack boyfriend and thought, *This feels right. I want to be as comfy as he is - maybe even more…*

The big question slipped out, like a future belly flowing out of a tight button-up:

"Mal… would you be okay if I got fat?"

The hyena blinked at the question in surprise and confusion, tilting his head with his mouth ajar, "Of course I would. You've seen me, yes? Who would I be to judge—"

"No, babe, like…*really* fat. I know I've bulked up for sports n' stuff but I've been feeling like—with my genes and how I eat—I'm gonna end up pretty big. I'm not gonna be the big jock around campus anymore…"

Malone had listened patiently; when Farid had something to say, he'd gather it up and say it; "I like being big and pushing stuff around, but I don't wanna keep doing sports forever. So I figured…why not go big another way? Get super fat and comfy. I want to settle down with you and…I dunno, I guess I wanted to know if you'd be okay with that?"

At that moment, Malone had known this was the turning point. He pulled the lion in for a gentle kiss and rubbed his small belly over his abs—a four-pack by now.

The hyena broke from the kiss and giggled, tracing patterns in the lion's curly mane with an ear to his pounding chest.

"I'd be more than okay, you big goof! You're a work of art no matter your size. I can hardly believe how beautiful you are—every curve like sculpted clay, every smile lighting up the room, every hug like an endless horizon, every colour stroke on a canvas, every fold and crevice like chiaroscuro and…!"

Malone caught himself amidst the sweeping wave of inspiration - and that's what it was; a sublime overwhelming presence of knowing exactly what Farid and Malone wanted to do. This was going to be the greatest collaborative piece of his life. Farid was staring, wondering what Malone would say next as the hyena took a breath and simply said,

"I would be *thrilled* to help shape you into a true masterpiece of fat; you will be my very own grand exhibit of lion lard."

And that was it. They'd ordered takeout that night and began a plan of bigger portions, bigger clothing sizes, bigger beds, bigger wedding rings, bigger doorways, bigger booths and bigger seats…and Malone saw it all reflected in those silvery eyes with new curls of silver in his mane. An entire body of work filled with love and care and food over the years.

"Hey hun, you spaced out there…" Farid called out. He reached around and stroked gently down the yeen's back, giving his rump a playful squeeze. Malone couldn't reach all the way around Farid to return the gesture, but he could hold those love handles.

"You're wonderful, Farid. Really…" He breathed, feeling the lion's weight push the words out.

"I know…" He smirked and licked the yeen's face, "and I wouldn't be this full without you, dearest."

Once again they kissed, with hints of cream and strawberry from the cake before, along with nuts and snacks the lion must have grabbed from the fridge. Paws exploring folds and rolls, old and new. The member poking into Farid's belly hadn't lessened as the two seemed to move in tandem. The lion shifted his hips and squeezed his thighs together around his member as Malone essentially fucked his fat belly. Waves sloshed through their bodies as Farid grunted low with each hump and gripped Malone's rump. The hyena had wrapped his arms around the lion's lardy neck and tried his best to thrust up against the immense weight bearing down, not aided by the licks and nips on his neck.

The pace grew quicker, fat folds rubbing and clapping as Farid grew louder and louder. After a pent-up day, neither were going to last long. Malone felt himself shoot up and smear against Farid's furry fat as he felt Farid's cum begin to leak in-between his thighs as the lion crashed down, panting and humming in satisfaction.

The two laid there, and Malone was grateful to have the foresight to put his towel underneath him on the couch. Rain continued to patter and fall, having lightened from the previous thunder and deluge. His muzzle nestled in between the folds of Farid's neck and whispered sweet somethings for every year they'd been together - and for every year to come. He could smell the vanilla shampoo fill his chest with every inhale, Farid's earthy scent underneath.

Eventually, the notification for the delivery began to buzz and the two fat husbands looked at each other, and then down to their scene of passion with a laugh.

"Another quick shower, love?"

Another kiss and a hum. Another leftover taste of sweetness.

"And then a whole night to indulge, darling..."

Manuel and Otis

Frances Pauli

Otis feels the years in his bones, lying deep in the spongy marrow and waiting to spring at him when he least expects it. He climbs down from the loft more slowly these days, placing each paw on a ladder rung tentatively, waiting for the twinge in his hip or the new, sharper pains that have taken residence in his ankles.

He is hungry, and his belly is not nearly large enough to see an old bear through the winter's sleep.

In the kitchen, Manuel hums a morning song, a low, rumbling churring that lifts Otis's ears from his skull.

"Come to breakfast," the younger bear calls. "Eat."

Otis shuffles in, his rear claws clicking softly against their floorboards. He finds Manuel already sitting, already heaping thick, berry-studded flapjacks onto both of their plates.

"Smells good," Otis mumbles.

He lowers his gaze, pretends to look at something near his toes while giving Manuel a sly examination. The younger bear's fur is thick and cinnamon red. His broad shoulders ripple when he shrugs, and the wave of that motion travels downward, jiggling the fat beneath Manuel's arms and crossing his huge, round belly like the tide's advance.

There is no doubt Manuel is healthy enough for the long winter. Otis eyes his friend appreciatively and can't hold back a smile. As he watches, Manuel makes liberal use of the syrup, drizzling the sugary liquid over their twin stacks of flapjacks.

Indulge

"You just going to watch me eat today?" When Manuel speaks, there is only amusement. Merriment and mischief light his dark eyes, then they narrow, and he grows serious. "You still need to put on weight."

Otis nods and climbs into his chair, pushing it way back from the table and noticing that his belly does not fill the gap. Manuel is right, but there is more on his mind than food this season. More thoughts circling in Otis's brain that keep distracting him from filling out his figure.

There is Manuel.

Otis looks up and catches the younger bear watching him. He drops his gaze quickly, picks up a rough wooden fork and pokes at the flapjacks.

"Eat," Manuel repeats.

But Otis wants more than food. He still shovels in the breakfast for Manuel's sake, all the while thinking of the long months ahead of him. Alone in a cold bed. Months when their amiable cohabitation will dissolve, and Manuel will seek his own den for sleeping.

"How are they?"

"Delicious." Otis thinks he should be brave enough to ask for a more intimate relationship, but the friendship has lasted too long. The window for an old bear to woo a young one closed many months ago. He is surprised Manuel lingers at all, but Otis is happy just to peer through his lashes and see the massive, rotund grizzly at the table opposite him.

Just the tread of Manuel's heavy paws on his floorboards is enough to soothe him. The sound of the other bear shuffling through his home. The comfort of his huge presence, a form that, even in his prime, Otis could never have matched.

He sees worry creasing Manuel's brow, and decides that the friendship, at least, is mutual. Manuel is worried, afraid to lose him.

"Old bears don't always make it," he says and watches the flinching, the way Manuel's ears fall to the sides. "It's natural. You shouldn't wor—"

"If you'd eat," Manuel says, and now there is a snap to his words, a thick quality that is not quite anger, not *only* fear. He gets up abruptly, shoving the table easily in Otis' direction. His deep breath lifts his chest, stretches his girth out and back. When he speaks again, he is calmer. "I'll make another batch."

There is no arguing with that tone, and Otis nods, does not want to fight in case…

"I'll eat," he says. Then, "I *am* trying."

Silence falls between them like a blanket, dense and fluffy. The pan hisses softly as Manuel adds more butter, begins to ladle out batter again. The sweet smell of baked goods permeates the kitchen, and Otis watches while Manuel's back is turned. He opens his muzzle enough to let his tongue gather the scents: batter, berries, butter, and one big, beautiful bear.

Manuel is humming again, and his hips move to the rhythm. His round rump seems to roll left and right, a ship rocking on the waves of Manuel's mood. It is glorious, and when the younger bear's tail joins in, Otis must look away for fear he'll make an audible sound of appreciation.

Slowly, the serving plate fills again. The flapjacks are a tower now, a fortress between Otis and survival, between his feelings for Manuel and his fear of the future.

"There we are." Manuel carries the plate all the way around to Otis's side of the table. He sets it all down in front of the older bear and chuckles.

The sound is physical. It shakes the table, trembles through the floorboards and up Otis's legs. Warmth spreads from it, heating the old bear from within.

"Thank you," he manages, but his voice is gruff with emotion. His lips curl above his teeth, and his nose twitches, filling with berries and syrup and Manuel's personal scent.

"You've got something on your muzzle." Manuel reaches a paw up, brushes at the short fur beside Otis's nose. His face is serene. The rolls around his jowls fold into a stack of their own, one upon the next. He brushes the fur again, then frowns. "Oh. It's just…"

"Gray furs," Otis says, swallowing hard. The touch of Manuel's paw against his fur is too much, and it lingers, heavy but gentle. A single claw traces a circle of fire against his muzzle. "More of them every morning."

"Silver," Manuel says. "Precious."

His paw falls away, but Otis can still feel it. There is heat in him now that swirls outward from the place the other bear has touched. His ears flick with it, and he shifts in his chair. He wants to say something, to reach out and place a paw against Manuel's body, to feel the roundness and the strength of him. Instead, he takes up his fork again. He eats.

To please Manuel. To make him happy.

"I've been thinking." Manuel rounds the table again, his rolling strides creaking the floorboards. "About this coming winter."

Otis mumbles encouragement from around a massive bite of flapjack.

"You're right about old bears," Manuel says. He sits with care, furrows his brow. "Sometimes…"

"It happens," Otis fills in the pause. "Nothing to do about it when the body stops storing so much fat. When the years catch you."

"But I don't want you to be cold," Manuel says. "Or hungry."

Something in his tone gives Otis pause. He sets down his fork, looks up and meets Manuel's gaze directly. The pity he expects is not there. The fear is, but there is something fierce about it, something else Otis has missed.

"I could stay," Manuel says.

It is a soft statement, and it slides between them, teasing thoughts to the surface, suggesting almost anything. Otis lives in the wake of it. He longs to roll in that sound forever.

"Only if you want," Manuel adds too quickly. He shifts, scratches at his round cheek. "I- I don't know what you want."

"I want you," Otis says, then panics and adds, "I want you to stay."

Flames rise in his ears, around the thin skin of his muzzle. He flushes with it, burns from the inside out. Miguel could not have missed that slip, could not miss anything now, with Otis bared and vulnerable before him.

Slowly, the younger bear smiles. Black lips curl merrily, and Manuel's cheeks plump, puffing with satisfaction. His eyes brim over, but all he says is, "Good." All he does is nod toward the tower of flapjacks and grin while Otis begins to eat in earnest.

He has put on more weight than he expected. Otis turns to the side, wrapping one arm around his circular belly. It is not as large as it should be, perhaps, but he isn't worried. He feels amazing, fat and strong and as secure as a cub in his mother's shadow.

His body is thick again, thanks to Manuel's fussing. His heart is full and fierce once more. He is ready, but only because he is not alone.

Manuel appears at the top of the ladder. He, too, has increased these past weeks, but he climbs into the loft with the ease and prowess of a bear in his prime. He is half again Otis's size, and his shadow weighs more than the old bear, even now.

"Are we ready?" he asks.

"Yes." Otis whispers, clears his throat, then tries again. "Yes."

Manuel thumps to the bed, the mattress piled with pillows and dense blankets they may not even need. His figure fills the loft, fills Otis's heart and spills over. Anticipation shivers through him.

"Are the doors barred?" he asks in a sudden fit of nerves. "I can't remember."

"I got them," Manuel answers.

"And the—"

"Windows all shuttered." Manuel's chuckle booms. "The stores are full, too. For when we wake."

Otis thinks he will be very hungry then. He believes an old bear should start a little earlier next year. Should take his health seriously, in particular when he has something to live for. Something wonderful.

"It's all good, then," he says.

"It's all good," Manuel answers.

The purr in his tone thrills Otis. He lets himself smile, crosses on shuffling paws to the bed.

It is already warm. When he climbs in, Manuel is there, waiting. He folds Otis into an embrace, supports him and encircles him. His wide chest is a better pillow than the downy ones they've thrown aside. His soft belly is warm and his snuggles are a whole-body affair.

Otis sinks against his lover. He lets Manuel hold him and knows that they will awaken together. He will wake up in the spring. He will make it. But for now, he has a long rest to look forward to, many days in Manuel's arms to enjoy.

The old bear curls around the younger one, sighs softly, and goes to sleep.

The Big Four Zero Zero

Indigo Rho

I lay in bed with my eyes closed, chasing after a wonderful dream I already had cloudy memories of. I remembered a feeding tube. And straps. At least, I think there were straps. It'd been a while since I'd last had a dream like that, and I wished I could pass out and fall right back into it. But even if I did fall asleep, there'd be a different dream waiting for me, one that might be less fun. So instead, I chose to get started with my Saturday.

I stretched, shifting the sheet that covered the dome of my belly and little else. Most of the covers had drifted over to Jordan's side of the bed again. My boyfriend hid under a mess of sheets, with only the zebra's messy, neon blue mohawk jutting out. I ran a paw through my mane, and my fingers snagged on tangled fur. There wasn't much a lion could do to keep his mane in check while he slept, and I wasn't the exception. Just another reason to get up. I added my lone sheet to his pile and slid myself to the edge of the bed.

My belly rolled onto my lap as I switched positions. The golden brown ball inflated and deflated with every breath, mesmerizing me. A mischievous thought in the back of my head imagined it swelling out and never shrinking, making me smile. As if I wasn't pleasantly big already.

I stood with a wobble and quietly gathered fresh clothes from the closet before sneaking into the bathroom. The walk-in shower called to me, and I answered. It was the first change I'd made to the house after buying it. Bathtubs haven't fit me comfortably in years, and the house's old tub and shower combo felt designed to exasperate me. I preferred the space the walk-in offered me. No worries about tripping over the rim of a tub or having my gut push away the curtain whenever I turned around. No knocking over bottles sitting on the rim with my tail. I'm not old old—I just turned forty-two last month—but being hefty comes with a few inconveniences to mobility that don't exactly enhance middle age.

Cool water rained on the back of my head. Since I wasn't in a hurry, I took my time massaging shampoo and conditioner into my fur. Working over my wide, round belly was the best part of showering. I kneaded every inch of it, following the beautiful curve as it bulged out into love handles and around my back.

My cock stirred down below, growing against my overhang as I fondled my gut. My breathing quickened a bit, and I suddenly regretted not waiting for Jordan to wake so we could shower together. Space could get tight—both of us were big men—but we had so much fun. There'd be plenty of groping and teasing as we cleaned. Sometimes, I pinned him against the wall, giving him a playful reminder of the dozens of pounds I had on him. We'd get ourselves so riled up that we'd have to jerk each other off before getting out.

But Jordan had already showered last night, and I couldn't wait for him to wake up, so I swiftly handled my pent-up desire for my own heft with a few jerks of my wrist. Once the soap suds—and everything else—had washed away, I turned off the water and turned on the dryers. Warm air gushed from nozzles on the back and side of the shower. Slowly, I turned in place, letting the air dry my fur. Just as there was a lot of me to wash, there was a lot of me to dry. My mane whipped about, gradually fluffing up. I held my tail up to the scorching heat of a nozzle while I wrung the water out of the fluff at the end. I followed up my shower with a towel and a blow dryer to handle the spots that resisted the nozzles, mainly the underside of my belly.

Smelling fresh and feeling only faintly damp, I was just about to dress when I caught sight of the bathroom scale. It was a sleek and sturdy slab of glossy black with a big digital display. High capacity, of course. Jordan had given it to me when we first started dating five years ago, and he'd always teased me with lofty weight goals. The scale handled up to something like 550 pounds, a weight I struggled to imagine myself getting anywhere close to, as delightful as it sounded. Characters in cartoons could balloon without effort, but in the real world, I had to deal with a decent metabolism, a balanced diet, food expenses, and a very mundane stomach that couldn't pack away an entire buffet in one sitting.

I realized I hadn't actually checked on my weight in a while. Maybe a month? No, two months at the very least. It might have been even longer than that. It was easy to forget since I'm more of a passive gainer than an active gainer. So, on a whim, I woke the scale with a tap and stepped on.

Looking down gave me a clear view of the curve of my gut and little else. Thankfully, the scale had the courtesy to beep at me once it was finished. I stepped off and couldn't believe what I saw.

406 pounds.

That...that couldn't be right. A smaller number on the right of the display showed what my weight had been the last time I checked: three hundred eighty-nine pounds. Below that was my weight from when I'd received the scale: a mere three hundred one pounds. The display went blank.

"No way," I said under my breath.

I tapped the scale and got back on. When I got off after the beep, the same reading as before stared back at me. 406 pounds.

I wasn't wearing anything. I hadn't had a bite to eat or even a sip of water since waking up. I was as empty as empty could be, yet I weighed four hundred and six pounds. A third check of the scale produced the exact same result.

My eyes watered, and I laughed. I'd never thought four hundred pounds was possible, even as I'd teetered on the edge of three-ninety for weeks. Then again, there'd been a point where I thought three hundred pounds was out of reach. And before that, a point where I never thought I'd gain much weight at all.

Ages ago, I was a scrawny kid who turned into a scrawny teenager. That didn't change in high school, but other things did. I figured out I had an attraction to fatter folk as a high school freshman and then that I liked both men and women as a sophomore. They were revelations I kept bottled up because high school wasn't safe for a queer kid in the '90s, especially one who mainly crushed on overweight former athletes.

A chance late-night internet search in college opened my eyes to a broad community of others with the same passion for pudge as me. I found a site dedicated to the celebration of bigger men and women. In it were stories people had written, fantasies where the protagonists gained incredible amounts of weight in all sorts of ways. I learned words like "feedee" and "feeder" and "gainer." I learned I wasn't alone; that I wasn't the freak I'd feared I was.

I entered the fat admiration community as just that: an admirer. I squirmed at the thought of eventually finding a big, beautiful soulmate, but I never thought for a second about gaining weight myself. Another thing that time changed.

My first gains occurred during college. Nothing significant—just enough pounds to turn me from slim to a little chubby—and certainly not on purpose. Like half of my peers, I gained a taste for beer and ate junk food at the dining hall too often. Working on my master's and preparing to become an English professor gave me plenty of time to establish lousy eating habits that wore down my old, lean physique. Whenever I felt plump, I exercised better, ate out less, and lost some of the weight. Then I gained it all right back. Then lost it, then gained it again, in a cycle that defined my twenties.

But there came a day when I checked my weight on a scale at the gym and saw I'd managed to inch past two hundred pounds, a new record. And just like today, pride followed my surprise. For the first time ever, I imagined myself with a large, round gut, and the thought aroused me. That was when I became a gainer.

Even then, I didn't actively gain. I overindulged plenty and embraced a new, heartier appetite, but I didn't set concrete weight goals for myself. I never have, honestly. I chose to accept whatever weight I accumulated and be happy no matter the size I ended up at.

406 pounds.

I may not have set goals, but I had plenty of fantasies, and four hundred pounds was one of them. I looked at myself in the bathroom mirror and smiled. "Four hundred pounds. Damn, Art, you got fat," I laughed.

The weight caught me off-guard. The changes to my body tended to happen at such a slow and steady rate that I didn't notice them. I only felt huge when I had old pictures of myself to compare to, which showed off how round my face had gotten and the growing curve of my doughy belly.

I ogled myself in the mirror for an embarrassingly long time. And when I finally put on my clothes, I thought about how each piece felt on me. My boxer briefs were snug, without much give between the elastic waistband and my waist. My shorts clung to my thighs tighter than I remembered; I guess I hadn't paid attention to it. Buttoning the shorts was a struggle, but that'd been true of all my pants for the last hundred and fifty pounds. A pleasurable tingle ran up my spine at being able to say that. I'd grown so massive over the years. My shirt fit fine, but it was stretchy athletic wear, my go-to style during summer. It'd only feel tight when it was a size too small.

Thinking about clothes reminded me of my work outfits hiding in the back of the closet, which I hadn't worn since spring semester classes had ended. I wondered if I'd outgrown any of them and made a mental note to try on everything well before the start of the next academic year. As horny as outgrowing my clothes made me, I couldn't teach a class with my shirt buttons threatening to pop off or my belly exposed.

I finished up in the bathroom as Jordan stirred to life in bed. I watched my boyfriend wiggle out from under his sheet fortress and sprawl across the mattress. He was gorgeous even half awake with his mohawk flattened across his eyes. He had a soft chest, modestly curvy hips, and a comically round belly that looked as if he'd swallowed a balloon. He weighed somewhere around three hundred pounds, and his gains gravitated to his ball gut, regardless of how he ate or exercised.

"Morning." Jordan waved at me.

"Morning." I took a deep breath. "Guess who's four hundred pounds?"

The sleep fled Jordan's eyes, and he perked up. "No way."

"The scale says I am." I couldn't contain my smile. My accomplishment still didn't seem real.

Jordan launched himself out of bed and zoomed over to me, wrapping his arms tightly around me. "Oh my God, babe, congratulations!" The zebra pulled up my shirt and placed his hooves on my belly, his fingers sinking into valleys between rolls of fat. He shook vigorously, jiggling my gut up and down, left and right, until my chest wobbled and my teeth clattered. "400 pounds!" he giggled.

"I'm not any bigger than I was last night," I told my boyfriend as he toyed with my middle.

"But last night we didn't know you weighed four hundred pounds."

"406, to be precise." I'm not one to brag about my weight, but saying the number sent an ecstatic surge coursing through me.

Indulge

"I should've known!" Jordan went to his knees and buried his face in my gut.

The loving attention stirred a tent in my shorts. If I'd asked him to take care of it, I'm sure he'd have jumped at the chance to nudge his muzzle lower, but I didn't want to clean up so soon after a shower.

Jordan eventually came up for air. He got to his feet, his smile as wide as mine was. "We need to celebrate!"

"We don't need to make a huge deal about me gaining a few pounds," I insisted.

"This isn't just a few pounds, babe. It's the big four zero zero! It's *literally* a huge deal! We're celebrating, and I'm pampering you, and I'm not taking no for an answer." Jordan tapped my belly and sauntered to the closet.

I admired his bubble butt as he went. "I don't want you to work on your day off, hon."

"Don't think of it as work, think of it as worship," Jordan teased. He squeezed into a pair of skinny jeans that fit like spandex and tried a couple of different shirts. I suspected he was aiming for a look that showed off his curves. Something that'd fluster me. "How about I cook dinner, and we have a toast to your spectacular girth?"

"Sounds wonderful to me."

"I'll put together a shopping list, then." Jordan bounced back to me with a jiggle in his step and a free hoof eager to grope my middle. "But first, we've gotta sate that gargantuan four-hundred-pound appetite of yours. I'm thinking breakfast at the Evergreen Cafe."

The name alone made my stomach rumble. "It's been a while since I've gone." The Evergreen Cafe was a breakfast joint a short drive away, famous for reasonable prices and absurd portions. It was heaven for gainers like us, as enticing as an all-you-can-eat buffet. I'd never refuse an offer to visit. "Let's go."

We left after Jordan tidied up his mohawk, making the short trip in record time. Fate must have wanted to stuff us. Weekends at the Evergreen Cafe were busy and loud, but the wait was always worth it. I actually *was* feeling ravenous by the time we were seated with coffee and menus. Choosing what to order only made me hungrier.

"Everything always looks so good," I complained. I'm fond of food in general—I didn't pass four hundred pounds being a picky eater—but breakfast has always had a special place in my heart. And stomach. I can't think of a single breakfast staple I dislike, and nothing at the Evergreen Cafe was below par. The omelets were always wonderful, the waffles had the ideal hint of crunch, and the pancakes were enormous. But then there were eggs benedict, biscuits and gravy, chicken fried steak, breakfast sandwiches, and a plethora of various breakfast combos. If it were physically possible for me to order one of everything on the menu, I'd do it in a heartbeat. Regret over the bill could wait until I was rolled out of the cafe later.

I forced myself to settle on a loaded omelet since I hadn't ordered one in a while. Jordan was less indecisive than me and had pancakes picked out while I still had half a dozen choices in mind. Once the waitress left with our orders, I felt Jordan's foot rub against mine.

"Feeling hungrier?" Jordan asked.

I looked around us. Every booth and table near us was occupied, so I kept my voice down. "In general?" My boyfriend nodded at me. "No clue. It's not like the, uh, change occurred overnight."

As much as I loved my weight, the average person didn't exactly understand or accept that love, so I refrained from openly talking about it in public. I refused to *hide* my weight, though. No horribly loose clothes that fit over me like a bedsheet. No wearing a shirt while swimming. No avoiding buttons or stripes or anything else that might become visibly strained by bulk.

Jordan was more willing to take his chances with thinly veiled innuendo, but my hushed tone got through to him, and he held off on further questions.

We talked instead of mundane things, like Jordan's boring shift at the bar the night before and how little I looked forward to having to move my office as the English department changed buildings. But even as we blended in at the Evergreen Cafe, thoughts of secret pleasures were never far from my mind. I very well couldn't ignore how the edge of the table dug into my globe of a belly no matter how far I sat back. Or how I felt the squish of my double chin whenever I glanced at my phone. Or the way Jordan's beautiful smile pinched his round cheeks.

Jordan sipped his coffee. "Hmm. I'll have to check the pantry when we get home and see what still needs to be picked up. I'm pretty sure we've already got about half the ingredients."

Indulge

"We *could* always order take-out to make things easier on you," I said, giving my boyfriend one last chance to avoid cooking duties. I was already fairly sure of his answer, though.

"Nope," Jordan replied without hesitation. "You're getting a grand meal fit for the king of the jungle. And if you try to get out of it, I can always tie you up." He winked.

I bit my lip, fending off blissful memories of my wrists loosely tied to a chair and a funnel in my mouth. "I don't think that'll be necessary. Today," I added.

Jordan's smile grew mischievous, and he wiggled in his seat as he typed something on his phone.

I've never known a more energetic person than my boyfriend. It's one of the things I love most about the bubbly zebra. His social battery is endless; he can dive straight into a conversation with strangers while running on little to no sleep. He gets me going places and nudges me along. He's a font of positivity who simultaneously makes me feel my age and a lot younger again, often in the same conversation. I'm sure the fact that he's a decade younger than me has something to do with that.

The teasing threats to bind me ended once our food arrived. Really, it was a feast. My omelet was a cheese-covered egg log sitting atop a plate-spanning bed of hashbrowns. Two thick slices of buttered toast fought the rest of my food for space. Jordan had a veritable solar system of plates before him. Large pancakes dominated the center plate, which was orbited by smaller sides of scrambled eggs, toast, and even more pancakes.

Jordan pushed the side dish of pancakes over to my side of the table with two fingers. "Can't let you starve," he said, as if I didn't have a monster of a meal, to begin with. Having more food shoved my way made me horny, though, so I accepted the pancakes.

I couldn't hold back my hunger anymore and dug in. My appetite shouldn't have been any different from the day before, yet I swore I felt hungrier than ever. I shoveled the food into my mouth, alternating between omelet, hashbrown, and pancake. Fantasies of being trapped at an endless feast flooded my head and drove me to gorge. They were an old favorite of mine. There'd be a table covered in dishes, which pushy servants promptly replenished whenever I finished something. An ominous tune would play in the background to signal the danger I couldn't escape. And I'd magically gain a pound with every bite, ballooning in my seat until I was too fat to reach the food I blindly craved.

It was a blessing to get so much pleasure from an act as simple as overeating.

I'd packed away the omelet and hashbrowns when a thought struck me. I tapped my fork on my plate. "I've been grabbing breakfast here for about fifteen years now." Almost as difficult to believe as my weight. "I always used to leave with a box of leftovers for lunch later. But I know I'm gonna finish every last scrap of breakfast today. I can't even remember the last time I needed a to-go box." Nothing else gave me a more solid feel for how my appetite had increased over the years.

"When you first started taking me here five years ago, I used to need a to-go box, too," Jordan said. "Though my leftovers were enough for lunch *and* dinner."

"It's really been that long?"

Jordan nodded, his mouth full of pancakes. He swallowed them down. "Five beautiful, bountiful years. For both of us."

I couldn't have described it any better way.

We cleaned off our plates, per usual, and made our way back to the car. I finally felt the full extent of my enormous breakfast as I slid into the passenger's seat. My belly was taut as a drum. I may have succeeded in finishing everything on my plate—and the extra one my mischievous boyfriend had snuck my way—but I knew I'd reached my limit while doing so.

Jordan reached over and traced a circle on my gut with his hoof. I leaned back with my eyes closed and groaned. "That feels so good." My boyfriend could turn me into a kitten with a touch, and he never let me forget it. "Maybe there is such a thing as too much, though."

Jordan laughed so hard his hoof jiggled my packed gut. "Nonsense. Every extra calorie you consume makes you rounder and rounder. Every nibble, bite, and gulp matters, babe."

"Is four hundred pounds not big enough? I mean, outside of the gainer community, I barely have any friends who weigh over three hundred pounds." I was the fat friend by default in those groups, an honor that gave me flustered pride.

"I'm sure those four-hundred-pound friends would feel fit and trim beside a five-hundred-pound lion. Only ninety-four pounds to go."

Indulge

I don't know how Jordan made that sound like a small number, but he did, and that got me squirming again. Five hundred pounds was a lot, a fine fantasy. But it wasn't impossible. I'd seen plenty of gainers online who weighed that much and more, some of whom had started their hefty journey at half that size.

I tried imagining myself larger, using memories of those immense gainers as my guide. There were enough superchub felines among them that it wasn't tough. I saw my belly spilling over my lap like a tidal wave of fat. Pecs so pillowy, they pushed at my thick, wobbly arms. A rump so wide I had to seriously consider the durability of any chair I sat in. Double chins and doughy cheeks framed by my mane for all to see.

A quiet moan escaped my lips. "We'll see," I said, unwilling to get my hopes up on a horny whim.

I practically had to lug myself into the house after the ride home. Inside, I caught my breath and wondered how close I was to popping the button on my shorts. Pictures cluttered the space around the entryway, hanging from the walls and propped atop the thin console table. They spanned the decades, from my freshman year of college to a friend's wedding Jordan and I had attended earlier in the year. They also spanned the gradual expansion of our waistlines.

I caught myself staring at a picture of me in the middle of a skateboarding trick from over twenty years before. My mane was painstakingly styled into thick spikes on the top—not covered by a helmet, of course. It took a concussion to convince my cocky younger self he wasn't invincible. I was shirtless because I thought it made me look cooler and a fraction of my current weight because I thought being thin made me happier.

Jordan saw me staring and slid up, sneaking a hoof around my back to grasp my love handle. "Babe, you've absolutely ballooned since college."

Ballooning was the most accurate way to describe my gains—and the horniest. It made it sound so wonderfully easy and got me thinking of funnels and feeding tubes. "The weight snuck up on me," I said, only half-joking.

"What would the old you in that picture say if he saw you now?"

"Nothing coherent. He'd probably cum on the spot." And then grope my belly before rushing off to stuff himself in an effort to make the hallucination come true. I was still shocked by what I'd achieved.

"Relatable," Jordan teased. "God, I can't believe my doughy professor used to be a total skater bro."

"I was a high schooler in the '90s, remember? Every kid on my street had a skateboard and a shaky plywood ramp to do tricks off of." And every last one of us was convinced we were one perfect demo reel away from getting sponsored and going to the X-Games. I spent so much time dreaming about getting rich and famous skateboarding that I was amazed I'd stumbled into a major that turned into a more feasible career.

"You always look pretty good in those old skateboarding videos you show me."

Emphasis on old. "That was a long time ago. I think boarding was the first thing I had to quit because of my weight. I still remember how it gradually grew harder and harder to pull off tricks. My timing was off. I couldn't get quite enough air. I lost my balance more. I miss it, but damn if not being able to ride anymore isn't horny as hell." I doubt I'd have kept skateboarding that long, regardless of how fat I got. My knees wouldn't have put up with it.

"And don't forget it's one less way for you to burn calories and shed the pounds." Jordan jiggled my belly. "The bigger you grow, the harder it is for you to lose all that weight, dough ball."

I bit my lip and moaned as fantasies bombarded me. I leaned my head against Jordan's and kissed him on the cheek. "You are *such* a menace, love. If I'm not careful, you'll fatten me to immobility one day." The funny thing was, I don't think I'd have tried to stop him.

"Just keeping you on your toes," Jordan said. "And eventually off them," he added with a giggle.

We left the memories behind and made our way into the living room. I plopped on the couch and fell right over, taking up most of the space. I yawned really big. "I've only been up for a few hours; how am I already this tired?"

Jordan knelt by me and massaged my belly. "Because your body wants to dedicate all its energy to churning your massive breakfast into beautiful fat. It's not like you're active enough to use that mountain of calories you consumed."

I scoffed. "I get out plenty."

Indulge

"Mhm."

"I do! It's just a matter of finding time between working on lesson plans and attending workshops." Summer was far from a vacation for me. "I hike regularly. And I still take the kayak out on the lake when I can."

"Haven't you been complaining about how tight your kayak's felt lately? I believe you said something about wiggling out of it being more exhausting than paddling. Everything has a weight limit, babe, and you might be about to outgrow that kayak. Are you sure you haven't outgrown it without realizing it?"

I glared playfully at my boyfriend. "You know for a fact I haven't because we went kayaking last weekend." And I needed his help getting out when we came ashore. How did I not realize I'd gained weight?

"A lot can change in a week. I wonder if they make kayaks in bigger sizes?" Jordan asked with a mischievous grin. He knew something I didn't. I suspected he had the answer to his question already.

"Probably," I replied with considerable doubt. Finding the current one had taken some time, and I didn't remember there being much in the way of variety. "You're riling me up talking about this."

Jordan's smile widened. "Oh, trust me, I know." I twitched as the zebra's hoof briefly poked my crotch. "So why don't you take a little nap to cool off? And consider getting in as much kayaking as you can this summer, just in case you have to add it to the rapidly expanding list of pastimes you're too fat to do anymore. Like skateboarding, snowboarding, and cycling." He kissed me before wandering off with a triumphant bounce.

I exhaled, my eyes half-lidded and my gut weighing me down like a wrecking ball. Jordan could push my buttons like no other. I was about to look up kayaks on my phone when I closed my eyes and nodded off.

I remembered a fair bit of my dream from that nap. Naturally, it was heavily influenced by Jordan's teasing and my own kinky desires. In the dream, I was at a store shopping for kayaks. But every time I tried one out, I grew a little fatter and couldn't fit. So the generic employee helping me kept bringing me bigger and bigger kayaks, and I kept growing fatter and fatter. The employee was lugging out a rowboat when sleep abandoned me.

The cheesy aroma of pizza fell over me before I opened my eyes. I rolled onto my side, smiling as I felt my belly roll with me. Two pizza boxes and a couple of two-liter bottles of soda sat on the coffee table.

Jordan walked up carrying paper plates and napkins. "Well darn, I was just about to wake you with a good old belly shake."

I stretched, making sure my shirt rode up and exposed my middle. "It's a good thing I foiled your plot, then."

"As if I'd let your belly get away that easily." Jordan set down the plates and napkins and grabbed the soft sides of my middle. I moaned faintly from the touch alone. Then he shook, jiggling my belly up and down like a fresh mound of dough.

I made a sound somewhere between a purr and a meow, giving in to my feline nature as my boyfriend played with me. "How long did I sleep, anyway?"

"About three hours," Jordan replied, ending his jiggling session with a hearty slap to my belly.

I winced. "I shouldn't have napped that long. It'll throw off my sleep schedule." I couldn't rebound from late-night weekends to early morning weekdays like I could in college. I had to spend a whole week adjusting my sleep schedule to match my class schedule before the school year started.

"The sleep was necessary to churn away all the breakfast so you'd have room for lunch." Jordan snuck in another rub of my gut.

"I can't even think about food right now, not after that huge breakfast," I groaned.

"Is that how you actually feel, or just how you *think* you should feel?"

It was a ridiculous question, but I humored my boyfriend by considering it for a moment, and by God, he was right. Despite passing out feeling utterly stuffed, I woke up not just feeling empty but feeling peckish. "But I just ate," I whined.

"Yeah, five hours ago. We chatted for a while after eating, then chatted some more after getting home, and then you went into a nice, long food coma. It takes a lot to sate a greedy four-hundred-pound tank like yours, babe," Jordan said.

"I don't normally eat this much, though. And it's not like I put on a hundred pounds overnight." I lazily maneuvered myself into a sitting position, adjusting my shirt and pants afterward to keep covered up. Jordan certainly didn't mind seeing more of me, but the habit came in handy in public and in class. The last thing I wanted was to go viral online because a student filmed my belly peeking out of my sweater vest the entire lecture.

"Babe, you're vigilant about a lot of things, but your caloric intake isn't one of them. Which is probably the reason your gains always catch you off-guard. Outside of the big four meals—and don't you dare try to claim that late second dinner you always have is just a snack—you graze on stuff all the time." Jordan's tone was borderline euphoric.

I didn't argue against the second dinner allegations. My meal before bed *had* started as a simple snack, but even I had noticed it growing more substantial. And I did tend to plow through entire bags of chips or cookie sleeves without realizing it. "I guess you're right," I admitted.

"Of course I am. No one knows your appetite better than me," Jordan smirked. "We're front-loading your gluttony today with larger meals, but I bet you'll barely consume more calories than usual. Don't doubt how exceptional you are at stuffing yourself."

I blushed at the compliment. I felt like all I'd done that day was blush and eat, and I was about to eat again. The two pizzas on the coffee table were larges—one for me and one for Jordan. My brain had the audacity to tell me I couldn't finish a large pizza in one sitting, but ravenous desire swept away that notion in seconds. Against the odds, I'd become the sort of glutton I'd admired in gainer stories for decades. It really was a dream come true.

I opened the pizza box before me. It contained a supreme pizza loaded with toppings and extra cheese. "My favorite."

"As if I'd get you anything else. You're more likely to overindulge on food you love, big guy." Jordan laid claim to his own pizza and tossed two slices onto a plate. "God, remember that time I dressed like a pizza delivery guy for that little roleplay we did? I 'forced' my way into the apartment, a menacing feeder intent on stuffing a tubby helpless lion."

I might have choked if I'd taken a bite of pizza a few seconds earlier. We didn't roleplay often outside of the occasional silly text or comment. But the few times we'd dressed up or portrayed characters had been special. And a little embarrassing. But so incredibly hot.

"I had to pretend to be backed into a chair at the dining room table by a sinister zebra half my size. Then I had to pretend I couldn't escape as you fed me slice after slice, all the while threatening to stuff me until I filled the room." For better or worse, I could visualize the scenario in a heartbeat. It was an old favorite I'd eventually commissioned a writer to turn into a story. And of course, there were the drawings. I shifted in place, trying to calm myself so I didn't blow my load while eating lunch.

"Don't forget we acted like every slice I fed you was a whole pizza. It was so cute watching you do an exaggerated wobble to imitate having a swollen belly." Jordan snagged one of the two liters and took a long gulp, which he finished off with a belch.

"It's fun pretending I can eat that much in real life." I couldn't help but notice how swiftly Jordan was wiping out his lunch. He was a slice ahead of me and not slowing down. I thought again about how my boyfriend had looked when we'd performed that silly roleplay session years ago and laughed.

"What's so funny?" Jordan asked between bites, side-eying me.

"I was just remembering how thin you used to be. You were a twink when you pretended to be that delivery guy. A fit twink, with slight abs and everything." Kind of like me during the early days of college.

Jordan flexed his chunky arms and pushed his belly out from under his shirt. "I sculpted my body into peak condition. People used to tell me I could be a model. Then a nefarious lion swooped into my life one day, and his horribly ravenous habits rubbed off on me. Now I'm ballooning out of control, with no hope of ever having washboard abs again!" He ended his tragic tale by chomping down on a third of a slice of pizza in one bite.

"For all the praise you've been piling upon me today, I'm still amazed at how fat you've grown in four years. You were just an eager feeder when we started dating." An energetic twink with a sweet smile who didn't mind dating someone over a decade his senior. My precious zeeb.

"I wasn't kidding when I said your bad habits rubbed off on me," Jordan said. "But I mostly blame the teasing. You joked a lot about pinning me down and feeding me junk food until my abs were buried under pudge. Then some of our online gainer friends started teasing me the same way. And what do you know, the idea of losing control of my diet made me stupidly horny." He shuddered so hard that his belly wobbled a little. "Literally doubling in size was a choice I made of my own free will, but it's so good pretending I was pressured into it and that the only thing stopping me from slimming back down is the bad influences I call my friends."

Jordan sat next to me on the couch and continued glutting. I placed a paw on his belly and rubbed it. "You're a natural gainer, babe. It's a fact you'll eventually balloon past me to become the fattest in the house—hell, the fattest wherever you go." I saw the flustered twist of my boyfriend's muzzle and knew I'd finally turned the tables on him.

"Don't get me thinking about being the 'fat friend' in a social circle where weighing three hundred pounds is the definition of slim. It's too fucking hot." Jordan wiggled.

As my wonderful boyfriend had insisted, I had enough space in my stomach to fit the large pizza and two-liter he'd ordered, though I had to force the last slice down. For the second time that day, I was utterly engorged. While the sleepiness returned to nip at me, I was determined not to pass out and throw my sleep schedule into shambles.

So I propped myself up, undid the strained button of my shorts, and found cooking shows to watch on TV. Despite my considerable heft, I wouldn't consider myself much of a couch potato. When I was younger, there was always something outside for me to do, from skateboarding to hiking to merely existing with friends. As I grew older—and fatter—I started to read and write more. TV was a sporadic treat reserved for relaxing nights with the boyfriend.

But that didn't stop me from imagining spending most of my days parked on the couch while my waistline swelled rampantly from a sedentary lifestyle. Some days off were meant to be spent horny.

My belly felt a little less like a doughy boulder by the time Jordan's voice freed me from the grip of a cupcake competition show.

"Dinner's ready, babe! I hope you're ready for a proper fattening."

"I'll be there in a second!" I shouted towards the dining room.

"You sure you're mobile enough to?" Jordan shouted back.

"I'm going to sit on you if you keep this up!" I laughed. Sitting up *did* take more effort than expected, but I blamed that on my hearty lunch and hunkering down on the couch rather than my weight.

Jordan darted between the kitchen and the dinner table, loading the center with large platters and bowls. The zebra had made a little of everything, cooking a personal buffet for us. There was ham, corn, mashed potatoes, scalloped potatoes, mac and cheese, macaroni salad, a casserole, butter rolls, and apple pie. Soda, beer, and water made up the drink selection. We were only short turkey and stuffing for Thanksgiving in July.

The full extent of dinner astonished me. Jordan had shooed me away any time I'd offered to help and had refused to give a single hint as to what he was preparing. "Babe, you didn't need to do all of this."

"I didn't need to, I *wanted* to, silly." Jordan set the table for two. "It took every ounce of restraint in me to resist turning this into a full-on feeding session. Bindings, tubes, funnels—the works! I only held back because I didn't have quite enough time."

The thought of being tied down and stuffed by Jordan made me feel lightheaded.

"You're the worst. I love *you* so much." I wrapped my arms around Jordan and kissed him over and over. My eyes watered. "Thank you so much for dinner."

"You can thank me by eating every last bite," he said.

"Or I can feed you everything here so we can celebrate you reaching four hundred pounds." I batted my boyfriend's belly and got him blushing.

"But what if I get too fat to cook?" Jordan giggled. "My ball gut already gets in the way from time to time."

"We'll just have to make do with takeout. It'll be worth it to stretch those stripes. And it's not like you'd be able to stop me." I added a growl to my voice, which I knew would work up Jordan. Sure enough, he bit his lip and wiggled, briefly rendered speechless.

"Less chatting, more eating. The food's getting cold," Jordan insisted.

We settled in and passed around dishes, loading our plates to the brim. Then we dove into the exceptional feast Jordan had cooked.

Once again, I happily stuffed myself to the very brim, intent on not leaving any leftovers. I savored the dedication and love Jordan had put into every bite. Nothing beat his cooking. I loaded up on seconds without hesitation the moment I finished my first plate. Jordan followed suit. I'll admit I pushed myself to my limit that meal. I embodied the mindset of the characters in my gainer fantasies, bottomless pits who could effortlessly clear out buffets. I ignored the fullness in my stomach and instead daydreamed of my belly ballooning across my lap as it became a food-filled globe.

I suspected Jordan's mind drifted to similar horny thoughts as we embraced the pleasures we typically hid from others. There was a tremendous joy in having someone you could be your true self in front of, whom you didn't have to hide any aspect of your being from. With Jordan, I could express my adoration of the larger side of life without fear of judgment. I could be as fat and gluttonous as I wanted to be. That was precious to me.

The few words spoken during dinner were in praise of the cooking. There wasn't time to talk with so much good food to glut on.

We didn't stop eating until we'd picked the expansive spread clean. Not a single bite remained of the grand dinner. Huffs and groans were all I heard at the table. I'd eaten so much it almost hurt to breathe, but I had no regrets. I rested my paws on my taut belly. Maybe I was just being optimistic, but I swore my shirt looked and felt tighter.

"Dinner was perfect," I purred. "I'm not sure I can get up after that."

"So you'll be helpless when I decide to bust out the funnel, then?" Jordan grinned, his eyes half-closed.

"As if you're in any better shape. I saw how much food you shoveled into your maw."

"Well damn, you got me there." Jordan winced from giggling. "Then again, I don't need to hold you captive to make you balloon. You're like a free-range gainer, always waddling back to the coop for more food." The stuffed zebra lugged himself out of his chair with some effort. While Jordan was lighter than me, he was far from slim and had admirably kept up with my gorging. He started gathering dishes.

"Let me handle that, babe. You already cooked for us; I won't make you clean for us." I tried to stand but immediately fell back to my seat with a grunt. My belly ached, and my body had no desire to move.

Jordan snorted and wagged a finger at me. "Don't you dare. I spent too much time cooking to have my favorite glutton waste precious calories doing work." He moved like he was trudging through a foot of snow, but at least he could move.

"I picked a winner," I told him.

"This winner's gonna make you immobile by the time you're fifty."

"Saying it won't make it true." I didn't see myself ever growing that fat. I didn't really think I *wanted* to be that fat. There was a vast difference between four or five hundred pounds and literally being too fat to move. But my weight preferences had changed considerably over the decades, and who was to say they wouldn't change again? "Honestly, I'm blessed with what I've got." I exhaled. "Four hundred pounds." *Four hundred and six pounds*, the proud gainer in the back of my head pointed out. Probably more after today's feasting.

"To four hundred pounds," Jordan declared. "And a hundred more. And a hundred after that," he snickered.

I raved about Jordan's cooking as he gradually cleared the table. He acted as if he'd won a Michelin star and thanked his ravenous taste-tester for helping him perfect his dishes. He also toyed with my belly as he cleaned, getting me to moan.

The last traces of the wonderful feast went away, leaving only our engorged bellies to remember it by. The inevitable food coma loomed over me. I yawned. "I can't thank you enough for dinner, love."

"Anything to pack you with calories." Jordan leaned in and kissed my middle.

I couldn't hold back the yawns. "I've done nothing today, yet I'm still exhausted."

Jordan rested his head on my shoulder. "Nonsense. You ate breakfast. And lunch. And of course, dinner. Your schedule was as packed as your gut."

I winced in anticipation of a belly smack, but Jordan merely traced a circle on my gut with a finger. "You gorged plenty yourself. Maybe even more than I did." I snuck in a kiss before he could yawn. "I think it's time for bed."

"Mhm." Jordan nodded.

We meandered to the bedroom and went through our pre-sleep routines with all the energy you'd expect from a pair of freshly engorged gainers. I sprawled on the bed once I'd disrobed. Jordan crawled in after me and doted on my swollen middle, running his hooves all over it. The gentle attention felt so great; he didn't poke or prod too hard. I pawed around until I found his belly and returned the favor with soft rubs.

"Congrats on passing four hundred, babe," Jordan murmured. His eyes were closed, and he was half asleep. I wasn't much better.

"Thanks, babe."

"I can't wait till we celebrate you passing five hundred. Maybe I'll order a cake when it happens." Jordan let out pleasant little giggles.

"Only if I get to feed it all to you. I can't let you fall behind." I thought of Jordan a hundred pounds fatter, then two hundred, then three hundred. I thought of us rounding out together, mutually fattened through years of

Indulge

loving gluttony. I thought of how lucky I was to be with someone who shared my passion for fat, who fed and encouraged and pampered me.

"Love you, babe," I said, squeezing Jordan's adorable belly.

A lazy hoof squeezed my belly right back. "Love you."

Drinks at the Sidebar

Faux

Dario leaned against the wall outside the Sidebar, studying the sole straggler in the pack of near-empty American Spirits before fishing it out. The Indian wolf fumbled for his lighter, the chill of Atlanta in mid-December biting at his cheeks. He managed to summon a timid flame before a gust of wind snuffed his Bic out. "God damn it," he muttered under his breath.

"You look like you could use a light," a sonorous voice murmured through the fog, recalling a late-in-life William Conrad.

"Please." Dario turned his head and was immediately confronted by an enormous tiger with a frame like the front end of a diesel locomotive. While the wolf was generally the tallest attorney in any given room, the tiger put him to shame. The warmth radiating from his sheer bulk was like a space heater that fended off the nippy air as he closed the distance between them. Dario extended his cigarette with a grateful smile. "I seem to have misplaced my Zippo."

"A pretty boy should never light his own cigarette." The tiger chuckled, a deep rumble that vibrated through his ample belly. His suit was expensive and clearly custom, stitched to frame his plush chest and the heavy swell of his gut. Dario couldn't help but stare as the tiger adjusted his jacket with slow, practiced ease, letting the fabric stretch and settle across his round middle as if to draw his eye. "May I?"

The tiger was enormous, easily clearing a head taller than Dario and twice as wide through the chest. Thick arms stretched the sleeves of his jacket, and his belly—firm, plush, and unabashed—shifted subtly with each breath, like a living monument to appetite. Gold glinted just beyond his shirt cuff: an Omega Seamaster Aqua Terra, its dial big enough for *hors d'oeuvres*. Everything about him radiated presence, a cultivated grandeur that felt less like vanity and more like gravity.

"P-please do," Dario squeaked, ears twitching as his free paw toyed with the hem of his button-down.

Gracefully flicking open a golden lighter, the tiger summoned a jet of blue-white flame that rivaled the glow of the nearby streetlamps. Holding the ramrod-straight fire in front of Dario's muzzle, he used his large paw as a windbreak for just long enough for Dario to puff his cigarette to life.

"Thanks. I never quite got into vaping or whatever the cubs are doing these days," Dario said, turning away to hide his blush.

"It's rare to find someone who appreciates the simple pleasure of a good cigarette anymore," the tiger replied, retrieving a gleaming Sobranie Black Russian from a gold case. He was an apex predator, his size as much a reflection of his place in the pecking order as the watch on his wrist. "Plus, it makes for a good excuse to sneak away from your desk and make new friends, right?"

"Right." Dario chuckled softly, a pleasant warmth spreading through his chest as the familiar nicotine buzz kicked in. "I suppose we're a dying breed, aren't we? Just two old-timers clinging to their vices."

"Mmm." The tiger took a long drag before exhaling, smoke forming a hazy halo around his muzzle. Dario judged him to be in his mid-forties from the touch of gray present in the thick stripes on his cheeks. "I'm Casimir, by the way," he added with a soft smile.

"It's a pleasure. I'm Dario." The neon glow of the Sidebar's "*OPEN*" sign spilled out onto the sidewalk, casting an intriguing green hue across Casimir's muzzle. "Do you come here often?"

"Oh, yes." Casimir's smile widened, revealing faintly coffee-stained teeth. The pavé diamond studs in his ears twinkled as he turned to fix his gaze on the wolf. "It's my usual after-work haunt," he said, voice low and velvety.

They shared the silence for a moment, luxuriating in the smoke-filled air that gently swirled around them. Taking a final drag that scorched the tip of his tongue, Dario let his cigarette fall gracefully onto the paving stones before grinding it out with the heel of his wingtips. "Would you care for a drink, then?"

"Hrm…" Casimir glanced down at his watch before nodding in agreement. With a quick flick of his paw, he extinguished his own cigarette and tugged at the lapels of his suit jacket, straightening them with practiced ease. "I suppose one drink couldn't hurt."

"After you," Dario said, sweeping one paw in front of him like a maître d'.

Casimir sauntered ahead, Dario close behind, past the Sidebar's red-brick façade and into a sleek interior with a curved bar to the right and half a dozen red leather booths lining the opposite wall. The wolf caught whiffs of sharp-sweet margarita mix as he passed the server station, several brightly-colored drinks with salted rims sitting ready on the dark countertop.

Once they reached the booth in the furthest corner, Casimir struggled to cram his sheer bulk into its tight confines. The tiger huffed and puffed, his dress shirt straining against the vast expanse of his belly. After he finally managed to settle in, Casimir let out a contented sigh, his plush form taking up most of the available space. Dario felt a stirring in his sheath at the sight.

Dario slid into the seat perpendicular to Casimir, the tiger's rolls squishing up against his side like well-kneaded dough. Despite the dim lighting, the wolf's muzzle glowed from a heady mixture of nicotine and arousal. He skimmed the drink menu's offerings with feigned nonchalance, trying to distract himself from the electric tension coursing through his thighs. "So, what's good here?"

"Do you like your margaritas strong?" Casimir replied, his amber eyes gleaming with a hint of mischief. "They don't go light on the tequila here."

"I've never been one to shy away from a double," Dario replied, voice laced with anticipation. Casimir's masculine musk saturated the space between them, erotic pheromones sending the wolf's tail into a fit of involuntary wagging. Dario's ears folded, and he cleared his throat to try to keep his composure. "I didn't manage to get through law school on just Bud Light and coffee alone, you know."

Casimir's velvety laugh filled the air. "Good. I prefer everything full strength."

Leaning back in the plush booth, Dario watched as Casimir summoned a server with a flick of his enormous paw. Dario couldn't help but be enchanted by how the tiger's sheer girth lent authority to even the smallest movement. Heart pounding, he shifted awkwardly in his seat as blood surged into his nether regions.

"Two margaritas with Sauza Silver and sub the sweet-and-sour mix for Grand Marnier, please," Casimir told the server, a young cheetah with a sleek black-dyed mane and an air of feigned indifference. Still, even he faltered for half a beat under the tiger's gaze—ears twitching, posture straightening—before jotting down the order with brisk efficiency. "And half a lime on the side, if you'd be so kind."

Once the server scurried away, the tiger leaned forward, his warm breath lightly caressing Dario's cheek ruffs. His eyes wandered, catching on the scent of grease and spice in the air. Casimir gazed intently at the steaming basket of chicken tenders being toted to the booth behind them, fries spilling over the sides of the parchment paper liner.

"I didn't come here for dinner," Casimir said, his gaze flicking back with a hungry glint. "But I wouldn't say no to a bite right about now. You?"

"Wasn't hungry a second ago," the wolf murmured, eyes drifting to the tantalizing appetizer at the next table. "But now? Yeah, I could eat."

A few moments later, their drinks arrived in oversized glasses rimmed with coarse salt that caught the light. The margarita was smooth on the first sip, with the tequila's bite lingering under the citrus.

"Oh, and while you're here...we'll take one of everything from the wings and bites, please—and two baskets of tenders tossed in Cajun Parmesan sauce." As Casimir leaned forward, the front of his shirt gaped just enough to show his stomach pressing against the fabric.

The server nodded, jotting without comment—no surprise, just a flick of amusement at the corner of his muzzle—then slid away toward the kitchen.

"'One of everything,' huh?" Dario asked once the cheetah was gone, eyes dropping to the gentle bow of the table under Casimir's middle. "Is that your usual?"

Casimir's whiskers tilted in a grin. "Big tiger, big appetite," he rumbled. "I like living large—and I don't want my appetite to deprive you."

He settled back, but the curve of his belly still met the table with an easy, unbothered confidence, as if the evening had already decided on indulgence. As they waited for their food, the air between them crackled with unspoken desire. Dario couldn't help but steal glances at Casimir's voluptuous physique, his Rudderbutts growing tight at the idea of sliding his paws beneath the vast expanse of linen and burying his paw pads in the tiger's flabby rolls. Breath hitching, heat flooded Dario's cheeks as he noted a telltale spot of precum forming on the front of his khakis.

With a knowing smile, Casimir reached for his half lime and squeezed it over his margarita, manicured claws working every drop from the emerald fruit. Discarding the desiccated lime, the tiger took a sip with controlled grace. "You'll have to forgive me. Most mixes don't seem to include quite enough of a sour kick for my taste."

Dario's mind slipped into a lustful haze as he watched Casimir's lips wrap around the rim of the glass. The way the tiger's tongue flicked out to catch the errant droplets clinging to the rim kept arousal buzzing in Dario's sheath. It was easy to imagine that hungry tongue rooting around at the base of his lupine shaft, firm knot resting on the ample padding of Casimir's triple chin.

"How about yours? Hopefully it's not too strong?" Casimir asked.

Dario took another sip of his drink, the sharp tequila scorching his throat as he swallowed. A hint of bitterness lingered on his palate, a reminder that the bartender didn't skimp on the Sauza Silver. The wolf's muzzle dried up as he hunted for the right words. "A little...but somehow, I don't mind," Dario murmured, voice husky with desire.

"Mrm...now try it with food," Casimir murmured, eyes lighting up at the sight of the cheetah returning with platters piled high with deep-fried delights expertly balanced on both arms. The tiger's belly audibly rumbled as the tantalizing and garlicky aroma of richly-sauced tenders filled the air. "Shared indulgence is always more pleasurable."

Their fingertips brushed as they reached for the same alluring piece, sending an electric jolt up Dario's forearm. His gaze darted up to Casimir's plush lips, imagining how they'd taste with a hint of lime and garlic lingering on their surface like a layer of Chapstick. Meeting each other's eyes, Casimir sliced the deep-fried morsel straight down the middle with his index claw.

"M-mrmph!" Explosive flavor accompanied by surprising heat detonated in Dario's muzzle, his enjoyment heightened by the tiger's satisfied chuffs. "God damn, that hits the spot."

"You're...mrm...telling me," Casimir grunted, tearing into the nearest platter. Dario's heart pounded as he watched Casimir stuff his muzzle with shrimp cocooned in oil-soaked breading. The tiger shot him a seductive smile as spiced garlic cream sauce trickled out of the edge of his muzzle like the aftermath of a stallion's cumshot. "Though something tells me your grin isn't just from an excellent meal."

Crimson warmth spread beneath the wolf's cheeks as he squirmed under Casimir's hungry gaze. "Well, that's the second time that you've made me blush," Dario replied. Reaching for a heaping plate of oysters on the half shell, he took one in each paw and greedily slurped down the salty morsels inside.

"Is that right?" As Casimir stuffed the appetizers into his muzzle as though his life depended on it, Dario swallowed hard, his throat dry and tongue twitching. Casimir's every movement, every word, and every bite of food seemed to be loaded with seductive intent. "Do you need me to dial it back?"

"N-no," Dario replied, biting his bottom lip as he reached down to adjust his swollen cock. While the piping hot food gradually eased his hunger, it did nothing to stem the bubbling desire rising in his loins. "Please, as you were."

"Mrm…that I can manage." Casimir's eyes gleamed as he impishly licked his lips, purposely dragging his tongue through globs of sticky sauce left behind by his voracious chewing.

Catching a whiff of sharp and smoky-sweet pheromones radiating from the tiger, Dario was overcome with need. He reached for a small tower of salmon bites, desperately trying to distract himself from the sensation of his quivering head being crushed-up against his fly.

"Don't forget to stay hydrated; that ice water of yours is looking awfully lonely over there," Casimir murmured playfully.

"R-right." Dario buried his muzzle in the plastic glass while Casimir's voracious appetite relentlessly teased him. Each muzzle-filling bite and sharp smack of his lips pushed Dario to keep up, the platters between them emptying at an alarming pace. "Are you getting full?"

Casimir chuckled, amber eyes twinkling with amusement. "Far from it," he replied, picking up the last of the deep-fried shrimp and slathering it in an ocean of sauce. "This was delicious, of course, but it takes more than just a *few* appetizers to satiate me."

"Well, let me make sure you don't go hungry." Staring at the wait station until he caught the cheetah's gaze over top of his iPhone, Dario summoned him over. In that moment, the wolf wanted nothing more than to see Casimir's soft and heavy gut crushing up further against the table between them. "My friend would like the Sidebar Burger, triple patties, and an extra-large side of fries. Put it on my check, if you would."

"Are you sure?" Casimir asked, the departing waiter's jingling keyring quickly drowned out by the dull roar of the bartender whipping up another batch of frozen margaritas. "I can always charge it to my tab."

"I'm sure," Dario replied with a wink. The wolf squared his shoulders in order to steal a glimpse at the alluring bulge in the front of the tiger's suit pants. "I did just get Uncle Sam's annual raise, so I have a little extra from my last paycheck burning a hole in my pocket."

"That's mighty kind of you," Casimir replied, flirtatiously licking his lips. The tiger reached down and adjusted his trousers, the bulge cresting as he brushed his paw pads across the silky fabric. "I'll make sure that you don't end the night without being *completely* stuffed as well. How's that sound?"

Dario's paws trembled with hunger despite a stomach crammed full of greasy appetizers. The thought of feeding Casimir's insatiable appetite while watching his belly expand with every eager bite sent a lascivious throb through Dario's needy cock. "Perfect," he replied with an excited shake of his muzzle.

Not a moment later, the cheetah returned with Casimir's towering plate, still steaming from the kitchen's hurried effort to keep pace with his hunger. Piled high with crispy onions, fried pickles, and bacon, only two bamboo chopsticks prevented the monstrous burger from collapsing under its own weight. Dario's knees bounced restlessly as damp heat bloomed through the front of his underwear.

"Mmm!" Stuffing his muzzle, Casimir let the rich juices dribble down his triple chin as the alluring scent of grilled beef and melted cheese wafted through the air. Dario bit his bottom lip, trembling as he watched the wide, round outline of the tiger's gut expanding with each gluttonous bite. "This is delicious. Would you care for a fry?"

Dario's breath hitched as he reached out to plunk a fry from the mountainous pile. The tiger's fingers, coated in a thick mélange of sauce and grease, brushed against the back of his paw as he reached for a fallen pickle. Dario dropped the fry in surprise as an electric jolt shot through his wrist. "Oh! My bad."

Indulge

"Need some help?" Casimir's lips curled into a teasing smile as he picked up the fallen fry and held it loosely between his fingers like a half-smoked cigarette. Their eyes locked just long enough to stoke the fire building in Dario's core, the wolf leaning in until his muzzle hovered inches above the tiger's chubby fingers.

"Mrm...yes, please." Dario inhaled sharply, hoovering the fry into his muzzle. A shockwave of salt washed over his tongue as his sheath throbbed sympathetically. Then, succumbing to his baser instincts, he brushed his tongue across the matted fur on the tiger's fingers, catching a hint of his masculine musk alongside the garlicky sauce. "Now that's a sauce worth savoring," the wolf murmured.

"Then I do believe seconds are in order," Casimir replied, skimming his fingers across the bowl of dipping sauce like a stone across a watersmooth-silver pond. With deliberate ease, he raised them to Dario's muzzle and slipped the sauced digits past his lips. Dario's cock buzzed with the energy of an electric eel as the tiger's fingers melted onto his tongue. The intoxicating blend of earthy spices danced across his palate, mingling with Casimir's musk and driving him wild with desire.

"T-thank you." As his hunger grew, Dario could barely contain himself. He wanted to ravish the tiger right then and there, to feel Casimir's bloated belly against his skin and bury himself in an expanse of soft fur and infinitely pliable fat. Dario licked his lips as he savored the ghost of Casimir's touch, still lingering on his palate like fine perfume.

As Casimir tore into the rest of his burger with grease glistening on his muzzle, Dario could practically see his girth expanding with every bite. The tiger's belly pressed harder into the edge of the table, his waistband visibly struggling to contain the growing swell. Dario's cock throbbed at the sight, at the idea of that straining dress shirt pulled tighter across a gut growing heavier by the mouthful. He imagined running his paws over those soft, rolling hills, each curve a decadent offering begging to be adored.

"Did that hit the spot?" Dario asked as the tiger took a final, gut-swelling bite. A blissful chuff rumbled from Casimir's chest as he leaned back, settling the full weight of his stuffed belly onto his thick thighs as each fold of soft fat formed a plush, natural cushion. Dario was only a breath away from creaming his Rudderbutts, undone by the sheer ecstasy of imagining Casimir growing heavier by the minute. Desperate to steady himself, he looked away and downed the last of his margarita in a futile attempt to cool the heat clawing through his body.

"Oh, yes." Casimir smacked his lips before dabbing at his muzzle with a fresh napkin. After a contented belch, the tiger slackened his belt by a few notches, the force of his expanding gut threatening to rend the polished Italian leather apart. Despite having just eaten a burger the size of Dario's head, he immediately moved to polish off the remaining fries. "But now I could really use a digestif to settle my stomach."

"Do you know a place?" Dario asked, heat building beneath his collar as though a sauna were hidden in the valley between his pecs. "I don't think the Sidebar specializes in *pousse-cafés*."

Casimir cocked an eyebrow, a sly grin spreading across his muzzle. "Know a place?" he echoed, his voice low and sultry. "How about mine? I have a bottle of Bunnahabhain 25-Year Scotch that I've been meaning to crack open. Just been waiting for the right company."

"You're really too kind," Dario said, patting his now-taut tummy. He handed the server his card with a trembling paw—to cover the burger, just as promised—while his gaze remained fixed on the tantalizing roundness of Casimir's gut. The tiger, meanwhile, slipped a few folded bills into the check holder to settle the rest of the tab before slowly sliding out of the booth. "Please, let me lend you a paw."

After steadying himself as an anchor, Dario drew Casimir in close. His paws slipped beneath the tiger's suit jacket, fingers brushing the soft curve of his love handles—a touch that lingered just long enough to betray its intent. Casimir let out a contented chuff and guided Dario's paws forward, encouraging him to fully cup the warm underside of his belly.

The weight of it in his hands—the plush give, the radiant heat beneath layers of fine tailoring—sent a tremor through Dario's spine. His breath hitched, cock throbbing against the confines of his underwear as his thumbs slowly traced the rise of Casimir's belly, reverent and hungry.

Casimir let out a low, velvety purr, leaning into the touch. "While I do appreciate the affection," he murmured, voice rich with amusement, "we'd best be off before things get too steamy. Though I think I've got a pretty good idea of what you're after now."

Indulge

"Uh...should I grab my car?" Dario asked, holding the door open as the tiger grabbed a pawful of chocolate-covered dinner mints on the way out. "I'm parked in the garage just down the block."

"No, my condo isn't far at all," Casimir replied. "I like the convenience of living downtown—close to the courthouse and even closer to the good food. Everything a gluttonous tiger could want, all within walking distance."

"I certainly see the appeal," Dario said, falling into step beside him. The crisp night air did little to cool the heat simmering beneath his collar as his gaze locked on the hypnotic sway of Casimir's belly with every step. Fortunately, they didn't have far to go—a single block brought them to the base of a Gothic Revival skyscraper.

"This is really something. You live here?" Dario murmured, trying to steady the tremor in his voice. Beyond the lobby, a neo-Gothic atrium stretched upward like a cathedral, its arched windows climbing toward a vaulted ceiling bathed in eerie crimson light. Casimir's presence seemed to fill the space completely, his steady footsteps echoing like distant thunder as they crossed the marble floor. "It's like stepping into another century."

"They film movies here for that very reason," Casimir said, taking Dario's paw and guiding him past an eagle-eyed concierge toward the elevator bank. He tapped a key fob against the security panel, then pressed the button for the penthouse. As the elevator began its smooth ascent, the erotic tension between them thickened, heavy as the fog that had been creeping across Atlanta all evening.

The tiger's apartment was a study in curated indulgence—plush leather furniture and sleek mid-century modern décor set against the warmth of antique mahogany floors. Along the far wall, a bank of tall windows framed a panoramic view of Atlanta's skyline, the lights of Mercedes-Benz Stadium glittering in the distance. Dario barely noticed. His eyes were locked on the hypnotic sway of Casimir's belly as the tiger led him toward the bedroom, each luxuriant jiggle sending a fresh pulse through his aching cock.

Dario swallowed hard as Casimir unbuttoned his shirt with a sly smirk. With a torso built like a cask of Amontillado and the sensual lower curve of his belly peeking out from beneath his undershirt, the tiger was everything he could possibly desire. The opulent rolls cascading down his chest rumbled with each heaving breath. "Do you like what you see?" Casimir asked.

"God… yes." Dario's tongue felt thick in his muzzle, his cock pulsing with unrestrained need. Lust flared hot in his core as his gaze followed the decadent swells and dips of Casimir's rolls. "Uhm…I could use that digestif right about now."

"You got it." With practiced ease, the tiger bared his belly to Dario, exposing the dense chub that padded every inch of his abdomen. Slick with sweat, his musky fur barely concealed the layer of fat that encompassed his torso like the glittering rings of Saturn. Sliding over to a globe bar in the corner, Casimir pulled out two Waterford glasses and filled them with a few fingers of amber liquor. "Please, enjoy."

Clinking the glasses together, Dario shot Casimir a soft smile as he savored notes of fig and leather with a long, smoky finish. The intoxicating scent of the tiger's Scotch-tinged breath filled Dario's nostrils as pleasant alcohol-warmth spread through his muzzle. Casimir's fur, stretched taut over his prominent rolls, glistened with sweat like beads of icing on a sunbaked cake.

A low ache built in the wolf's loins, curling tighter with every breath. The taste of the Scotch, the haze of heat, the visual weight of Casimir's indulgence—it all converged like gravity in Dario's gut. His cock strained against his waistband, desperate and leaking, and he felt his restraint slipping with every heartbeat.

"You're…" He swallowed hard, voice low and rough. "You're fucking beautiful."

Casimir tilted his head slightly, amber eyes gleaming. "Am I now?"

Dario nodded, breath shallow. "You are. I've never wanted anyone like this. I want to touch you…all of you. No, nix that—I want to get *lost* in you."

Dario set his glass down with a soft clink and stood, paws trembling as he stepped toward the tiger. "I want to taste your sweat. Feel your belly against me. I want to straddle you, take every inch, and ride all of your glorious heft until I'm utterly spent."

Casimir's smile deepened, slow and knowing, as he rose from his chair with the deliberate grace of a predator who knew exactly how much space he took up and how much Dario wanted every inch of it. "Careful, pup," he purred, voice low and silken. "Say things like that, and I just might give you everything you're begging for… and then some."

Indulge

"Good," Dario breathed, his muzzle now inches from Casimir's chest, the heat of the tiger's body washing over him. "Then take me. I want to bury myself in that plush belly of yours while you fuck me senseless." The words tumbled out raw and unfiltered—pure hunger, laid bare.

Casimir chuckled, a low rumble that vibrated through his entire body and rattled the pendulum of the mechanical clock on the nearby dresser. With unhurried ease, he peeled off his undershirt and let it fall aside, baring the full breadth of his striped torso. His belly drooped into the space between his legs, coming to rest just above the prominent bulge in his underwear. "Are you sure?"

"Never been surer." Dario placed a tender paw just below the tiger's navel, exhaling slowly as he luxuriated in the warmth of Casimir's plush chub. With only a little pressure, his fingers disappeared into the soft, squishy expanse, completely swaddled by layers of fuzz-covered fat. "Oh...oh, fuck."

His paw pads settled on the tiger's soft and sensitive underbelly. Giving it a gentle squeeze, he savored the rolling slope of Casimir's belly—each succulent ripple of fat a testament to a life lived richly, shamelessly. The tiger's paw moved with practiced ease, hooking his thumbs into the waistband of his underwear and sliding them down to free the thick, pulsing length beneath. While the soft overhang of his tummy partially obscured the base, there was no mistaking the sheer presence of his engorged cock—veiny, barbed, and already twitching with anticipation. A lascivious smirk curled across Casimir's muzzle as he caught the widening of Dario's eyes. "Well? Go on, slick me up. You asked for this."

Breath hitching as he complied, Dario reached for the half-empty bottle of Astroglide on the nightstand beside a few crumpled bags of gummy bears. Dario struggled to contain himself as he rubbed the greasy gel onto Casimir's straining girth, paw trembling with anticipation. "How's this?" Dario asked, the sheer magnitude of the tiger's shaft making him easily the largest beast the wolf had the honor of bottoming for.

"Good. Now bend over," Casimir ordered, pushing forward like a living wall until Dario was braced against the comforter draped across the bed. Clenching the sheets, the wolf moaned as the tiger squirted a hefty dollop of frigid lubricant onto his tailhole. Experienced fingers worked methodically to spread the goo around Dario's tight entrance while his tail flagged up and out of the way. "There's a good pup."

Dario grunted, breath catching in his throat as Casimir's low whispers urged him to relax. The tiger nuzzled against one of his taut cheeks while Dario's lupine cock dribbled precum onto the bed below. Casimir's lips followed the curve of Dario's spine, planting soft, reverent kisses along each vertebra. Below, his thick fingers pressed inward with slow, deliberate precision, stretching Dario open with a steady rhythm that spoke of a mélange of experience and lust.

"That's... that's me," Dario whispered, voice trembling.

Moonlight filtered through the tinted windows, casting a soft silver sheen across Casimir's immense form as he climbed onto the bed. With his radiant smile and bountiful belly, he looked every bit the living echo of Budai—equal parts joy and indulgence. "Now, come here," he rumbled, drumming his paws against his gut with a deep, resonant *thwump* that seemed to vibrate through the bedframe.

Dario grinned, the prospect of burying himself in the overstuffed tiger impossible to resist. Heaving himself upright, the wolf scrambled into Casimir's lap like an eager Bichon Frisé. With a low purr like the idle of a well-tuned engine, the tiger wrapped his paws around Dario's waist to guide him into place. Dario bit his bottom lip, moaning as his sensitive head was pressed up against the tiger's voluptuous rolls.

"Ready?" Casimir asked, his voice low and rich with promise.

"More than ready," Dario gasped, his body trembling with anticipation as he squirmed atop Casimir's ample girth. His tongue flicked across his lips, tail wagging in eager, uncontrollable bursts at the sheer promise of what was to come.

"Nice and easy now," Casimir murmured, his voice a soothing rumble as he cupped Dario's hips in his steady paws. He guided the trembling wolf downward, slowly easing his entrance onto the glistening head of his cock. Dario gasped as the engorged tip breached his tailhole, the slick barbs gliding over his inner ring like the textured surface of a puffer ball—strange, soft, and electrifying. Their eyes met, locked in a raw, breathless gaze as inch by inch, Casimir's thick shaft disappeared into him, claimed by taut, yielding muscle.

Indulge

"Mmm… there we go," Casimir purred, his eyes fluttering shut as he sank deeper. The upper curl of Dario's tail brushed against his trunk-like thigh, twitching with every pulse of pleasure. "You're taking me beautifully."

Clinging to the tiger's plush fur, Dario gave in to the decadent weight pressing down on him, each breath hitching as his body stretched to accommodate the slow, deliberate thrusts. His cock throbbed with every inch that sank deeper, nerves singing with pleasure. "Fill me up," he growled, voice ragged. "I want to be just as stuffed as you are."

"Go on, show me how bad you want it," Casimir grunted, his heavy paws clamping onto Dario's hips to guide him into motion. Silhouetted against the moonlit cityscape, the wolf began to rise and fall in a steady rhythm on Casimir's enormous cock, his tail swishing with each driving thrust. Muscles strained and flexed with the effort, the silver light tracing every ridge and contour of his toned form. "Mrmph…just like that."

The bed groaned under their combined weight as Casimir pressed Dario firmly into the mattress, pinning him against the vast swell of his gut. The wolf let out a guttural cry as the tiger's cock filled him to the hilt, barbs dragging deliciously across his inner walls and leaving sparks of torment and pleasure in their wake. Ecstatic moans echoed through the room as they fell into rhythm, each rocking thrust underscored by the heavy slap of flesh on flesh. Casimir's sheer mass bore down on him, overwhelming, inescapable—every nerve in Dario's body bent toward him.

"F-fuck… squeeze harder," Casimir gasped, his voice dipping into a timbre both feral and commanding. His paws gripped Dario's hips with steady force, claws grazing the skin just enough to make the wolf shudder beneath him.

Dario clenched down, his tailhole gripping hard around the tiger's throbbing shaft. Tilting forward, he ground his needy cock against the yielding softness of Casimir's belly, smearing precum into the plush fur with each desperate thrust. His ragged breaths tangled with the squeak of the bed frame as the pressure in his sac coiled tighter, building steadily with every guttural cry that tore from his throat.

"That's it, pup… you've earned this." One heavy paw slid down to seize Dario's cock, guiding it into the crease of a velvety roll. The wolf moaned as the soft chub swallowed him whole, burying his shaft up to the swollen, apple-sized knot. Precum gushed freely, slicking Casimir's fur in hot rivulets that seeped deep into the tiger's stripes.

"Mrmph… yes!" Dario moaned, his voice growing ragged as Casimir's formidable girth stretched him wide. Lubricated barbs dragged across his tailhole, each pass sending white-hot jolts through his nerves. His cock leaked in steady pulses as he bounced on the tiger's cock, grinding against the heavy softness of Casimir's gut and painting his gray-black stripes with slick streaks of precum. "I want all five hundred pounds of you, Casimir!"

Casimir's muzzle curled into a slow, knowing smile as he tightened his grip on Dario's hips, guiding each downward plunge. "Five hundred and twenty," he corrected in a guttural rumble that shook the wolf's inner thighs. "All of it right here for you to ride."

The number hit Dario like a shockwave. His breath caught, his knot swelling as the sheer thought of straddling all that mass—and riding every inch of it—drove him past reason. Sweat and musk thickened in the air, mingling with the slap of their bodies, feeding the feral heat coiling in his belly.

"You like knowing that, don't you?" Casimir teased, hauling him down harder with each thrust. "The fact that you're riding every inch of my cock while straddling five hundred and twenty pounds of tiger—it drives you wild, doesn't it?"

"Don't you know it?" Dario growled, clenching hard around him. His body trembled as Casimir pumped faster, fur bristling with each brutal stroke. Spurt after spurt of precum smeared across the tiger's belly as the wolf's shaft leaked desperately under the weight of his own need.

Casimir's muzzle split into a hungry grin. "Greedy pup," he rumbled, his voice rough with exertion. "You can't get enough cock, can you? Just like I can't get enough food." His thrusts grew heavier, each word punctuated by a bruising slam of his hips. "Two gluttons, each feeding a different hunger…no wonder we fit so perfectly together."

Dario's ears flicked back, breath shattering into ragged gasps as Casimir's words seared through him. "Fuck—yes," he panted. "I'm greedy for all of you. Every inch, every pound… I need it all."

Casimir's laugh rolled out low and guttural, hot against the wolf's ears. His grip tightened, bruising as he hauled Dario down to the base, impaling him on every inch and holding him there. "Then take it," he snarled, amber eyes blazing. "Take all of me, pup."

Dario rocked back and forth, his cock trapped in the pliant heat of Casimir's belly. Each flex of the tiger's soft chub stroked him just enough to keep his shaft throbbing, nerves alight with pleasure. Above him, Casimir drove in with a carnal rhythm as steady and inevitable as the rising of the sun, every thrust wringing gasps from the wolf's muzzle.

"Mrmph... you getting close?" Casimir growled, punctuating the question with a series of powerful thrusts. His heavy balls swung forward with each motion, slapping against the close-cropped fur of Dario's cheeks with wet, resonant *thwaps*.

Casimir tightened his grip on the wolf's hips, hauling him down flush against his belly. He ground in deep, holding him there for a long, punishing moment, making sure Dario felt every veined ridge pulsing inside him. A growl rolled from his chest, low and primal, as his thrusts slowed to a deliberate, grinding rhythm that teased at the brink without letting him fall.

"Finish in me!" Dario cried, voice breaking with desperation. Casimir pulled back just enough to gather his strength, the cords of muscle in his thighs flexing like drawn bowstrings. Then, with a single devastating thrust, he drove himself to the hilt, his cock burying deep and stretching Dario's tailhole to its absolute limit. The wolf cried out, a raw "A-ah!" torn from his throat as pleasure and pain fused into one shattering release.

"Here it comes!" With a feral snarl, Casimir erupted inside Dario, spilling hot torrents of seed that filled him to the brim. The wolf clung to the tiger, muscles locking as sticky warmth coursed deep through his core, each pulse marking him from the inside out. Dario's breath broke into ragged cries, his own climax rushing toward him like a runaway train. "M-mrmph!"

"Unnh!" Dario convulsed as orgasm overtook him, pleasure ripping through his body in relentless waves. His cock jerked violently, unleashing thick ropes of cum that painted Casimir's plush belly and streaked across his dark stripes in milky arcs. All the while, the tiger's barbed shaft throbbed deep inside him, prolonging every spasm until Dario could do nothing but repeatedly cry out, "Fuck!"

With a final grunt, Dario slumped forward into Casimir's embrace, the tiger's immense body wrapping around his lithe frame like a living fortress. Their breaths came in ragged syncopation, hot and uneven, as they lay entwined in the heavy stillness of spent desire. Still adrift in the hazy afterglow of a mind-melting climax, Dario let his paws wander, tracing the soft arcs of Casimir's rolls and luxuriating in the yielding warmth that cradled his pads.

Casimir's cock remained buried deep inside him, still snug within the wolf's slick passage, twitching faintly in time with the steady beat of his heart. A low, resonant growl rumbled up from the tiger's chest, the only sound to break the thick silence, a primal reminder of the power that still lingered beneath their shared exhaustion.

Tugging open the deepest drawer of the nightstand, Casimir drew out a wicker basket lined with linen, brimming with indulgent treats—dark chocolate truffles, wax-sealed miniature wheels of imported cheese, and strips of artisanal jerky. "You, uh… want a snack?"

"I could go for a little somethin' somethin'." Still catching his breath, Dario let out an exhausted chuckle. He plucked a foil-wrapped truffle from the basket and unwrapped it, holding the rich morsel up to the tiger's muzzle. Casimir accepted it with a rumbling purr, and Dario grinned. "Mrmph… we should do this again sometime."

"Oh, we will, pup. A bottom of your caliber is wasted on one-night stands." Casimir smiled softly, savoring the truffle as it melted on his tongue, rich and bittersweet. He peeled a hunk of Grana Padano from the basket and pressed it to Dario's lips, rumbling with approval as the wolf obediently accepted the bite. His paw drifted to the wolf's tummy, caressing the taut fur with deliberate slowness. "Though I'll have to fatten you up a bit more. I like my boys with some meat on their bones."

Dario plucked another truffle from the basket and popped it into his muzzle before leaning forward to kiss the tiger's whiskered lips. "It's a deal, then. I'll work on filling out while you keep getting bigger, hrm? The power your size commands is like nothing I've ever felt before. I want more of you…if that's even possible."

Casimir chuckled, the sound rolling from his chest and belly in a low rumble that made the bed tremble beneath them. "I'll take that as a challenge," he said, eyes gleaming. "And one I'll happily rise to…as long as you keep the Sidebar Burgers coming my way." He pressed a lingering kiss to Dario's cheek before reaching for the remote to the Harman Kardon system. A moment later, the room filled with the soothing soundscape of a tropical rainforest—chirping frogs, rushing water, the susurrus of distant leaves. "Now close your eyes and rest, pup. You've earned it."

"Mrm hrm." Dario closed his eyes, letting the warmth of Casimir's body wrap around him like a heavy quilt. He barely stirred as the tiger slipped a towel beneath his hips to catch the slow trickle of seed that followed when his cock finally slid free. The thought of their bellies growing together made the wolf smile faintly, even as drowsiness tugged him under.

And as gentle darkness carried him off, Dario knew he'd never crave anything less than Casimir's fullness again…

Scout's Honor

Ash Cinder

On average, how many people who went to camp as pups eventually make the transition from camper to counselor? Probably not many, especially now that most pups' images of camps include a hockey-mask-wearing beaver dragging a bloody sleeping bag around.

I was never one for camping as a pup. I was a scrawny, nerdy beagle growing up, who always preferred to be inside playing video games instead of outside getting dirty or getting whacked in the face by branches. I definitely would have preferred spending my summers alone in my room getting to the next difficulty in *Guitar Hero* instead of summer camp every year because my parents couldn't afford a regularly scheduled babysitter for me.

So, why is it that I returned to camp almost as soon as I was old enough to apply to be a camp counselor? Did I suddenly gain a newfound appreciation for the great outdoors? Did I really need the money and had good enough recommendations to get the job? Or was I just looking for an excuse to see my first childhood crush again?

The third one. It was the third one, if you hadn't already figured it out. Though this was a crush I couldn't exactly pursue, for a number of reasons. Most camp kids develop silly, little, secret crushes growing up for other campers, sometimes a councilor. I don't think most get the hots for their scoutmaster, and if they do, they certainly don't pursue a silly old schoolboy crush when they're in their twenties.

Despite all the negative things I dreaded every summer about camp, if there was one thing that made the entire stay there tolerable it was Scoutmaster Chase, Ralph Chase. The old Great Pyrenees was like a second dad I only got to see during summer. He always wanted to make sure everyone was having a good time, even campers like me who he knew were only there cause their parents made us go. My first impression of him as a pup was him offering to teach me a little guitar, after I was honest, when he asked if I was having fun.

"Not really," I believe were my exact words.

He taught me to play "Wouldn't It Be Nice," by The Beach Boys that day. I still can't help but think of him whenever I hear or play that song.

It didn't take too long after hitting puberty to realize I was very into dad types. Warm, kind older men with bellies that looked like would make good pillows, and Scoutmaster Chase was certainly the definition of that. He was a typical big, floofy Great Pyrenees, with thick white fur, who always wore a scoutmaster uniform that never seemed to be the exact right fit for him, but was never too small to where it looked ridiculous either.

I'm not sure what I expected when I decided to take that summer job. It's not like I thought I'd be confessing my crush to Scoutmaster Chase and hooking up with him all summer. I guess I just sort of thought the pay was decent, and I'd at least get to see him again while I worked. I'd stopped going to camp around the time I turned fourteen when my parents finally let me decide if I wanted to keep going every year, or if I could be trusted home alone. But once away from camp I couldn't get Scoutmaster Chase out of my head. It was even harder not to once I reached dating age, and realized the number of gay dads wanting to hook up in my area was dangerously low.

I guess part of me did come back to camp with the silly intention of trying to hook up with my old scoutmaster, as unlikely to happen as I knew it was. At camp everyone growing up were like ninety percent sure Chase was gay. He'd never been married, or had any pups, he never mentioned having a girlfriend or any real significant other of any kind, and at least one counselor claimed they saw some kind of rainbow mug or flag in his office. This had been only my first week back at camp and already my gaydar was going off every time I was around the canine.

"Thinking about the dad of your dreams, again?" My friend Josh asked.

"I *was* until your voice broke the fantasy," I snarked.

I leaned against the outside wall of the cabin while the kids inside slept and looked at the raccoon approaching me, his eyes glowing in the moonlight. I'd been relieving him for his break and now he was back. He gave me a teasing smirk before leaning against the wall next to me.

"You going to poke him about it already?" He asked.

"You can't just ask your scoutmaster to hook up with you."

Josh was the only friend I'd had at camp who ended up taking the job alongside me. He was also the only one I'd ever told my secret crush to and while he wasn't the type to go telling everyone, he loved bringing it up in conversation to play matchmaker.

"You're both adults, Kyle. Besides, you and I both know if you don't find a dad to bone by the start of fall, you're going to explode from all the pent-up sexual frustration."

He hushed his voice on the word "sexual" as we usually did when cubs were around. I chuckled and gave him a playful push.

"I was the last one you had to relieve for their break, that means yours is next," he pointed out. "What better time to bump into him and have a little 'encounter'?"

"We don't even know for sure if he's gay. It's just a rumor that started around camp, like that other one about *The Blair Witch Project* being filmed in the woods around camp."

He placed his paw on my shoulder and squeezed firmly. I turned to meet his gaze; his eyes gleamed with excitement.

"What?" I asked.

"Yes, we do."

"We do, what?"

"I *know* he's gay," Josh said confidently.

I looked at him skeptically.

"What? Did you catch him jerking it to dad and son porn on his office laptop?" I snarked.

"No," he shot back, "but I did see a photo in his office..."

My ears perked up.

"What kind of photo?"

"Just a slightly younger Mr. Chase with some male friends dressed in some... interesting attire."

"Interesting?"

"Nothing revealing or anything, and you know I'm mostly straight, but I think he looks a lot sexier in leather than his scoutmaster uniform."

"H-He just had that in his office?" I asked.

"He didn't have many pictures, but that was one of the few I saw in there when I had my evaluation earlier today, looked like it was taken at one of those festivals in San Francisco."

Man, this changed everything... Maybe I could try approaching him now?

"Seriously, bro, just go sit down with him on your break," Josh insisted.

"And what? Ask him if he'd like to follow me back to the woods and fuck, like two soon-to-be-dead horror movie extras?"

"I was thinking more along the lines of striking up a normal conversation and seeing where it leads."

"Right…"

"Don't make it weird, Kyle," Josh scolded.

I began to walk away from the cabin.

"Right, don't make it weird…" I repeated, trying to relax. "See you in the morning."

"Have fun!" he teased.

I looked back and playfully stuck my tongue out before continuing down the path to the main lodge.

I walked down the dirt path and sighed thinking about what I might say to him. It was like Josh said, just a normal conversation… what was normal? Uh, movies? Did Mr. Chase like movies? Video games? Was he a gamer? He was, like in his mid to late fifties, maybe he had an Atari or something growing up?

This is ridiculous, I thought to myself. What if we're both wrong, or even if we're right, what if I end up getting in trouble… or getting him in trouble. Man, the idea of hooking up with my old scoutmaster was so wrong… but that's part of what drew me to it. As I continued up the lodge steps I couldn't help but start getting lost in the fantasy again, imagining Mr. Chase stripping off his uniform in the woods and revealing a leather harness underneath. I could feel my underwear tighten as I imagined it: *him holding me close and pinning me against a tree with his white floofy belly, forcing me to my knees and shoving his cock into my muzzle before grabbing ahold of my ears and fuck—*

"Evening there, Kyle! Or 'night' I guess."

His voice brought me back to reality, as I had walked right into the lodge and sat at the lunch table, across from him, filling out some final first-week paperwork. My body had been on autopilot for the last half of the walk. Okay, Kyle, conversation time… don't make it weird.

I smiled at him. He definitely looked more casual at night, with his shirt not tucked into his shorts, making his sexy white belly more visible, with his shirt even slightly unbuttoned for good measure. If I didn't know better, I would have thought he could be a small polar bear.

"Uh, hey there sir. I thought you'd be asleep by now."

"Nah. Now that I'm done filling out the logs for y'all's breaks, I'll be up for at least another hour. This is my 'me' time," he said, casually stretching his arms out and pulling up his feet, propping them up on the table.

"Aren't we not supposed to put our paws on the table?" I asked.

"We're the adults, we can do what we want when the kids aren't watching," he said casually.

What he said sounded very suggestive, but I didn't yet detect any flirtation in his tone.

"Besides," he continued, "we have to wipe them down in the morning before breakfast anyway."

"Alright."

I followed his example and propped my paws up on the table.

"It's been a while since I've seen you, I almost didn't recognize you when you and the other counselors arrived the week before the cubs did. Same with Josh. Believe it or not, not many former campers return as adult counselors."

"I guess I'm not most campers."

Man, that was lame!

"I'm a little surprised you did return," Chase said. "I always got the feeling you weren't much of a camper as a pup."

"Oh yeah?" I asked. "Was I that obvious?"

"Well, you always preferred being in the cabins instead of outdoors, you never did successfully make a fire, and you were always afraid of getting hurt while doing something."

"You could have just said 'yes,'" I chuckled.

"What I'm getting at is, what made you apply for the job?"

I felt my face heat up under my coarse fur, I guess I did come to finally tell him, but man, was this awkward.

"If you want me to be honest," I began, "it was you." He raised his eyebrow, but the slight smirk he had told me he'd already figured it out. I went on, "Yeah, I wasn't a very good camper, but you're what made every summer here not totally awful. You were a good scoutmaster, we all looked up to you, some of us even more than the rest of us…"

"Kyle, just come out and say you've had a crush on me. I'm not gonna judge."

I gave him a surprised look, not expecting him to have me pegged like that.

"Wow, I *really* am that obvious… Josh didn't tell you, did he?"

He just chuckled and walked over and sat next to me, patting my shoulder firmly.

"I'd suspected it when you were still a pup," he went on, patting my head. "You used to jump at the chance to go with any group I was leading on some sort of camp activity. I caught you, more than once, making some googly eyes at me, the final summer you were a camper. It wasn't until you showed up here again, all these years later as a camp counselor that confirmed it for me. We all have our childhood crushes when we're growing up."

My ears perked up a bit as he stroked the fur of my cheek with the back of his paw.

"I've certainly caught your gaze more than once during this first week," he whispered.

I could feel my face heat up again.

"I hope I'm not making you uncomfortable," he inquired.

"N-No, sir, I'm just…"

"Scared out of your mind?"

"Yeah, I think that describes it pretty well."

"Well, don't worry son, I don't bite… unless you want me to," he said with a slight growl that sent a tingle down my spine that worked its way right around to between my legs, making my crotch noticeably tense up.

"So, you're not like freaked out by this?" I asked, starting to relax. "That we've kind of known each other since I was a pup and now we're having this conversation."

He just kept smiling and patted my shoulder again before standing up.

"Wanna go on a walk with me?" He asked.

"S-Sure…"

I followed him outside and down the stairs of the main lodge, my head still spinning from what just happened. Scoutmaster Chase really just flirted with me… like brazen flirting. I'm glad he was taking it slow, don't get me wrong, I eventually wanted to be handled roughly by a DILF like him, but not right away.

"So," I tried to converse as we walked, "you hook up with other counselors?"

Chase just laughed, a few birds scattering out of the branches right above us.

"This place is definitely scenic enough to get any animal, feral or otherwise, in the mood, but you can't exactly let loose easily with pups around."

I laughed in agreement,

"Yeah, I've certainly had to tone down the gutter mouth I've developed since I grew up."

"Haven't caught you slipping up, yet," he replied, patting my shoulder. "Let's see where the night takes us, pup."

I couldn't help but wag my tail when he called me "pup."

"You have much experience with guys?"

"Just a little... but I've never been with the types of guys I'm interested in."

He looked down at me while we walked, raising his park ranger hat.

"And what type is that?"

I giggled nervously, I still couldn't believe this was happening.

"I-I like dads..." My voice cracking a bit.

"Dads?" He asked with a smirk.

"Yeah, you know, older types with noticeable bellies, who are bigger than me... and stronger," I added, looking up at him.

I could see a bit of a grin spreading across the side of his face.

"Ever given a blowjob out in the open before, son?"

I felt my cock twitch in my pants.

"I-I haven't."

"I haven't had one outside in a while, if you want to help 'a dad' out?"

He pulled me close to him as we approached a wooded area just off the path.

I let out a nervous, but excited whine as we stopped in front of a large oak tree, I was about to drop right to my knees before he stopped me.

"Hey," he said, taking a more serious tone. "Don't feel pressured to do anything with me that you're not comfortable with."

My tail continued to wag as I nodded.

"If things are getting a little 'too much,' just say the word." He assured.

"What word?"

"Snipe," he answered enthusiastically. "How's that for a safe word?"

I chuckled. "Do we still do those 'Snipe Hunts' here at camp?" I asked.

"Nah, your generation eventually told the younger one that it was bogus, and ruined us adults' fun," he teased, booping me on the nose.

I couldn't help but giggle, enjoying letting myself relax enough reach out and brush my paw against his. He took the hint and gently took both my paws in his.

"Let me get a good look at you, in the moonlight," he said with a warm smile.

He looked me up and down, then held me close so that I was against his belly. I trembled with anticipation as he slid his paw down my back.

"Still a bit nervous about how big I am compared to you?" he asked.

"Not as much as I was," I admitted.

"Don't worry, pup, we can start off slow."

Indulge

My tail began to wag faster as I heard him unzip his shorts and my eyes widened at the sight of his erect cock, for the first time. It was so bright red compared to the white fur all over his body. It looked about as long as a soda bottle, with noticeable bulge where his knot was clearly trying to reveal itself.

"Yeah, you wouldn't believe how pent up I get maintaining my squeaky-clean scoutmaster image," he panted with a chuckle.

I could already smell the musk radiating off it, so pungent and manly. If he told me to drop to my knees, I don't remember hearing it, I just remember diving right for his cock and began lapping at it with my tongue. My tail wagged wildly when I felt him place his firm paw at the top of my head and rubbed it.

"Mmmm, that's it," he growled above me. "Eager boy, aren't you?"

I looked up at him and watched him unbutton the rest of his shirt, putting his big soft belly on full display. I wrapped my muzzle around his cock and reached both my paws up, gently rubbing his belly while I sucked him off. His grip on my head tightened and he let out a pleasured growl.

"Belly rubs? Fuck, pup!" He gasped. "You're going to make daddy cum already."

I moaned back and savored the hot musky cock I was slobbering all over. I'd always wondered if musk from older men was different from guys my age. It's true, it's like a fine wine, makes a younger pup ready to submit to his alpha and lift his tail. At this point I was operating on pure animal instinct, doing my best to take in as much of it as possible. By now his knot was all the way out of his sheath and I was lapping at it with my tongue, each time I pushed myself forward. Then Chase started to take control.

He'd said he'd take it easy on me, but once he saw how eager I was he started getting more rough and soon I wasn't even bobbing myself on his cock anymore, it was all him face-fucking me like a fleshlight, and doing it out in the middle of the woods? So fucking amazing. I had never experienced sex this intense before, but I didn't dare try and tell him to tone it down, I was loving every second of this.

I continued holding onto his belly, running my fingers through his thick, snow-white fur. I bet if I slept with him in bed, I could use his belly as a pillow all night. I could feel my underwear wet with pre as I pleasured the old Pyrenees above me. I hoped he'd be ready to breed me after this, judging by the noises he was making above me, I wouldn't have been surprised if he held me down on the ground and buried his knot in me until I lost consciousness.

We must have been tuned into the same wavelength, because suddenly he grabbed onto my shoulders and quickly picked me up as much as he could while his cock was still in my mouth and pushed me against the tree before humping my face, my eyes rolling back in my head.

"Good boy, that's it!" Chase growled. "Daddy likes a tight muzzle."

I began to relax my body and just let the big dog take control. This was my dream, being handled so roughly by the dad I'd been crushing on since puberty. I didn't care that I had to time my breaths right, as he rammed his cock down my throat, I just wanted to feel his big, warm load fill my belly. I wrapped my arms around his hefty waist and clutched both his ass cheeks, while he grabbed ahold of my brown floppy beagle ears and used my muzzle as a fuck toy.

"Almost there, pup. Daddy's got a big load for his eager good boy."

My tail thumped against the tree I was pinned to, even as I struggled to breathe through my nose in between moments of his cock clogging my windpipe. I let out muffled pleasured moans and whines as the Great Pyrenees shoved every bit of his meat into my greedy mouth.

"Take it all, puppy," he moaned deeply, "enjoy your treat."

I squeezed his fat ass tightly as I felt his warm, virile seed shoot down my gullet, with Mr. Chase shoving his member as far as he could fit it, I continued to do my best to lick his thick knot. I happily sat still and enjoyed my "reward." The musky, salty cum tasted better than anyone else's I'd tasted. I just closed my eyes and focused of his throbbing member in my muzzle, each pulse shooting more of that thick, Pyrenees seed down my eager throat.

"That's right puppy," he panted heavily above me, "don't waste a single drop."

I firmly squeezed his cheeks again, enjoying the feeling of his firm paws caressing the back of my head while he held me there, continuing to feed me. I heard the daddy Pyrenees let out a deep chuckle.

"You like daddy's fat ass, boy?"

He pet my head affectionately.

"Mmhm..." I managed to choke out.

"Didn't used to be this big," he huffed, patting his belly. "Been wanting to try losing some weight, but you really seem to like it..."

He pushed his weight down more on me, pressing me against the tree. I managed to still weakly breathe through one nostril, inhaling his mature, manly scent. Fuck, all I wanted after this was for him to pin me down with all his weight and shoot a litter of pups into my tailhole. I wanted to be powerless to push him off me.

Soon, his pulsing cock got weaker and weaker until after a few more tender caresses against my head, he released his hold on me and pulled his wet cock out of my muzzle. I gasped deeply, now that I could fully breathe. I licked around the outside of my mouth to make sure there wasn't any leftover Pyrenees cum.

Scoutmaster Chase patted his belly again before reaching down to help me up. I reached up, still catching my breath, and let him effortlessly lift me to my paws.

"Woof," the Pyrenees huffed, "looks like we were both a bit pent up."

I leaned back against the tree and let out a happy sigh.

"Yeah. Th-Thanks for the treat, Mr. Chase," I panted.

"Oh, you can call me Ralph now, I think we've crossed that bridge."

I giggled and he gave me a warm grin, giving me another pat on the head.

"You've still got a little something on your mouth?" he teased.

"Where?" I asked confused.

I walked right into that one, as he pinned me to the tree again, this time to lock muzzles with me. I moaned into his mouth and happily allowed him to push his tongue past my teeth to explore. My body trembled as he slowly slid his paws up and down my body, feeling me up under my shirt. Meanwhile, I was aggressively feeling up his belly, enjoying how soft and thick his fur was in contrast with my traditionally coarse beagle fur.

I felt him slide his rough paws down my back before firmly squeezing my ass. I pushed against his paw to tell him it was all his to squeeze. He took full advantage, taking it up a notch by shoving his paw down the back of my pants to grope my bare beagle ass. I moaned louder into his muzzle when he did that, beginning to relax in the powerful daddy's arms as he began to use me as his toy.

"Mmmm, you're a natural sub, pup," he growled through the kiss.

I continued to run my fingers through his white fur, moving up from his belly to his chest. Oh my, I thought to myself, his chest is a lot more well-toned than I thought. He clearly took a little time out of each week, taking care of his upper body. As he continued to feel around the inside of my mouth, I felt around his chest until I found what I was looking for. I took his nipple in my pawtips and pinched tightly.

Chase let out an even more animalistic growl, tightening his grip on my ass and holding me so close that he lifted me up at least an inch off the ground, all the while his tongue was all the way down my throat, probably tasting some of his leftover cum lingering around there. It was so hot, not only to be handled this roughly, but out in the middle of the woods like this! I wonder what the other counselors would say if they caught us?

Josh, I thought to myself, *you enjoying the show somewhere behind a tree?*

I found his other nipple with my free paw and pinched that one as well. Chase responded by digging his claws into my ass cheeks a bit.

I must have let out a whine that sounded concerning because he quickly pulled his muzzle away from mine and let me fall back to my paws.

"S-Sorry that I got a little aggressive," he said with a nervous laugh, "I haven't been with a sexy young stud like you in quite a few years."

"No, it's okay," I reassured, "I actually really like it rough… but I like a little tenderness too, like when you were petting me."

"Good to know…"

My gaze couldn't help but drift back down to his cock, which was still fully erect and dripping drool and precum.

"Looks like you're still up for some action," I teased.

"Just wondering if that other hole of yours is as good as your muzzle."

"W-Wanna find out?" I asked.

He gave me a sly smirk, letting his unbuttoned shirt to fall to the ground and displaying his full naked dad bod before me. It was then I realized that I was still fully clothed. I decided to give him another chance for some added fun.

"You want me to strip down, or do you want to… unwrap me yourself?" I asked in a seductive tone.

His cock twitched when I suggested that. "Did I ever tell you there's a new policy for counselors here?"

"What's that sir?" I asked, playing along.

"Gotta inspect your uniform to make sure they're up to code, starting… now."

He reached down and casually unfastened one of the buttons on my shirt with his black claws, making me blush under my fur again.

"Well, then I guess I'd better let you frisk me then."

He had a toothy grin on his face as he slowly began to unbutton the rest of my green uniform shirt. My body vibrated with excitement as he undid the last button and let my shirt fall to the ground, revealing my young, twinky, college boy body.

"Well, well," he flirted, "no undershirt, that's a dress code violation."

"Is daddy going to punish me?" I asked innocently.

"Up against the tree," he ordered.

I did as he said and placed my paws against the tree, wiggling my ass teasingly. I let out an excited yip, as he gave it a playful slap.

"I think you're starting to become a bigger tease than me," he added with a chuckle.

I looked down as he reached his arms around my waist and began to undo my shorts, my cock throbbed in my underwear as I felt the large elder canine press his soft body against mine, I shivered with anticipation when I felt him grinding his shaft against my crack through the shorts. I moaned, feeling his heavy breathing against the side of my neck, before he slowly licked it affectionately.

"But first I gotta lube you up."

He removed my shorts and underwear.

"You ever had your ass eaten out, boy?"

That got my attention, as my brown floppy ears perked up.

"N-No, sir," my tail starting to tap against his belly. "No one's ever offered."

"Then you're in for a real treat," he said, licking the side of my neck. He presented both of our underwear to me. "But that means you're going to be pretty vocal, so we'll need to give you something to muffle it. Now, which underwear would you prefer?"

I couldn't help but laugh at how casually he explained this, but I imagined he'd probably had this conversation with other inexperienced submissive bottoms in his life.

I smiled back at him and picked up his sweaty underwear, my tail wagged excitedly as I looked at the undergarment. I held it to my nose and took one last whiff of his manly scent before shoving the musky briefs into my muzzle. I resumed my position against the tree, presenting my ass to him. I felt him kneel down and grip both my ass cheeks firmly in each of his paws.

"Try not to get too loud," he warned. "We're pretty far off from the cabins, and the underwear should muffle it enough, but no howling."

I nodded before lifting my tail.

"Mmmm, what a yummy looking tailhole," he commented, petting my ass. "Don't mind if I do."

I gasped, feeling him drag his wet tongue across my entrance. I dug my claws into the tree, my heart pounding in my chest. I was really about to go all the way with my old scoutmaster. I looked down to see my cock dripping with pre and twitching with anticipation.

I froze stiff as I felt Chase's tongue slide past my anal ring and worm its way inside me. I began to let out muffled moans and whimpers through his underwear in my mouth. He growled deeply behind me, digging his claws into my ass and pushing his way deeper inside me.

I'd never felt anything like this before. I'd bottomed before, but none of the previous guys I'd hooked up with had offered to eat me out. My legs and arms started to feel like jelly as I struggled to hold myself up while the Pyrenees behind me began to tickle my prostate. I could feel tears form in my eyes, the pleasure I was experiencing was just so intense, and the fact that it was my childhood crush giving it to me made it that much hotter.

I did my best to not whimper too loud and continued to hold myself up, but everything was so intense. I couldn't even hear him growling anymore as he ate me out, I was lost in the bliss I was feeling, I wasn't touching my cock, but each lap of his tongue to my g-spot made me feel like I was about to explode all over the tree.

I'd tried poppers once before at a party and I remember my head spinning the whole time during sex. It was incredible. This was a whole different kind of high. It was the best kind of sensory overload; I didn't want him to stop until... he did.

All my senses came back as I suddenly felt him yank his tongue out of my hole. I hung my head down and began to pant heavily. I stared wide-eyed down at my twitching cock, along with the cumshot splattered all over the tree. I'd cum from him eating me out and hadn't even realized it! My mouth was hanging open so far, I watched Mr. Chase's underwear fall to my feetpaws.

I watched him reach around and gently stroke my dripping cock.

"Looks like Daddy's still got it," he said with a chuckle.

"H-Hell yeah, he does..." I panted.

My limbs were buckling as I recovered from the intense pleasure sequence.

"Hope it wasn't too much for you. Your legs were shaking so much, I was a little afraid you were about to pass out."

I chuckled as he patted me on the shoulder.

"N-No," I stammered, "that was incredible!"

"Good to hear."

I felt him place his paws on my hips and push up against me, resting his rock hard member in between my cheeks. He ran one of his paws up from my belly to my chest.

"You ready to be my good boy tonight, son?" he asked in the warm, fatherly tone I was used to from him.

I practically melted into the dirt, my tail ceasing wagging and just lifted itself for him.

Indulge

That was all he needed, letting out a deep sigh, before pushing the tip of his cock against my entrance. He let out a soft growl, slipping past my anal ring, running his big, strong paws down my chest and belly at the same time.

I cringed and let out a soft moan of pain and pleasure. Fuck, he was big. He stopped pushing for a second and affectionately licked the back of my neck.

"Just relax, puppy," he whispered. "Once you've relaxed, daddy will slide right in."

He continued to rub his paws up and down my smooth body, tenderly holding me close to his soft, fluffy belly as his cock continued to slip into me, inch by inch.

"Yes, daddy," I moaned softly. "Just do what you need to do so you can breed me."

"Good boy," he growled.

He placed his paw against my cheek and leaned forward, turning my head to meet his, before kissing me deeply, while giving me a reach around with his free paw. This helped me relax as I focused on our tongues dancing around each other's mouths, while more and more of his shaft was forced inside me. He pulled out of the kiss again and yanked my hips back, making me yelp as he shoved himself all the way in, just stopping at the knot.

"It's going to be so tempting to knot you," he growled lustfully in my ear, "remember, I don't want to push you too hard."

"Yessir," I panted. "Now, please, breed me, daddy."

He firmly gripped my hips, growling deeply, withdrawing himself from my tailhole. I let out a shaky moan, doing my best to keep my voice down, before gasping when he slowly forced it back in. He leaned forward past my shoulder again and licked the side of my muzzle. I accepted his invitation and we passionately kissed again. I shivered as he pushed his tongue deep down my throat at the same time he thrust his cock into my tailhole. It was like he was fucking me from both ends at the same time.

I felt him continue moving his paws up and down my body, eventually gripping my cock again and stroking it at a nice and steady pace. This was a dream come true, getting fucked at camp by the dad of my dreams in the middle of the woods. It was so risky, but that made this even more fun.

He broke the kiss again and began panting in my ear, increasing the pace of his thrusts. I did my best to move my hips in rhythm with him, loving how full I was feeling with him inside me.

"Let me tell you, pup," he panted, giving my ear a nibble, "it felt real good to see how much I made you cum just by dancing my tongue on your prostate."

"Th-That was one of the most intense orgasms—ah! I've ever had," I said in between thrusts.

"Makes an old dog feel like he still knows his way around a twink."

I giggled, feeling him playfully nip my ear again.

"Th-This is—OH! Amazing, sir!" I moaned.

"I think you and I are going to have some more 'catching up to do' during our breaks this summer," he grunted.

I gasped, feeling him go even faster, increasing the strength of his thrusts.

"I'm sure—Gah! You could teach me a thing or—*huff*! Two!"

"Oh, I *know* I can, pup."

He removed his paw from my cock and placed both paws against my chest, pulling me close against him, his floofy white fur engulfing me while he roughly pulled my hips against his. I let out pleasured whimpers as he licked the side of my neck again.

"Such a naturally submissive pup," he whispered. "How many wet dreams have you been having about your old scoutmaster, just like this?"

"T-Too many to count!"

"Who'd have known you'd grow up to be such a naughty pup?" He asked.

"I have a weakness for daddies..." I panted.

"Oh, I'd hardly call it a 'weakness.' You *love* pleasuring big-bellied, pervy old men," he growled in my ear, "and this old Pyrenees has been needing a good 'son' in his life."

Before I could say anything else, the Great Pyrenees jammed his fingers into my mouth, and I began instinctively lapping and sucking on them.

"Mmmm, that's a good beagle boy."

I let out pleasured whines and whimpers as the scoutmaster began bucking his hips against me while continuing to hold me off the ground against his floofy chest. I looked down to watch myself bouncing against his cock, my own bobbing up and down, strings of pre sliding off the tip and landing on the ground or the tree.

Fucking hell, I thought, *he's really going at it! I hope he doesn't accidentally shove his knot in.*

"Mmm, I could have a lot of fun with you, pup," he continued to talk dirty, not breaking stride in his thrusts. "You ever get bred tied up in a sling before? How about worshipping and licking my feet paws?"

Wow, I thought, I always suspected Chase had been gay, but I didn't think he was this hardcore. The dog was the most hardcore dom daddy I'd met in person. He was even sexier than I expected him to be. I wanted to be dominated by this big sexy dog, over and over. I wanted to give him belly rubs in the morning while I sucked him off in bed.

"Mmm, just thinking about all the things we could do together is getting me even closer to blowing my load inside you, like we both want. You should come visit me at my place once summer's over."

I moaned longingly. I wanted to feel his warm seed fill my belly and mix with the first load I swallowed. Did he really mean it when he said he wanted me to visit him off the clock sometime?

"I think you'd like my place, got some toys there I haven't used on anyone in a while."

I gasped as he removed his fingers from my mouth and moved them down to my neck, caressing me as he whispered,

"How much do you want daddy's pups, boy?"

"I want them! Please!" I whimpered.

"You want all of them?"

"Give me your pups, daddy!" I panted, trying not to yell.

"Then take them!"

He pulled my hips hard and held me in place, his knot straining against my hole, but not slipping in. He hit me just right in that moment, I felt his cock spear my prostate, hard, causing me to yelp and whine as I came a second time, both of us cumming in unison. I began to clench my hole against his thick cock, trying to match the rhythm of its throbbing.

"That's it, puppy," he gritted through his teeth, "I'm not pulling out until my cock stops pulsing! Milk daddy dry."

I looked down at my belly, feeling as full as I wanted to feel. I thought about all that Pyrenees cum that was inside me now, I couldn't help but fantasize about my belly swelling with the older canine's litter. We just stayed there, both panting heavily while his orgasm lasted. He slid one of his paws down my body and felt my tummy.

"How's that belly feel, boy?"

"Nice and warm."

"That's how I like to leave my pups after a good breeding session."

He tenderly caressed the side of my face with his other paw, making me let out a relaxed whine.

"You wanna head back to the lodge and spend the night with daddy?" he asked.

I giggled, my face heating up again. "Can I, really?"

He gave me a warm smile.

"Wanted to ask if you wanted to go skinny dipping tonight, but we should head back after I go soft, we've been out here naked long enough, and you gave me quite a workout tonight."

"I'd love to try skinny dipping with you another night, though," I reassured.

"Sounds like we're going to have a fun summer. I can introduce you to all the special, secluded spots in the woods."

He patted my full belly before squeezing me in a tight bear hug.

"I think you've just about milked my cock dry, tonight, boy." He tugged a bit on his cock in my hole before gently letting me down on my feet. "Ready for the pullout?" he asked.

I grabbed the tree firmly before he slowly slid his shaft out of my sore tailhole, making me moan with relief before gasping once it was finally out.

I could feel a bit of cum leaking out, and trickle down the back of my leg, and my own cock was still dripping. I certainly looked like I'd been very well used.

"Boy," I muttered, "I'm pretty messy right now. Not sure I want to put my uniform back on…"

"Don't worry, we can carry them back a discreet way through the woods that will take us right back to the lodge."

He gathered up our clothes, insisting to carry them all, probably because he noticed I was having a bit of an issue walking after such an intense breeding. I followed him to the secret path, which was just off the one along the lake. We continued to flirt and chat a bit as we walked.

"Thanks for working up the courage to pursue me, pup. I didn't realize just how much I needed that back there."

"Don't tell me a guy like you doesn't get any," I asked in disbelief.

"Used to, at least in my neck of the woods," he explained, "before I *got this*," he said bitterly. He smacked his belly.

"Really?" I asked. "I think it's sexy."

"A lot of people expect my breed to be pretty fit, but I only really enjoy maintaining my arms and chest." He flexed a bit for me. "I know there are plenty of young guys who are into older chubby canines like me, I just got unlucky in the part of the country I settled in."

"That's a bit where I'm at too. There's not too many older gay guys where I live, so I haven't hooked up too many times, it's probably why I seemed so—"

"Virginal?" he asked with a smirk.

I gave him a playful look back.

"I was going to say 'inexperienced' but I guess that's accurate."

"You really let me take control," he growled, nudging me playfully with his arm.

"I thought I might faint. The pleasure was just so overwhelming."

"Good to know I can still make a young twink tremble in my arms. I'd almost forgotten how good that feels."

We made it back to the lodge and I let Chase unlock it and lead me up to his quarters. He suggested we both take a shower before settling down together in bed. As he helped wash his lingering cum out of my fur, I couldn't help but comment on how nice it was that he could be both tender and rough with me.

"I didn't realize you could be so dominant, Mr. Chase."

"You can call me Ralph outside of work, Kyle," he said in an almost scolding tone. "If you had my cock in your ass, you don't have to be afraid to use my first name."

"That'll take some getting used to… Ralph." I said with a giggle.

"I'll also accept 'Daddy' as a compromise," he added.

I let out a small yip as he gave my wet bottom a playful grope.

"I think your cute little ass is clean now."

Before finishing up, he wrapped his strong arms around me and rubbed my belly. "You like having your old scoutmaster's cum in you, son?" he asked, licking my ear.

"Was it that obvious?" I asked.

He chuckled at me before flicking his tongue out and licking my nose. I giggled and let him kiss me again, enjoying the feeling of the warm water running down my lean body while this sexy manly dog kissed me passionately. It felt so good to finally be in the embrace of a daddy, it was so tender, but so dominant at the same time.

"I would have never guessed you would grow up to be such a naughty boy," he teased.

"I wouldn't have either." I nervously giggled and scratched the back of my head. He gave me a quick pat before turning the water off and drying ourselves off. Being a beagle, it didn't take me long to get dry.

His bed was just big enough for the both of us. I let him hold me close to him, with one arm, while I rested my head against his floofy chest. My tail thumped against the mattress when I felt him nuzzle the top of my head with his nose. Part of me still couldn't believe this was real. If this was all just a dream, I didn't want to wake up, ever.

"Did you mean it earlier when you said you wanted to hook up sometime after summer is over?" I asked.

He gently slid his paw down my body and rubbed my ass, still sore from the fantastic fucking he'd given me. "I have to admit, pup, we sure seem to have what we both want in a dog," he said, giving my head a lick. "I'd love to see how you'd look with a leash around your neck."

My ears perked up and I looked up to him smirking.

"Oh, does puppy like that?"

I snuggled up to him even closer, rubbing the side of my face against his chest fur.

"I'll put it this way," he went on, petting my head. "You won't have to apply to work as a counselor just to see little ol' me anymore."

I looked up at him, flicked my tongue out and licked his nose, making him chuckle before opening his mouth for another passionate make out session between us.

"Does that sound like fun, pup?" He asked through the kiss.

My tail wagged through the blanket, thumping against the mattress. I whined happily like a feral puppy.

"You want to be Daddy's puppy when summer's over?" His voice, like butter.

Our canine tongues danced together, in and out of each other's mouths as he gently ran his big, strong paws up and down my naked body, letting me relax in his embrace. I'm not sure when I fell asleep in his arms, but looking back, if there was a way someone could be "kissed to sleep," I think he did it to me.

Inexorable Ascent

Al Song

Everyone needs to sign a waiver to get into a climbing gym. Unwise decisions lead to some awful consequences, especially when people don't know the gravity of the situation, heh, sorry. Whenever I went bouldering, I tried to not to push the envelope or risk my safety—especially since bouldering didn't use ropes or harnesses. I just wasn't a gambling rat as well, especially after a dozen losing scratch-off tickets on my eighteenth birthday and a strict econ teacher who also taught stats made me feel awful after I went to a casino for the first time. Generally, I also had a lack of stamina when it came to anything physical, but my desire for accomplishment got the better of me. At that moment I felt myself slipping.

With a loud thud, I fell onto the padded floor from ten feet off the ground.

"Ugh," I groaned as I opened my eyes to the sight of a large brown rat loping toward me.

"Stan!" I heard a booming ring fill my head followed by the sounds of footfalls smacking against the plastic-covered padding. "Are you okay?" Florian asked, offering a paw with an expression filled to the brim with concern. A few fennec foxes glanced over with their large ears pointed toward me. They then turned their attention away after confirming I wasn't dead.

"Yeah, I think I'm alright," I replied while taking the fellow rat's pink paw and sitting up. His brown fur and my gray fur meeting as he sat down next to me. My gut and upper back ached from the impact. It was nothing compared to the first time I went climbing. When I was practicing falling correctly during that time, I somehow ended up rolling my ankle.

Indulge

I sat in a canyon of gray walls with small, colorful stones sprinkled on them as if they were shards of candy scattered across the surface of a taupe cake. The climbing routes were color-coordinated at this gym. Some were as easy as climbing a ladder, and some facilities had difficult, world-championship ones that were like trying to scale the side of a greased-up skyscraper.

When it came to climbing, I was lucky to be a rat. The ability to chalk up my entire paw instead of just pads aided me with hanging onto holds with impeccable efficiency, though my weight didn't help. My tail was never able to support my heaviness, and using it felt like trying to do a pushup with my pinky. Despite all the advantages, I still lacked in the endurance department.

"Gonna try it again?" Florian asked as I handed him the faded chalk bag, which was in the shape of a twenty-sided die.

"Maybe I'll do some easier routes to make myself feel better," I sighed plopping down on the cushy floor.

"I believe in ya. Mind showing me the green route over there?" the brown rat asked.

"Sure. You're taller, so it might not be the same way for you to tackle it," I said, sizing up the problem.

"It's cool. It'll help me see what I should be doing."

The route started with me standing with both feet on one foothold. I maneuvered a across the emerald holds as slowly as I could while explaining my moves to Florian. Eventually I made it to the top of the rock and stood tall with my paws on my hips.

I was hoping that Florian would be able to 'flash' it with my help, and yes, climbing had some terms that sound outright dirty: like smearing, edging, and don't get me started on harnesses. There's also something called the Alpine cock ring, but that was an outdoor climbing term. I wondered if anyone had climbed in the buff there before.

"Fuck me. You make that look so easy," he said once I got close to the ground as I down climbed.

"This route is all in the arms, and I know you've been working on those big guys. You can definitely do it. I think you just need to go quickly so you don't expend too much energy at the beginning."

"Maybe I need to do more weight-lifting," he sulked.

"You're plenty strong, Flor."

I attempted to conquer the problem, another term for 'climbing route' a couple times more. Unfortunately, I kept falling off while becoming more and more fatigued and frustrated.

"Wanna call it a day?" Florian asked as he sauntered over to me.

"Yeah, I give up…for now," I sighed and glared at the problem. The bigger rat pulled me up again and led me to a bench with stone tiles beneath my feet.

"Hey, uh, Stan?" he asked, steadying himself to sit down on a solid surface.

"What's up?" I asked, taking a swig of water from my HydraFlask.

"I wanted to ask if you'd like to go to grab a coffee or something." Florian scratched the back of his neck and gave me a small smile.

I wiped the residue off my chin, smirked up to him, and said, "That'd be great! Is your neck itchy? Does it hurt?"

"I'm fine! Don't worry about it." I could see the anime sweat fountaining behind him for some reason.

My muscles were sore, and I was ready to flop on my bed and watch movies on my laptop, but I knew spending time with friends was more important. We headed out of the climbing gym as the sun was setting as the sky was painted hues of pink highlighted with burnt orange.

It was about a year ago, after a bad break up, my friend and fellow third culture cub and Lao-American partner-in-climb, Angela, convinced me to go bouldering with her. I knew she was trying to get my mind off Keith. She was a lithe tiger who'd been climbing for years and put all my accomplishments to shame, and if she could read my thoughts she would tell me to stop comparing myself to others.

Florian and I met at Scalare a few months later, and he came to this climbing gym with a friend, who also wanted to introduce him to bouldering. I remember him telling me that he was worried about going to the gym while also existing on the heavier side. He disclosed to me he was afraid that he'd be the only gay guy there, so I let him know he wasn't alone.

We arrived at Bubble Up Tea House, which was a bubble tea café with an upstairs area containing board games. They tried to get a fantasy JRPG vibe out of the décor. There were tree stumps that served as stools. Most of the furniture was made of reclaimed wood or recycled materials. The air always smelled fresh and floral due to all the plants. The ceiling was painted blue with clouds in the shape of non-copyrighted anime characters, and they served the boba in flasks and beakers decorated to look like potions. The staircase leading up to the gaming area had vines intertwined between the balusters, and the walls had decals of pixel trees with hearts, apples, and roses in their branches.

"What shall we play tonight?" Florian asked as he rubbed his paws together like a card shark.

We decided on a deck building game called, 'Scales of Life,' which had a muscled Anubis on the cover and a Rainbow Games Award sticker next to his handsome face.

We went head-to-head, mano a mano, vis-à-vis, tit for tat. It was a cardboard massacre, with neither of our troops budging. We each garnered more cards from the shuffled pile and stole them from one another. In the end we tallied our points, and I made the announcement. "It looks like we've tied."

"And we're not even canids," the bigger rodent said as he grinned. Bigger both in height and his burliness. That wasn't a critique on his weight. My little black book mostly had guys on the bigger side.

"Seriously?"

"I'm sorry," he said, but his visage revealed other motives.

"You're so cheesy."

"We can asiago, if you want."

"Do you really think this is funny?" I said, trying to drain the giddy emotions from my mind and body.

"You're smiling, aren't you?"

"I guess I can't deny that," I said as he smirked at me.

"Hey, uh, Stan?" he asked as he started to put away the game.

"What's up?" I said after a sip of my tea.

"We've been doing this for a while."

"Doing what?" I asked as he put his paws on the table and clasped them together.

"You know, after I get off work at my parents' bakery and you leave your shift, we go bouldering, and then we come here and play board games."

"Yeah?" I put the a few of the matching card types together into the box.

"You're able to speak to my parents in German, you're really fun and nice, and I like you… so, can we go out on a real date?" he asked with a small smile, and I reached out for his paws.

"Flor, I think you're awesome."

"Oh," he said as he retracted his arms and crossed them around his large stomach as I folded my paws over my own big belly.

"You're really incredible, and I definitely think you're hot, but I don't know if it's a good time for me."

"If you think I'm awesome and handsome, then why don't you want to go out with me?"

"You know I went through a pretty bad breakup last year."

"Yeah," he said, looking down at his lap and fidgeting.

"I just don't know if I'm ready for another relationship yet," I said packing up the game.

"Okay," he said, and I felt my stomach churn.

Florian left as I placed the die in its slot and shelved the game.

Later that night when I got home, I hopped in the shower and put on some senseless, catchy pop song to get my mind off of the evening. I tried to sing along to cover the remorseful, jeering voices in my head and the queasiness in my stomach, but I only succeeded in singing the chorus for the few songs that played before I left the shower.

I stood under the fan as the warmth embraced me. It felt especially good on my groin and butt as I widened my stance feeling the heat funnel to my loins as I felt myself stiffen. When the hot air stopped, I opened my eyes to a blurry, gray aberration in the mirror and turned away. I threw a towel around myself after drying up the harder to reach areas and headed to my room.

Feeling thick under my towel I admired how much of a bulge I could make, but I also understood cock size wasn't usually a thing people could affect themselves. Nonetheless it made me smile to see how much of a towel rack I could be.

I started up my laptop and put on a video featuring a heavyset, mature coyote in nothing but an olive-green jockstrap flexing for the camera. He had nipple piercings along with rings running down his right ear. The coyote stood in front of a short cliff face in the desert showing off his rotund belly and began to scale an easy section of the orange and brown rock.

His muscles were enormous as he lifted himself so easily as he wiggled his voluptuous cheeks. He clung to the wall with one hand as he spread one of his cheeks and lifted his tail to show off his pink pucker.

Indulge

I didn't know how people showed themselves off on the internet. Weren't people afraid of loved ones or coworkers finding their videos? And weren't they afraid of how it could affect their future careers? Maybe. All I did was help manage a music store, and the owner probably didn't even know how to access porn.

The coyote's bulge was enormous. He made grunts and monosyllabic sounds like "yeah" and "unh" as he posed showing off his biceps and tweaking his nipples while he scaled the rock. Soon he made it to the top, and I quickly lowered the sound, since my parents were just a few doors down. He got on all fours and lifted his tail to reveal the bottom of his green bulge and to show off his pucker again.

The handsome, bulky canid then sat atop the ledge and began rubbing his bulge. The jockstrap hugged his giant package, which throbbed as he groped it. With each pulse it threatened to tear the tight fabric apart.

My towel flew off of me as I began to stroke my cock witnessing a sight of bulging grandeur before me. I dug through my laundry and grabbed my jock from the pile, shoving my snout into the pouch as I put the elastic waistband around the back of my head.

I pulled my foreskin back and thumbed the head of my cock. I felt a spurt of pre burst from my tip while watching the coyote turn around and remove the jock. He threw it off the wall as he squatted on the ledge and showed off his heavy sac. The rough skin on my paws felt great against my cock, though after climbing I sometimes had trouble gripping and closing my paws tightly.

I had a solution.

Rushing to my closet I grabbed two toys: a sleeve and a dildo. I lubed them up, then coated my cock and slicked my tailhole.

Fletcher was a canid dildo, and what I really enjoyed about him was the giant knot. It was great that they could also act as butt plugs. This was a birthday gift from Florian, but I tried not to think about that too much. Having a pleasurable distraction didn't make me a bad person, right? I just needed some stress relief. That has always been something everyone needed in life. Florian has always been a great friend and climbing partner, so telling him the only thing I actually wanted for my birthday was this new toy after knowing each other for a just for a couple of months wasn't that strange. That was just me being silly and random with a friend I could make sex jokes with. But yeah, it always feels great having a thick cock inside me, but taking the swollen knot and keeping the dick inside me always felt incredible. The porn star he was based off of was this giant dingo with a massive muscle gut, and he was impressively well-endowed. I lubed up the toy, slipped the tip between my cheeks, and then forced myself to relax as I pushed it in and slowly drew it out of me. I started off gently with a relaxed pace, and then sped up my strokes as I watched the coyote on the screen jack himself off.

Callum was a cock sleeve with an entrance in the shape of a tailhole. He was the tightest toy the company had, and he was definitely my favorite. He was so soft, and the snugness did great things to my foreskin and glans as he massaged my cock. My foreskin was pulled back as I thrusted forward, and the soft, slickness of the sleeve felt incredible against my head. When I motioned back the skin rolled over my tip, and I felt the urge to thrust forth again.

These were some of the nicest parts of my day. I loved that I could have some self-care time, allowing me to bring myself to climax without having to worry about someone else doing it and then breaking my heart. And I didn't have to think about how I also joined the gym because a part of me wanted to improve myself fueled by spite, and how maybe doing this with a certain other rat could ruin our friendship and make me even lonelier. What kind of person would ever have thoughts like that?

The coyote was grunting harder and faster. I was just as close as he was. The image on the screen, along with the sleeve and dildo, helped me scale the cliffs of desire and lust within me. I huffed my own scent through the jock on my face as I pushed the knot hard against my pucker. It banged against my prostate after each push, and I buried my own cock inside the sleeve stroking my leaky shaft. I shoved the plug inside me and saw the coyote squeeze himself behind his scarlet knot. His load erupted from him off the top of the rock wall. It soared in an incredible arc as he howled in ecstasy. Fletcher's knot pushed against my prostate. I then thrusted myself balls-deep into the sleeve. The intensity of it all sent me directly to the sensual zenith of elation as I moaned and grunted, taking in my own musk while waves of pleasure shook me to my core. It all knocked me off the peak as I pumped Callum full of my hot spunk. It spurted and leaked out the little hole at the end.

I twitched and exhaled sharply into the jock. After a few breaths I pulled the pink sleeve off of my cock as it slid against my overly sensitive glans.

Fletcher and Callum were the only ones who could ever make me this happy. It was fun to imagine them being my lovers as I hugged my pillow tightly, burying my face into it while enjoying my afterglow, my jockstrap still against my muzzle. I hugged one of the pink toys tightly against my chest, and gave the one inside me a big squeeze as well. I'm glad toys didn't judge me or tell me what

Indulge

I was doing wrong in bed, but they also weren't the same thing as having someone to hold.

At least they couldn't break my heart.

I squeezed the knot lodged within my rear again as I rested my eyes, and then thoughts of Florian flooded my mind. His sad look drowned every ounce of relief in me. I worried if he never wanted to speak to me again. He was my friend, and was always there for me. He usually wanted to hang out and do fun things together, like escape rooms and trivia nights. Did I just lose another friend?

The worst part was that I really did want to go out with him. Oh fuck. What did I do? Why did I have to let a jerk run my life? A constant whisper creeping up my spine making me sabotage my own life. I had to metaphorically destroy him because the alternative wasn't legal.

I decided to text Florian, since I wasn't going to let Keith continue to ruin my life. I also kept Fletcher inside of me that night as a good luck charm.

"Two chamomile milk teas with soy with grass jelly," the red kangaroo announced as he placed the drinks on our table.

We thanked him, and I pulled out an escape room board game and placed it on the table.

"'Escape the Box'? I love those, but I thought you weren't into co-op board games?" Florian cocked his head, examining the game.

"I just bought the 'Escape the Matterhorn' level, since we like climbing and all that," I said, tearing the plastic veneer off the game.

"Are we just going to pretend nothing happened yesterday?"

"I-" I had no idea what to say. Yes, I thought we could just play a game and see where things would go, because I honestly didn't know how to handle this. "I, uh, I don't know?" I then shrugged and felt my face contorting into a painful smile.

"Let's just play." He let out a sigh as I pushed the avoidant button in my head.

I took out the instructions and read them aloud. We had an hour to solve a variety of puzzles in the box, and we could get help from the app if we needed it. The app told us we were trying to scale the Matterhorn, but got separated from the rest of the group during a storm. We found ourselves at an abandoned ranger station, and needed to find a way to contact help before we froze to death. The first folder had a couple cards and documents. There was also a mess of numbers written on the backs of postcards with formulas and phrases.

I was squirming as the menacing red lines of the clock ticked on the app, and my stomach was in knots trying to tangram a painting of celestial bodies. At least it wasn't the only part of my body dealing with a knot.

In unison we said into the phone, "S.O.S. Lima-Alpha-Kilo-Echo Constance!" The app stated we won and were saved with five minutes to spare.

We laughed in pure elation as the rabbits at the other table gave us a funny look.

"That was awesome," Florian said with a grin.

"I'm glad.." I then looked him in the eye as our gazes faltered.

"So…?" he cocked his head trying to make contact with me. That made me stomach churn as nausea threatened to knock me over.

"I'm sorry," I said, looking down. Eventually my eyes slowly went up to meet his. "You know… Like yesterday."

"You don't have to apologize for not wanting to go out with me."

"But the thing is…" I felt my face becoming hot, and I felt knots forming in my stomach.

"What's up?" he asked gently.

"Maybe we could try top rope at some point."

"Oh?"

"You know. We help each other climb the taller walls and build up some endurance." I was trying not to be the anime character pushing their index fingers together.

"Sure, I guess." He was fixing his shirt as I admired his large chest and belly.

"I just wanted to show you that I've learned some things about trust, and I think the game showed it."

He nodded grabbing one arm with the other.

"I do want to go out with you," I said trying to swallow my fear. "I- I really like you too."

"Why didn't you just say that?"

"I was scared, and honestly, I'm still scared."

"Of what, me?" He lifted a brow.

"No, I'm afraid of breakups. I don't want to go through one again. The last one really messed me up," I said, looking down at my drink. "I just really don't want to lose another friend because of a breakup."

"I can understand that," Florian said softly

"But I do think you're definitely a lot nicer than him, and you make me laugh, and you're way more handsome than he is."

"You like all this?" he motioned to his belly, which made my groin twitch… Well, that and something deep within me helped as I leaned forward to take in the sight.

"First of all, I'm not the skinniest guy in the world either." I patted my own round paunch. "And second, I'm more into larger guys, like us. You're also older than me, which I really like."

"By like, what? Five years?"

"I'm not saying you're old. I'm saying that I really like you," I stammered, and then exhaled a sharp breath. "Do you actually want to be with all this? I'm just a sad gray rat who should really be going to therapy and makes a little above minimum wage."

He paused looking down at our paws, and I realized we were still holding each other's. Florian continued. "After college it's really hard to make friends. No matter what stage of your life you're in, it's tough asking someone out. When you ask a friend out, you risk the chance of ruining the friendship. It's not like you can un-ring a doorbell."

"Again, I'm sorry," I said and everything inside of me just felt like discomfort, even the knotted toy that was supposed to make me feel pleasure.

"I'm just so tired of rejection. I thought you liked me too, and that's why I was able to gather up all the courage inside of me to ask you out."

He paused again, and I stared back down at my tea.

"I think you're amazing and you're a really good friend," he said with a calm, steady tone.

"Okay, I see where this is going."

"I promise that I'll try my best not to hurt you, and to make sure that we stay friends even if we do break up. If that's what you want."

I froze, and when the ice around my heart melted, I looked him in the eyes. "Wait, so you do want to…"

"Yes, yes! I want to date you. One million times over the answer is yes!" he shouted, and the rabbits looked over at us again. "Mr. Vongsouvanh, you and I are labelled in the dating category now."

"I'm glad to be there with ya," I said and ran around the table giving him a kiss. It was so warm and the chemicals bubbled and ascended in my brain as

I felt his lips on mine and his tongue swirling in my muzzle. We smiled at each other as our mouths parted.

"You make me so happy."

"Likewise."

"Bottoms up to us!"

The drink was actually pretty good. The cheese was creamy and tasted more like cheesecake rather than cheddar. It went well with the chilled strawberry rooibos.

"I'm more on the vers side," I said with a grin, and Florian snickered.

"I think you're un-brie-lievable?"

"Flor," I said as flatly as possible.

"Yes?"

"You're the best."

A few hours later we walked down the stairs to his basement bedroom as he held my paw. I told him he didn't have to do that since I'd been to his bedroom before, but he told me he wanted to.

He held me close after we made it to the bottom of the stairs, and I took in his scent as I rested my head against his soft chest.

Looking around, it was messier than usual. A few books on the shelf were resting on their covers, and a couple papers were scattered on his desk alongside a small plate and a mug. Maybe we were both spending more time than usual in our rooms. I was glad he still had the small vinyl collection of baroque pieces I got him for his birthday. He told me months ago he wanted to learn more about classical music in general, but I just realized ever since we started hanging out he wanted to learn more about things I cared about.

Florian rubbed my back as I nuzzled his chest and looked up at the large, brown rat, inhaling his gently salted scent. He turned his gaze down to me and our lips met. His hot breath intermingled with mine as our tongues caressed. As his paw dove under my shirt, I slid mine down to cup his heavy bubble butt. I gave his roundness a nice squeeze, and I felt a smile form when our whiskers touched.

We broke for a moment and he smirked at me. I unbuttoned his shirt as he removed my pullover. In return I tugged his undershirt off of him, and admired his muscular arms flanking his sexy belly. He had broad shoulders and a patch of white fur in the middle of his chest.

Indulge

"You're gorgeous," he said to me as he felt up my muscles and played with my chubby, gray-furred stomach. I flexed my forearms and biceps for him, and he happily squeezed them. I witnessed his bulge twitching.

"I feel the same about you," I replied as I put my palm on the white patch and dragged it down his soft belly until I made it to his waist.

Placing a finger on his zipper, I undid his fly as I lowered myself to my knees. I pulled down his pants and grinned up at him.

"You're wearing a jockstrap?"

"I remember you telling me how much you liked them, so I decided to check them out, and it turns out I like wearing them. Heh…" he said, rubbing the back of his neck. "It's nice the way they frame big butts."

"And I like how they show off hefty bulges," I said as I cupped the straining pouch. The way they conformed to the cock and balls did things to my own jock. The fabric of the bulge before me had an evergreen tree on it, almost resembling a ribbed arrow. I nuzzled the 'wood' as I inhaled the musk and pheromones emanating from his groin. I began kissing and groping it as he sighed, and I took a moment to admire his cheeks before I removed his jock to get to the main event.

While I knew my balls had a nice heft, it seemed to be true that rats in general had big balls. Florian was no exception; his were the biggest pair I'd ever seen outside of the internet. He sported a thick boner, and I could see the outline of his glans underneath his foreskin.

"Let me grab something," he said as he pulled a climbing harness from his closet and started to put it on. "Ever since I bought this, I wanted to try having sex while wearing it."

"I didn't know you climbed top rope."

"I like, uh, topping," he said with a grin, and I knew he was trying to suppress a chuckle. "You like what you see?"

I dropped my pants and showed off my own bright, cherry red jockstrap to the tall rat before me and said, "I think he speaks for himself." I motioned down to my crotch, which had a pool of pre staining the front.

"Damn." He looked mesmerized by my throbbing bulge. "It almost looks like the shape of Germany."

"Komm her," I said as deeply as I could. "Or should I say, komm rein…" I then turned around and spread my cheeks to show him a surprise.

"Is that the canid toy I got you?"

"I named him Fletcher." I grinned as I wiggled my cheeks and the base of the toy at him. "The shaft works a wonderful dildo, and the knot turns it into an incredible butt plug."

"You wore this to game night?"

"I wanted to be ready just in case things went smoothly, and if you wanted to top something smooth."

"You kinky, little…" he growled as I faced him, reaching down to my stiffness and stroking it as it bobbed in its pouch. I then pulled it forward and down to reveal my own firm cock pointing out at him.

I stood as our muzzles met again. I then grabbed the straps of the harness and ran a trail of warm kisses down his cheek to his neck, then to his bulging pecs and belly. I then buried my nose in his pubic fur taking in his scent, and then looked up at the handsome rat.

I turned my attention back to his warm desire.

I cupped his hefty sac with one paw as I grasped his throbbing length and pulled his foreskin back, revealing an engorged tip. A single strand of pre leaked from his thick cockhead. His glans were so shiny and smooth, and I couldn't help but stick my tongue out to lap at his sensitive flesh, tasting the salty pre on my way there.

He exhaled with a groan at the contact between my muzzle and his cock. I felt his paw between my ears on the top of my head, gently guiding me on the speed he desired.

I stroked my own dick a few times and felt pre coat my glans and foreskin. While swirling my tongue around his head, I worked his balls with my free paw. I bobbed my muzzle back and forth across his thick length, and at times I would pause to bury my nose and whiskers in his tuft of pubic fur to take in his delicious musk.

"Your mouth is magical," the bigger rat sighed.

I hummed in response, which elicited a shudder along with a muffled "unf" from him, and I was rewarded with a spurt of pre on my tongue. I pumped myself faster and I felt myself bucking into my paw.

"Shall we get on the bed?" he asked between breaths.

It was a struggle for me, but I removed his cock from my muzzle and said, "Sure, if that's what you'd like."

We got on top of his sheets, and I was lying down on my back as he started playing with my sac and stroked my cock with his rough climber's fingers. It felt exquisite as my foreskin glided across my glans with the help of Florian's paw. He knelt down to kiss my tip and proceeded to suck on it.

123

Indulge

I sighed in delight as I reached for his package, and he got down on his side as we formed that magical number. I turned, and with one paw I worked that throbbing cock into my muzzle while the other played with his balls. I pushed my nose into his furred sac and kept his thick cock earthed within my throat as I moaned and hummed against his exposed glans. I felt his long, pink tail curl around me.

Florian motioned his head back and forth against my dick as he squeezed my ass with his strong paws. He elevated the levels of pleasure within me, bringing me higher to the point of no return. His hips thrusted as he started to grunt, and I decided to bob my muzzle again around his shaft.

Florian's muzzle made a loud popping sound as he removed my cock from his muzzle. He asked, "I know it's rude to play with a present I gave you, but would you like me to fuck and suck you at the same time?" He wiggled the base of the toy as pleasure spread through my prostate and groin.

"You know how to take pleasure to new levels." I relaxed my pucker, and with a little effort on both our ends, the dildo also emerged from me with a pop.

He slid Fletcher in and out of me slowly, but soon his pace matched that of his muzzle against my cock. My prostate thanked him by leaking more pre into his hungry maw. Everything was looking up as he went down on me.

We kept at this for a while, enjoying the sensations between our legs and the ones in our cheeks—between all of my cheeks. Shortly, Florian started to snarl and moan more audibly. Soon a fountain of salty sperm gushed from his cock, filling my muzzle with his essence as he shuttered and moaned around my dick. It was all becoming too much for me as all the sensations pushed me up and over the edge. My body started convulsing, and I felt my stomach muscles tighten up. I bucked into Florian's muzzle as I emptied myself into his hot throat.

He then jammed the knot back into my sore and needy hole.

The pressure against my prostate made me erupt even more as I cried to the ceiling. I felt whole again; harmonic completion through his moans drinking me down along with my whines of elation, our music surrounding us ascending to the apex of pleasure. Nothing missing, nothing broken, only wholeness between my mind and body, and between Florian and me as we reached the summit of serenity together.

We flopped on our backs panting as the afterglow washed over us.

My harness felt snug as I stared up at the insurmountable wall before me. I found another intermediate route in the top rope section of the gym. I took some breaths as Florian helped clip me in and made sure the ropes and carabiners were all in check. Climbing with a harness required more endurance than bouldering, but I knew this would help me with my wall stamina. This would be a way for me to finally conquer that red route in the bouldering area. I squeezed the toy in me for good luck.

The route started off fine. I was in an awkward squat, threatening to lose my plug, but I was able to reach up to another hold to get myself in a more stable stance.

I had been doing some of the easier routes for the past week to get comfortable climbing with a harness. If I let go during bouldering I would fall and be at the mercy of gravity. Here, the walls were much higher, and at any point I could just let go, and trust that the person holding the other end of the rope was paying attention. When I slipped the other day—sixteen feet in the air—Florian immediately stopped the rope as my heart pounded, and I floating in midair. My life was in his paws, literally.

About two-thirds of the way up I tried to reach for a hold above me, but it was still a good foot or so away from my reach. I didn't see anything else above me I could grab and started to panic.

"I might need to come down! What do I do next?" I shouted to Florian.

"There's a hold on the right side of the volume," he yelled pointing to the parts of the wall that jutted out.

"Thanks," I called down and groped around the protruding cube and finally gripped firmly onto a small hold. I knew I had to keep going. This wasn't my original goal, but it helped me. Solo climbing was fun, but this was important too. It taught me to learn how to trust. And I needed that when it came to love and sex. Florian somehow knew when I needed more or less slack before I even asked for it, both on the wall and in bed.

After getting myself up I was able to get back into the groove, and I found my momentum returning. Soon the two pieces of tape attached to a large hold signifying the end of the route were in front of me, as sweat flooded my face and my muscles were inundated with pain.

I squeezed Fletcher behind the knot and thoughts of Florian and pleasure rushed into me. I put one paw on the hold followed by the other. Florian cheered for me along with some applause from other spectators.

Indulge

"Ready to go down," I shouted, giving him a thumbs-up.

"You always are," he called back and laughed.

"We're in public," I yelled, trying to stifle a chuckle. Unlike most of my life I was being let down slowly and loved every second of it.

Florian gave me a hug after the descent, and I wished him luck on his white whale of a route.

I sat and cheered him up the wall. He'd been doing cardio for the past few days, both in bed and at the gym. I rooted for him on as he passed the most difficult section. Soon he was there! He grunted and let out a cry grabbed the final hold and placed his other paw on it.

"I did it!" he shouted.

"I knew you could do it!" I shouted.

"I'm too tired to climb down."

"Just try to rest there!"

"I can't!" He was standing in an awkward position. His legs were trembling, and soon one of his toes slipped and he fell onto the padding with a thunderous crash.

"Are you okay?" I rolled over to him.

He gave me a thumbs-up and relief washed over me.

"I'm so proud of you! Fletcher really is a good luck charm," I said as I put out a paw to lift him up. He grabbed it and yanked me down.

"You're wearing *him* in public...again?"

I just nodded while grinning.

The larger rat hugged me tightly as I squeezed him back. He flipped me onto my back and kissed me tenderly. I looked up at him and smiled. At that moment it felt like I was on top of the world.

Conversations and Cream

Pendoggo

The sky was a light gray as snow continued to fall over the sleepy town, the night slowly approaching as the light began to fade. Small apartment buildings lined the streets as a bulky figure quickly walked home, his weathered, dark brown sweatshirt and black scarf in contrast to the white snow that blanketed the streets. His brisk pace kicked up the freshly piled snow that blanketed the streets in a fine, white powder, leaving one of the few trails through the town as he went. The sidewalk was surprisingly empty for the hour; it was usually bustling with students rushing to the various apartment blocks and eateries nearby. This late in the semester many of them had already gone back to their hometowns, giving the town a few weeks of sleepy quiet. Rounding the corner, he walked up the front porch of a small apartment and fumbled with the keys, his breath steaming out from the cold.

The warmth of the old room greeted him as he opened the door. The earthy scents filled him with a sense of comfortable familiarity as his nose began to warm. The apartment was nothing out of the ordinary, nothing to write home about. Yet he had come to appreciate the smaller things that made it decidedly his; from the class group portraits and thrift shop paintings that he chose to hang on the walls, to the small, ornate table in the corner that he found at a flea market and tinkered with a few years back. The mastiff glanced to his side and noticed the thoughtfully arranged group of succulents and pothos plants at the windowsill. A few letters were sprawled messily on the windowsill too, one with the logo of a quite prestigious company, though not addressed to him. The mastiff looked at it curiously. The home wasn't just his anymore. He pulled off his sweatshirt, wet and

Indulge

heavy from the snow, and rolled his shoulders to adjust the thick, striped polo shirt that he wore underneath. His polo and undershirt were damp from sweat and his brisk walk through the snow. He shivered lightly as his moist clothes clung to his hefty body and contoured his soft chest and belly. Removing his scarf, the black muzzle of a tired, brown mastiff poked out. He idly rubbed his wide belly as he peeked into the dimmed hallway.

"Art?" He called out, as he sniffed the air. With his nose adjusting to the warmer air, he picked up the scent of home, old books, and spiced beef.

"You're back!" A voice called out from the kitchen. Two short, pointy ears popped out before the fluffy head of a gray, striped, tabby cat appeared.

The chubby tabby cat ran happily to the hefty mastiff and leapt up to give him a big hug. Tom growled happily, returning the hug and squeezing tight as he greeted the hefty feline in turn. He let out a deep sigh as their embrace let out the tension that had built up inside him for the day. Looking down, he nuzzled the top of the feline's head thoughtfully.

The cheery tabby cat was only supposed to stay with his mentor for a few weeks while found his footing, but weeks turned to months. Neither seemed to be in a rush to bring it up at first as they enjoyed each other's company. And eventually, months turned to years. The mastiff soon grew to know his younger colleague even more: both as a dear friend and, after the cat noticed him checking him out after a jog, even more intimately.

"Tom! Welcome home," Arthur said, giving the mastiff a peck on the cheek. The chubby cat just wore a loose shirt and fleece shorts, his fur and padding doing most of the work to keep him warm. "Forgot your coat again, didn't you?"

"I didn't think it'd snow this much," Tom reasoned, resting his head on the tabby cat's shoulder as he enjoyed the dry warmth of the pudgy tabby cat.

"I'm just glad you got home safely," the tabby cat replied, his paws roaming the mastiff's cold back to warm it up. "Lots of papers to grade, professor?"

"Just finished them," the mastiff grinned back. "I didn't want to take home any distractions tonight."

"So that's why you stayed behind," the tabby purred as he rubbed the mastiff's belly playfully.

"It's a special day!" Tomas replied. "Happy birthday, Art."

"You already greeted me this morning," the cat laughed.

"Can't a dog greet his lovely cat again?" the other replied as they finished their hug. He rummaged through his worn-out canvas messenger bag and

128

fished out a blue, wrapped box. He held it out to the feline, smiling awkwardly. "I got you something this time. You… you wanna open it?"

The cat gasped as he held the box in his paws before giving the dog another kiss. "I'll open it later. First go and get comfortable so we can eat."

The tabby cat hopped back to the kitchen while the old mastiff sighed in relief and got comfortable. He unbuttoned his polo shirt and pulled it off. The bulky mastiff shivered slightly as the remaining heat under that had kept him warm was released. He took off his belt and unbuttoned his pants, sighing in relief as his belly was freed from its tight confines. He untucked his undershirt, his belly finally released as he gave it a thoughtful pat. With his comfort worked out, Tom walked down the hallway and peeked in the kitchen to see what the tabby had whipped up.

The tabby cat hummed cheerily to himself as he stirred the pot he was cooking. He swayed to the tune as he let the pot simmer, carrying his bulk with a hint of nimbleness. Even through the loose shirt, the soft curvatures of his belly and moobs showed as the cloth draped over his generous body, teasing that soft, yet masculine, body underneath. One side of his shirt was casually raised, resting atop an invitingly squeezable love handle. The gentle curves of the tabby cat swayed to his little dance, adding to the warmth of the kitchen during the dreary winter night.

"I should really get a new belt," Tom said absentmindedly. "This one keeps digging into my gut."

"I told you to try wearing some suspenders," Art replied, not looking up from the pot he stirred. "Or just wear more sweatpants."

"But wearing sweatpants is your style," the mastiff complained with a scowl as he scratched his white undershirt. "And I don't like suspenders."

"Why not? I think it'd suit you. Give you a vintage look." the cat said, finally looking up.

"I'm not that old yet," Tom grunted. He gave a slight smile as he watched his younger colleague check him out. The mastiff was broad, typical of his breed, and the addition of muscle and a healthy layer of fat only added to his heft. With his pants unbuttoned, they slid down slightly, and his t-shirt rode up untucked to show a bit of belly as he leaned his arm up at the doorway. Below, his white briefs peeked out invitingly.

"S'not about age," the tabby cat slurred, distracted by the massive mastiff at the doorway. "Just would give you a nice look. Sexy farmer?" Art's eyes looked the chunky mastiff up and down, before slowly settling on the peeking white undergarment. "Though on second thought, you can keep the belt off too."

Indulge

The mastiff woofed playfully as he lifted his heavy arms and flexed. He used to feel a lot goofier posing like this, though the tabby cat's sincere enthusiasm made him feel less conscious about it. Confident, even.

"If you join me in finding a better belt after our jog tomorrow, I'll keep it off for longer."

"Hmm," the tabby cat pretended to ponder, a sly grin on his face. "Before I agree, I want one more thing."

Art looked at Tom and pointed a paw down playfully. The mastiff blushed. He knew what the tabby cat wanted.

"Aww, come on, for me?" Art asked playfully, giving the canine that sweet smile that made him fall for him in the first place.

The mastiff blushed and decided to go with it. Ears red, he forced a cheeky smirk and turned slightly to the side. The big mastiff raised his arm once more and gave it a big flex. His other paw went below his belly and tugged his pants lower to reveal even more of the bulge that lay wrapped in his white underwear. He glanced at the watching cat, giving him a rumbling, seductive growl.

"Okay, okay, you've convinced me. We'll go shopping next time. You've distracted me enough," Art said with a funny grin as he unabashedly adjusted the front of his shorts.

"You're paying for the belt," the mastiff grunted. The dog acted annoyed, yet a smile crept up his muzzle as he pulled his pants back up.

"Worth it," the tabby cat agreed. He purred as he approached Tom, holding the old professor's paw down to keep a bit of that white bulge showing. "You look like such a tasty treat."

"Easy there," Tomas said, as he felt Arthur nuzzle into his chest.

"Mmph, I could eat you up, big dog..." the tabby cat muttered, his nose rubbing at the mastiff's nipple while his other paw went for the warm bulge below. "Just a big, tasty dog coated in chocolate and marshmallows..." Tom yelped lightly as he felt the a warm breath, followed by a playful bite on his chest. The mastiff's eyes met with Arthur's as the cat snapped out of his fantasizing, his small, pointy ears slightly red.Now both of them had a quite visible tent. The cat chuckled a bit abashedly. "Let'sget some stew to fill that belly up nice and warm."

The two sat together at the kitchen table, each with a bowl of hearty beef stew and some slices of buttered sesame sourdough bread. Another succulent plant sat in the middle of the table, decorating the plain wooden surface with a phone leaned on its pot. A video on mountain climbing played quietly on Art's phone, just loud enough to add some noise while they ate.

"...and so I told the boar he could buy some doughnuts, and he really did!" Art laughed.

"So that's why there were a few doughnuts on my desk," Tom chuckled. "I was so confused, you know. I thought you trying to hint something at me for tonight."

"Stop!" Arthur blushed, bopping the mastiff's muzzle lightly. "I swear, he's always just looking for an excuse to show off his favorite bakery," the feline replied. "My birthday was just another jackpot for him."

"That sounds sweet," the mastiff replied. "I should visit the lab more often."

"You should! People miss you, you know." Art replied as he sipped some warm tea.

"I'm just swamped with consultations right now," the professor sighed. "I'm glad you guys are fine without me."

"You're a good advisor, the data can gather itself now. Maybe next semester you can take it easier," the tabby cat answered. "Though you didn't miss much recently, other than the birthday doughnut party."

"So, what are your plans?" Tom asked between bites.

"Plans?" Art inquired, as he took a spoonful of soup.

"For the future. You turned thirty today, after all," Tom clarified. "You got a lot of experience here as a researcher. Sustainable bio infrastructure is highly sought after. Or perhaps a doctorate?"

"I haven't really been thinking about it," Arthur replied, "I did get some job offers though I haven't really considered them yet. One was all the way up north! It's cold there. Or I guess a doctorate is always an option."

"Job offers, huh?" Thomas said a bit softly, before giving the tabby cat a smile. "That's a good way to grow!"

"That's true, though I'm not sure if researching for a private company is something I'd like. Maybe it'd be fun? Try out a few years there and try not to freeze. " The cat stabbed a carrot with his fork and chewed thoughtfully.

"A few years, huh?" Thomas replied wistfully, kind of regretting he brought up the question at all.

"Hey, I didn't say I'd take the offer yet," Arthur replied, sensing the drop in his lover's mood. "Maybe I can go full time into teaching here if there aren't any projects left."

"Teaching here? Really?" Tom laughed. "Why?"

"Why not?" The cat shrugged, laughing in return. "I suppose it would be more ideal for me to get a doctorate first. How about you?"

"I don't know," Tom replied, "When I was thirty…" The mastiff pondered, his jowl slowing down as he chewed a small bit of meat. "I guess I was doing what I'm doing now. Teaching here." The mastiff frowned. Silence settled in the room as the video they were listening to came to an end. "I've been here for a long time," He muttered to himself. "Has it really been more than a decade?"

"I've only known you for five years," Arthur commented. "You really need to tell me more stories about the campus and your projects."

"You didn't miss anything," Tom joked. "Same apartment, same old dog."

"Same big dog?" Arthur grinned, poking his finger into the mastiff's soft pec.

"I was thinner back then! A bit," Tom laughed back. "Your cooking doesn't help."

"I'd say your diet improved when I arrived," the grey-striped cat mock-pouted. "I *actually* buy veggies."

"Yet you make me eat more," the mastiff replied, as he looked in the feline's eyes softly. "You really are a cat of many talents."

"Buttering me up on my birthday, I see," Art laughed, his ears red. He looked back at Tom with a smirk "Is my *good boy* trying to be sneaky..?"

"I- ah- errm-," the mastiff blushed, covering his muzzle with his paw as his tail wagged enthusiastically behind him. "Maybe?"

"You're so cute," Arthur chuckled.

"You're cuter," Tom replied, reaching across the table to give the cat a kiss as he tried to recompose himself. "You done with dinner?"

"I suppose," the cat answered curiously. "You have a plan in mind for later?"

The mastiff grinned cryptically as he took their finished bowls and got up . "Stay there, I'll be back."

Arthur waited curiously as the mastiff headed down the hallway,his tail wagging behind him. After a couple of minutes, he heard Tom call him from the bedroom.

"Alright, come here!" Tom said, a hint of excitement in the old dog's rumbling voice.

"What is it, big guy?" Art asked as he rounded the corner into the room. He gasped as he felt a large arm wrap around him. The cat was spun to his side as a large paw pulled him into the mastiff's wide bulky body. Another large paw gripped his love handle tenderly, giving it a gentle squeeze. He felt the mastiff's muzzle brush against his, and he closed his eyes as their muzzles locked together in a passionate kiss.

"Happy birthday, my sweetheart," Tom said huskily as he withdrew his muzzle, keeping the tabby cat's plush body against his. "Are you ready for dessert?"

"Oh, dessert? What did you have in mind?" Arthur asked as his paw ran down the mastiff's soft pec. The big dog gave a silly grin as he reluctantly pulled away from their light embrace.

"Come here and get some, then," the mastiff said, his ears red as he gave a big, awkward smile. He turned to the bed, his movements slow and smooth as he stripped off his shirt to give the tabby cat a view of his broad, sand-colored back. The yellow light of the desk lamp gently lit the contours of the massive mastiff's back. The big dog rolled his shoulders as his body was freed, muscle causing shadows to appear beneath the warm layer of fat. Age may have weathered the mastiff's physique, but the strength was still very visible within. The tabby knew that the big guy could still lift him up and toss him with ease, from actual experience. Though he was only able to convince the gentle giant to do it once. He watched those broad shoulders roll slowly before Tom climbed onto the bed. The mastiff looked back, a blush on his face as his tail wagged, his position stretching the pants he wore around his well-formed, soft buttocks. The mastiff grunted as he flipped around to lie on his back, which caused the bed to creak from his weight. His paws raised up and rested behind his head, showing off his pits and chest before he looked back at the tabby cat. "All yours to feast on!"

Art's ears perked up in a mixture of surprise and lust as he looked back at the splayed body of the old dog. The professor had a sheepish grin on his face and his ears were red. Even up to now, the old dog still wasn't used to displaying himself so brazenly in such a way. He felt the tabby cat's eyes roam up and down his wide body, watching his belly rise and fall with every breath. Art's feline eyes shimmered attentively in the dim light as he looked at the blushing dog. The warm light shone over the large pecs and belly of the mastiff, which lit the fur over the soft curves and left the underside of his pecs and belly in deep, sultry shadows. A light sheen of sweat coated his generous chest and stomach, a result of their kiss as well as from being trapped within the damp shirt. His pecs flexed subtly as the large mastiff shifted his arms, which caused a jiggle to ripple gently across his hefty chest. Atop those pecs were two prominent dark brown nipples, which quickly perked up from the cool air in front of the feline's eyes. The furless nipples glinted softly in the light, silently inviting the tabby cat's muzzle closer. The bulky frame of the dog commanded an aura of respect, weighty and strong. Yet above the massive frame was a muzzle so gentle, one that Art knew would keep him safe and loved. A muzzle right now that was blushing coyly.

It was then that Art noticed the array of cans and containers that were assembled in a small box on the nightstand; suddenly he realized why his partner looked more embarrassed than usual. A can of whipped cream and a few syrups and sweet toppings were carefully assembled in the box, clearly waiting to be used. Art felt his ears and cheeks warm up in appreciation of the dog's effort. He grinned, stepping toward the bed. With graceful feline dexterity, he smoothly crawled over the topless mastiff. Their bellies touched as muzzles met. The tabby cat purred loudly as he gazed with passion into the mastiff's kind eyes.

"This is the perfect gift, stud."

The cat purred as their muzzles met once more, and they resumed their kiss. The tabby cat's warm paws roamed the sides of the canine and gave his love handles a squeeze, which got Tom to grunt into his muzzle. The other paw ran up the mastiff's wide arm, feeling it flex to his touch. The two broke their kiss, grinning at each other as steam rose from their breaths.

"Let's see, where to start…" Art pondered. The tabby cat slid his paws down the mastiff's strong arms, feeling the muscular armpits while his eyes wandered the various sweets that were put together. His ears perked up and he raised the can of whipped cream. He licked his muzzle happily and gave it a shake.

"I knew you'd choose that first," the mastiff chucked, his chest and belly shaking slightly.

"Oh, you know, cats and their cream," Art replied as he popped the cap off. The tabby cat watched his lover shiver as the cold cream hit his nipple, coating the dark spot with white. Content with the small foamy mound, Art sprinkled some chocolate chips on top. He grinned to himself as he examined his small creation atop the large canine with lustful eyes, which made the dog blush. With a loud purr he dug in, lapping at the thick cream to get to the hard nub below.

Tom gave out a moan as he was finally touched. His arms flexed in desire to hold the frisky cat, but he kept them behind his head. He wanted to let the birthday cat have free reign. The cold of the cream slowly went away as it was replaced by the cat's warm tongue. The feline's short muzzle had a small coating of cream as he dug into the white mound and eagerly lapped at the canine's brown nub buried within. He groaned, his chest flexing in response to the coarse tongue, which was just textured enough to intensify the feeling. He felt the tabby cat rest his other paw on his cheek. With a low whine he leaned into it, where he nuzzled into the soft, warm paw for support.

Art purred as he tasted the mastiff underneath all the cream, the hard nipple fun to toy with atop the big, soft moob. He carefully licked up every trace of the cream, giving the mastiff's nipple the most attention before he got back up, his thighs spread on the sides of his partner's wide belly. His own dick twitched in his shorts, squished between his own generous belly and the one below him.

"Such a treat," Art purred as he gave the mastiff's cheek one last rub. He leaned down and gave the dog a peck on the nose before turning his attention to the other nipple. He gave it a lick, purring softly as he savored the mastiff's natural taste. His paw kneaded the other pec as he took a cold strawberry and rubbed it in circles over the old dog's nipple. The wet fruit put a shiny glaze over the brown nub and caused it to perk up from the cold. Tom's moans encouraged him further, and he placed the cold fruit down on Tom's nipple before coating it with whipped cream.

Tom closed his eyes and moaned, giving in to the tabby cat's stimulation. The soft cat was thorough and delicate with his licks as he savored each beefy pec. Even after the cream was gone, Art gave a few more licks to the husky nipple before he got up. He scooted himself down the mastiff's body until he sat down on Tom's groin, huffing as he felt the warm bulge below. The feline then took a small strawberry and coated it with some cream. He looked down and gave a sultry grin as he placed it between his teeth, before leaning over to meet the mastiff's muzzle. Tom eagerly took the offer, biting the creamy fruit and sharing it with the pudgy cat. The two kissed once more, slow and soft. Their tongues savored the taste of fruit and milk as they danced against each other in their muzzles.

"Enjoying yourself?" Tom asked as he felt the tabby cat's paws on his belly.

"I always do," the cat replied with a grin. "I can't believe you actually went through with this."

"It's been on my mind ever since you brought it up," Tomas replied. He rumbled as his belly was gently kneaded. "You seemed pretty interested to try it out and I got curious."

"Well, it's sweet," the cat replied, his face bunched up in a pleasant smile. "Sweeter than cream covered nipples. I love you, big dog."

The mastiff blushed, a warm smile appearing on his own muzzle. "I love you too, big cat."

Arthur took a small bottle and grinned. He held it up. The golden liquid within glowed in the dim light. Opening the bottle, he slowly drizzled down thick honey onto the bearish mastiff's belly. The honey slowly poured out, and created shimmering lines on the soft, ample belly that it lay on. The thick, high-quality honey and the cold kept it from dripping. Instead, it clung to the fine fur and created an artistic web of sweet nectar as it followed the cat's curvy strokes.

Tom hummed, finding the feeling of the sticky fluid novel and odd. He sniffed. His sensitive nose smelled the remnants of the cream on his chest and the sweet smell of the honey. Mixed in all of it was the unique scent of his partner. His nose focused on the hint of musk and caused his heart to beat faster. The cat had a glimmer in his eye as he looked down at the dog's bulk. His eyes wandered up and down the powerful chest and ample belly that he slowly and meticulously painted honey on. The mastiff blushed. Arthur appreciated his body with a lust and passion that he had never thought he'd feel. The cat was able to make each and every curve and mark feel beautiful.

Licking his chops, Art put the bottle away to look at his handiwork. Honey ran across the wide frame of the mastiff with a few glimmering trails on his biceps and chest. His belly was crisscrossed with golden honey as it met with his torso, which all shimmered in the light. From above, the mastiff looked like he was dressed and bound in golden strings.

"You've given me a perfect excuse to taste your belly," the tabby cat giggled.

"As if you ever needed an excuse," the mastiff replied, giving it a seductive shake.

"That's true," Art laughed. Leaning down, he brought his muzzle close to the warm belly and started to clean it.

The mastiff felt warm breaths wash over his stomach as the cat began to lick. His tongue was slow and careful, making sure to take out all the honey from the short fur that it clung to. Tom's chest and stomach rose and fell as he felt the cool air in the room in contrast to the warm tongue that swept over it with care. He shuddered as he felt the cat's tongue roam higher, licking up the honey that pooled in the valley between his pecs and belly.

Art purred loudly. The cat was clearly enjoying the tastes and sensations of the soft body that he intimately knew and was so closely exploring. He took a few passes through each side of the pec and belly valley, getting the taste of honey and mastiff before going lower.

As the cat continued to scoot down, Tom felt a warm paw hold on his inner thigh for support, which kneaded the tree-trunk like thigh lovingly.

The cat continued to trail down the large, brown hill before arriving at the honey in his belly button. He looked back at Tom. Their eyes met and the cat gave him a knowing grin. Before the mastiff could react, he stuck his tongue into the pool of honey and began to lap at it.

Tom shivered as he felt his belly button get teased, that rough tongue doing wonders as it took the honey that pooled inside it. All the stimulation made him begin to pant and his belly rose and fell quickly, meeting the cat's thirsty muzzle. Art looked back at the panting dog, admiring the lusty big dog's chest, armpits, and belly, all exposed with his arms behind his back.

"I know what to do to make you moan," Art said mischievously.

"Oh really?" Tom asked. He grinned back as he flexed his arms. "Let's see you try."

"Oh, I don't need to try," the tabby cat replied, his paw creeping further up the dog's inner thigh.

Tom blinked. He suddenly felt the cool air on his thighs and realized his pants were already around his ankles. His mind briefly pondered when the fluffy cat was able to pull his pants down, before the cat's paws quickly brought his thoughts back to what was right in front of him.

"Confident, huh?—" the mastiff began, before his ears perked up and he lay his head back in a low, satisfying moan. "Ooooh, that's the stuff…"

Art grinned smugly as he worked the big dog, his paw scratching the belt marks on his underbelly. He interchanged between short, quick scritches and long passes below his belly, relieving the itch after a long day.

"A little to the side…oooh, yeah, that spot right there," Tom groaned, shaking his belly to the cat's paws. Art grinned as he complied, giving the belly a good scratching. "You sneaky bastard…"

"That's it, see?" Art replied, as he felt the tension leave the big dog. The dog's tongue lolled out happily as the itch that had been mounting up for the day was satiated, his tail dragging on the bed between his legs. The gray cat giggled as he continued to scratch the dog's underbelly, watching his big belly jiggle happily.

It was then that his paw trailed higher to grasp at the soft tool between the dog's legs.

"A-ahh", Tom groaned, the warm paw a reminder of his ignored member as it slowly got kneaded behind his briefs. Each knead pressed deeper on the mastiff's bulge, coaxing a heavy throb with each press.

"Feeling good?" Art asked, his voice deep and husky as he slipped his paw up the warm undergarment's leg. Finding his prize, he grasped it and squeezed. Tom didn't reply, except to continue a deep, rumbling moan. He fondled the thickening shaft slowly, his paw getting wet as he brushed against the tip. Once it was hard enough, the thick tool began to insistently push his paw back, and the mastiff's cock peeked out tastily.

In contrast to his light brown body, Tom's dick was cut and dark brown, almost the color of dark chocolate. The difference seemed to emphasize it further, showing a decent length and weighty thickness. It jutted up and throbbed softly as it continued to harden. The glans was a dark pink and brown, and its slit began to grow wet as the dog got even further excited. The cat grasped it and brought it close to his muzzle, getting a good view of the hot, throbbing head. Grasping the shaft, he helped it further. The cat fished out the dog's heavy, dark brown balls and rubbed a thumb up the underside of his shaft to push out a small bead of pre, getting a quick whine out of the big mastiff. He snuffled as he got a whiff of the earthy, sweaty scent of the dog's cock and balls.

"Looking good, big guy" Art grinned, watching the pink head throb every stroke. His thumb toyed with the extra skin on the underside of the shaft and gave it a few tugs to watch the member throb in response. His belly scratches slowly changed to belly rubs, his paw running circles around the big dog's navel.

"You're too skilled with those paws," Tom replied breathily. He felt the cat's paw sink down into his fat pad to get a longer stroke as he grasped the buried length within.

"Of course I am," Art said mischievously, his strokes slow and teasing. "I know what you like, don't I? I really know what you like…"

The dog groaned, peeking over his belly to see the tip of his dick.

"Maybe I should put some chocolate syrup on this dick. Make it taste the way it looks," the tabby cat said, his strokes in a slow, steady rhythm as he ran a thumb over the top of the dog's glans. "You'd want that, wouldn't you?"

The old dog whined softly, his ears hot and red as the tabby cat continued to talk to him sultrily.

"I should give this dick the treatment it deserves," the fat cat said. He gave the shaft slow, long strokes, squeezing at the head as it tightened in his grasp. With a sultry purr, he brought his muzzle right next to the tip of the dog's cock. His warm breath washed over the throbbing head as he looked the dog sensually in the eyes.

"Because you're such… a good boy," Art said, feeling the mastiff's thick tail wagging intensely below his pecs. "A good… good boy."

WOOF!

Art jumped as Tom barked excitedly. His cock throbbed in the cat's paw. His tail also raced,thumping beneath the cat's soft moobs as it wagged uncontrollably.. The dog panted, and a big blush quickly formed on his muzzle. "Excuse me," he said, coughing. He looked away, clearing his throat as he rubbed the front of his muzzle. "You knew that would happen," Tom said, still looking away. His voice was professional and refined, the tone he used in his classes.

"I didn't know you would be that loud!" Art replied, giving the mastiff's belly a rub. "That was the most full-bodied bark I've ever heard."

"I—you..." the mastiff replied, still clearly embarrassed. "You know I can't control that."

"I'm sorry," Art laughed, patting the dog's belly. "It was really cute though."

"Hrrm," the dog said, crossing his arms.

"I'm not kidding!" the tabby cat laughed as he felt the semi-hard cock twitch in his paw.

"I'll let it slide this time," the mastiff replied, "It's your birthday after all."

"Thank you, big dog," the tabby cat beamed, and gave the thick cock a few strokes in response. He felt the mastiff's heartbeat begin to quicken once more as they got back into the mood. Squeezing the chocolate-colored shaft firmly, he gave the slick head a very soft rub. "Just tell me what you want to do next, big guy."

"It's your gift, you decide," the mastiff said. He began to pant as the tabby cat wiggled his dick playfully. The cat resumed his strokes, easily bringing the dog back into a lusty haze.

"Well, I want to make you a very horny dog," Art replied, jostling the dog's heavy, dark brown balls. He leaned forward to give the tip of the dog's member a small peck.

"I want..." the dog answered, his voice tapering off.

"Yes?" the cat asked, nuzzling into the underside of the dog's sensitive glans and feeling up the frenulum with his warm nose.

"I want..." the dog huskily muttered, "...you!"

The tabby cat yelped as he felt two paws snake into his armpits, and he was quickly yanked from between the dog's legs and onto his belly. He met muzzle to muzzle with the lustful dog, who pulled him into a voracious kiss.

The mastiff could smell himself on the cat's muzzle, which only made him even hungrier for the beloved tabby cat. His paws roamed all around the warm cat's soft body, feeling the gentle curves and warm folds before he reached the hem of his shirt. Their kiss only broke momentarily as the tabby cat's top was pulled off, giving the mastiff more access to the uncovered, plush body of the cat on top of him. He growled, giving the cat's generous love handles a firm squeeze which caused the cat to groan into his muzzle. The sudden passion from his lover overwhelmed the chubby cat, and he felt himself go slack in the protective dog's arms. They broke the kiss and panted heavily, their breath washing over each other.

"You're so fucking sexy," the large dog growled as the tabby cat sat back on his belly.

Like his partner, Arthur's body was wide and heavy. The tabby cat's belly fur was light gray ivory, with bits of the slate-colored fur of his back and some stripes blending in at the sides. The curves on his body had a softness that gave it a friendly feel and look, comforting to the touch and even better to hug. His chest and belly were plump and welcoming, like a warm blanket during a cold winter night. The tabby cat wasn't as keen to exercise as the mastiff once was, and this gave his bulk a plusher form, easy to hold and sink your paw into. Yet he carried his weight well, from his bulky arms to his plump pecs and the light grey nipples that topped them. The tabby cat exuded an aura of friendly, welcoming, manly sexiness, and one that the mastiff couldn't resist.

Growling lustfully, Tom quickly yanked Art's shorts and slid them down his thick, warm thighs before tossing them across the room. He panted at the sight, the tabby cat now in just his black briefs. The small piece of undergarment hugged the cat's body intimately, squeezing his thick thighs just right which left little to imagination of his bulge and ass. The mastiff ran his paws through the tabby's soft belly before cupping the underside of his heavy pecs. He gave them a squeeze, growling in enjoyment as Art purred in pleasure, leaning into the mastiff's eager paws. His plump moobs made the mastiff pant faster, soft and bouncy yet they still held a good form from the muscle that was underneath. He patted the tabby cat's belly a few times, watching it shake before he went back to cup his soft butt cheeks. With the plump buns as leverage, he pulled the cat up to his belly till he felt the warm, cloth-covered package rest below his pecs. He gripped the tabby cat's broad chest, kneading them lustfully before pulling them down.

"Big dog!" Art purred as he was pulled down by his chest. He grasped the bed frame for support as his plump pecs hung down right in front of Tom's muzzle for him to play with. The mastiff nuzzled the soft warm chest as relished in the cat's innate scent. He sighed as he felt the warmth weigh down on him, before finding one of the gray nipples and suckling. Art groaned, his sensitive nipples enthusiastically sucked by the hungry dog. He began to instinctively hump at the mastiff's chest, which made his belly roll against his partner's pecs. The mastiff growled happily, his muzzle latched onto the soft chest as he switched from nipple to nipple, making sure to give each one ample love. When he was finally done, he looked at the soft cat's pecs and his handiwork. The feline was panting, his nipples and the fur around it shiny and puffy.

"You're so fucking sexy, Art," the mastiff repeated, still sometimes in disbelief that he had the plush, manly tabby cat in bed with him.

"So you've said," Art replied, his mind muddled from lust. He leaned back, he gave the mastiff a full view of his front as he grasped the underside of his belly and pec and jiggled them seductively. The mastiff growled, wanting to ravage and worship the cat's beefy body even more. Yet right now, he had a yearning for something else. He slowly pulled Arthur closer until the cat straddled his chest. Holding Art's love handles, he slid his paws down and grasped the black briefs underneath with his thumbs, tearing it off those thick thighs with a hungry growl. This got a gasp from the tabby cat as he was suddenly stripped. Tom huffed as he felt his chest get wet as the last of the cat's clothes came off. He gave the cat's underbelly a quick rub before he pushed it up. This made the feline lean further back and use his arms to prop himself up, his chest and perky nipples pointing up and putting what lay underneath his belly on display for the big dog to see.

The musky scent of his partner was the first to hit him, the mastiff letting out a deep whine as he took in the distinct scent of male musk and arousal. He then came muzzle to muzzle with the tabby cat's familiar, uncut dick. The shaft throbbed lightly, the color a light gray, like his fur, with enough skin to keep the sensitive head covered even when erect. The tip was moist with thick precum which had trailed along the mastiff's heavy chest, a fine strand still connecting the dick to his fur. Underneath were some tight, greige balls. Tom started to drool. The tabby cat wasn't that long or thick, but his dick was just the right size for the mastiff to enjoy. Snug enough to fill his muzzle nicely, but not thick enough to tire his jaw or hurt his throat. A dick he could enjoy sucking for hours, one he could leave in his muzzle to edge the cat for as long as he could last. But there were other things to explore first.

The mastiff followed his nose and pressed it into the cat's warm fat pad above his dick. He took a whiff, filling his senses with the cat's heady, male scent. He nosed into the plush pad happily, taking in the mix of the cat's musk and pre. The cat's underbelly plopped down on his muzzle as Tom let it go, quickly covering him with its comfortable weight and warmth. Tom nosed down and ignored the hard member as he pressed his nose between Art's dick and balls, giving the sweaty nook long, hard whiffs. Tom let out a loud sigh of pleasure, which washed the balls with his warm breath as he enjoyed the comforting, earthy scent of his lover.

"You really like sniffing there," Art commented as he took a paw and rested it on the part of the Mastiff's head not covered by his belly, as he understood the dog's affinity for scents. "You should have let me put some whipped cream on first."

"You know your scent is just as distinctive to you as your face is to me," Tom muttered into the feline's balls, feeling pre wet the bridge of his muzzle. "Adding some whipped cream would be like adding the cream to your face. Besides…"

The mastiff took a deep breath, pressing his nose into the tabby cat's fat pad. "I like it natural."

"It wouldn't be the first time you put something white and sticky on my face," the cat replied. He rubbed his large nipples happily as he felt the dog's warm, wet tongue give his balls a few laps. "You just need to lick it all up afterwards."

"Perhaps later," Tom replied, his nose twitching as he finally got to the main prize. As he pulled his muzzle back from the cat's plush groin, he watched the cat's member throb right in front of him, the covered tip nearly touching his nose. He gave it a few sniffs, smelling the scent of the cat's groin, but also traces of the distinct scent of the cat's member. While one paw kept the feline's belly up, his other paw finally grasped the member, squeezing the bunched-up skin at tip and getting a drop of pre to leak out. He gazed lustfully at the leaky member before his paw slowly pulled the skin back, exposing the shiny, pink head to the cool air.

The cat shivered with pleasure as his cock head was revealed. He blushed as he looked down and watched the dog stare intensely at his cock. Tom snuffled, taking in the unique, heady, and distinctly male musk of the cat's glans. He rolled the foreskin back and forth, watching the head pop in and out, the skin silky and soft to the touch as it gleamed in the light. The captivated mastiff pushed the skin back fully, his paw pressed into the cat's warm fat pad as his pink glans strained and shone in the dim light which caused the cat to grunt and tense up. Fascinated, the big dog ran a thumb gently over the top and slit of the cat's head, carefully as he knew that the feline didn't like it if he was too rough on the bare, sensitive glans. His thumb traced gently over the exposed head, not too fast or pressing too hard, as he learned the nuances of the tabby cat through experience. He snuffled once more, enjoying the thick dick similar to his own, yet with such a different handling and scent.

"Having fun down there?" The tabby cat asked, his mind hazy with lust as he felt the mastiff cover his member once more.

The mastiff only rumbled in approval and leaned forward to nuzzle the tip of the musky dick. Muzzle drooling, he slowly pulled the foreskin back with his tongue to lick at the slick, silky head within. He rolled the hard shaft around in his muzzle, enjoying the throbs and twitches as he took in more of the cat's cock. He eventually reached the base, and the throbbing member rested comfortably on his tongue.

"Big dog…" Art purred as the warm maw enveloped his member. He took a paw that squeezed his own chest and placed it on the dog's head. Tom rumbled in approval with the warm, heavy paw, and sank deeper, pressing into the cat's fat pad to get more of his malehood and musk. He stayed there for a while, enjoying the feeling of his muzzle full and nose filled with the scent of his partner. After some time, he pulled off with a wet slap and watched as the excited member rolled back into the soft plush and the foreskin covered the head once more. He gave the soft skin a few gentle nibbles which caused the cat to moan.

The cat blushed harder at the old dog's sincerity. "You make me feel so special."

The mastiff rumbled approvingly. Instead of replying, he decided to shove Art's dick back in his muzzle as he kneaded the cat's soft belly. This quickly got out a deep moan from the tabby cat.

"Fuck, Tom," Art moaned, the dog's warm mouth and broad tongue quickly bringing him to the edge. The dog's broad tongue lustfully slipped into his foreskin, licking at the pre that covered his glans. He began to thrust gently into the mastiff's mouth, his belly rolling on the dog's muzzle like a plush, warm, wave. "I'm getting close…!"

The mastiff didn't stop. Rumbling loudly on the cat's throbbing shaft, he encouraged the feline by burying his dick further down his muzzle, his nose pressed deep into the cat's soft fat. Soon, he felt the slick cock throb hard, and a wave of warm cum flooded his maw. The cat thrust harder, moaning as he rode the waves of his orgasm. The strings of cum that hit the dog's tongue and throat slowly grew weaker, until it finally came to an end. Tired, the pudgy feline's arms gave out and he fell on his back and his dick slipped out of the mastiff's muzzle. Tom licked his chops as he gulped down the rest of the warm seed and took a deep breath, finally getting some air after being surrounded by so much fur and fat. He watched the fluffy, towering belly heave in front of him. The stiff cock in between leaked the last of its load as it throbbed in the middle of two thick thighs, slowly softening and balls loosening with every throb.

Art panted, his head landing right next to the mastiff's hard cock. He slowly collected himself before he grasped the thick member and gave it a couple of strokes.

"Thanks, love," Art grinned, facing the leaky dick to tease the tip with a finger.

He felt the bulk beneath him shift as the mastiff slid out from under, which left him on his back on the warm, slightly sweaty bed. The dog plopped down at his side and wrapped one arm around his belly as he cradled in the fat cat preciously. They shared a small kiss, the cat tasting his own seed on the dog's tongue.

"Glad you enjoyed it," he grinned back. The dog glanced at the cat's member. Though it was slick with spit and cum, the shaft still throbbed at half-mast. "Anything else you want to do tonight?"

"Hmm… we can go shopping online for a new pair of briefs."

The excitement slowly died down in the dim room. The warmth of lovemaking began to settle into a cozy atmosphere, with the light from the lamp mixing with the occasional light of passing cars. Heat still lingered in the bedroom, the remnants of their previous activity, as well as the scent of honey and cream, all mixed together with the sweaty musk of two big males tussling together. The canine and feline lay beside each other. The mastiff rested on the cat's chest, his eyes closed as he felt the big cat's chest rise and fall. He wrapped his arms around the cat, sharing each other's heat as he lay snug in the crook of the cat's armpit. Art purred contentedly. His belly and chest rose up and down, careful not to drop the assortment of chocolate bits and fruit that lay on top of his belly for them to snack on. He popped a chocolate chip in his muzzle and flipped through his phone absentmindedly, the short videos he was watching making noise in the small room.

"Hey, love," Tom muttered, deep in thought.

"Yeah, big dog?" Art asked, swiping down to watch another thirty-second video about the history of curry.

"How much longer do you think you'll be staying here?" the mastiff asked.

"What do you mean? In bed? I do want to brush my teeth before sleeping," the cat replied as he swiped through another video. "Oh! We should make sushi next time."

"No, not like that," the dog muttered. "I mean in this town... in the university."

"Oh! Like I said, I have no plans yet. I'm still enjoying my time here. Why, do you have any plans to leave?" Art replied as he glanced down at the mastiff in the crook of his arm.

The dog shook his head in reply. The tabby cat frowned as he sensed something off. Placing his phone on the bedside table, he put a paw on the mastiff's cheek.

"What's on your mind?" Art asked.

"Well," the dog began, "you... just have a lot of potential! You're young, smart, and have a bunch of experience and publications under your name. You can go far, Art."

"Tom..." Art replied, holding the dog close. "You know I got a couple of those publications and experience due to you."

"And I'm happy I was able to help," the canine replied. "I just want to make sure... I want to make sure that nothing's holding you back. The dog looked away from the cat's eyes, peering at his gray belly instead. "I want you to go far and not stagnate." The dog's voice trailed off. "...Living in a small apartment with an old professor."

"You're not holding me back, big dog," the tabby cat said gently, running his warm paw between the dog's ears.

"I wish I could have given you more," Tom continued wistfully. "I wish I had more to show. Yet you were the one who ended up opening up so many more experiences for me. I felt ashamed. How could you love an old dog who spent so much of his life stuck where he was?"

"How?" the tabby cat pondered, "I don't know, honestly. Though does that matter?" Arthur looked at him, his cheery eyes glinting in the lamp light. "All I know is you've made me so, so happy."

"Love... I'm sorry for suddenly bringing the mood down," the mastiff apologized. "I just think you deserve better."

"We both deserve better," the tabby cat replied, bopping the mastiff softly on the head. "If I do something, it would be with the both of us in mind. We both still have time to change things up." The cat leaned down and placed a finger on the mastiff's nose with a smirk. "Though you like it here, don't you?" the cat asked.

"I..." the mastiff muttered.

"The way you handle your students, the familiarity," the cat replied softly, his voice with a hint of admiration. "This is a place close to your heart. And you welcomed me and brought me into your life with open arms. I don't wanna take that away from you."

"Art," the mastiff sniffed, his ears red.

"Anyway, we don't need to come up with a decision right now. We still have time," the cat continued, giving the mastiff his sweet, reassuring smile. "We still have a lot of time together, right?"

"Yes..." the mastiff replied, a twinkle appearing in his eye. "We still have a lot of time."

Paws intertwined, the two hefty men sprawled out in a big embrace.

Snow continued to fall over the town, blanketing the roads and rooftops with a thick white cover as shops began to close and people rushed home. The night grew dark and cold, yet in one of those windows there was warmth. A warmth that, no matter the circumstance, would still be there. And from that window a second loud, deep, WOOF boomed out, causing a few nearby windows to light up as well. And so, the night continued, preparing for the next dawn to arrive.

Paying Your Dues

Renard Avec-Histoire

I stand there, my maw slightly agape as I read tonight's match card posted on the locker room's bulletin board. I can hardly believe what's written on that piece of paper.

'Diamond Dust vs Wrecking Ball'

It's my very first wrestling match live on air, and I'm being put in the main event! Not only that, I'm about to have it with my favorite wrestler! I've been watching Raging Underground Fighting Frenzy since I was just a pup. Wrecking Ball debuted a few years ago, quickly becoming a fan favorite. His brute strength and charisma captivated the audience. Every time his music played in an arena, the crowd would erupt. He had them eating from the pads of his paws the moment he stepped out onto the stage. The people ate up his bully heel persona. They would pop every time he would chuck his opponent across the ring or slam them straight down to the mat. But the one thing the fans would go absolutely nuts for was when he would shove his rear in his opponent's face to completely dominate and humiliate them. And I was one of those awestruck fans.

I've only been signed to the roster for a few months at this point. I'm basically still a rookie, so I don't have much say in who I wrestle on any given night. It's going to be some time before I'll be booked to win some televised matches. So, for a while at least, I'm going to have to get used to being flattened by the seasoned wrestlers on the roster.

147

Indulge

Everyone else in RUFF has had their snout wedged between Wrecking Ball's cheeks, and now it's my turn. The rookie has to pay their dues, after all.

My chest is burning with anticipation. This is my only chance to make a good impression on the rest of the roster. The stakes are high and the pressure is on, but I refuse to let it distract me. There's no room to be nervous.

I start putting on my gear and stretching, trying to focus on the fact that I was getting a match on TV. I'm one of the smaller guys in the promotion, and we usually don't get a lot of screen time. The boss has always favored the bigger, stronger wrestlers. It's a little annoying, but I understand why. Something about watching these larger-than-life men beating the snot out of each other is borderline mesmerizing. I'll take what I can get. Being tossed around the ring by a behemoth is better than spending yet another show stuck in catering.

As I'm bending over to touch my toes to warm up, I hear a voice come from behind me.

"Hey there, fox!"

Assuming that 'fox' means me, I turn around to see 350 pounds of Rottweiler towering over me. I'd been watching Wrecking Ball on TV for a few years before I started wrestling for this promotion, but I've never had the chance to actually meet him. Good lord, he's so much bigger than he is on TV! I stare up at him, my muzzle hanging open like an idiot, completely unable to string two words together.

"Are you Diamond Dust?" he asks.

All I can do is nod silently. He smiles genuinely and extends his paw to me.

"Nice to meet you! I'm Doug, but everyone calls me Wrecking Ball."

I'm taken slightly aback. This man is easily twice my size, but he seems very nice and laid back. I return his smile and shake his paw.

"It's really nice to meet you, too! I'm a big fan!" I say back, completely starstruck.

He lets out a hearty chuckle, "We'll see how much of a fan you are after this match!"

He gives me a playful clap on my shoulder. I give a timid laugh in return, almost not believing that I was talking with one of my favorite wrestlers of all time. I almost want to pinch myself to make sure I'm not dreaming.

"So, the boss wants this to be a quick little squash match," Wrecking Ball explains. "We'll go out there, I'll throw you around for a few minutes, and we'll send the audience home happy. Sound good?"

I smile and nod. "I can do that!"

I take a moment to look at my opponent tonight. He stands at least a foot and a half taller than me and easily has two hundred pounds over me, most of which gathers in his round, ample belly. His biceps are almost as big as my head, and his thighs look as thick as an anaconda. His muscle-to-gut ratio is proportioned perfectly. He's already got his gear on: black boots, elbow and knee pads, and tan trunks with an image of a wrecking ball plastered on the back. Which, if all goes to plan, is an image that I'm about to get very familiar with. His dark fur is sleek and shiny. Looking up at him, there's only one thing that crosses my mind.

'God, he's so handsome!'

I'm so lost in ogling at his large frame that I almost don't register him speaking up again.

"Since it's your first match on TV, I want to let you show off a few of your moves. Is there anything in particular you'd like to do?" he asks.

I look at him in shock. He's going to let me pull off some of my own spots! That's way more than I was expecting for this match.

"Oh, wow, that's really generous of you!" I say with a sheepish smile, "Uh…well, I'm kind of a high-flyer. Would you be okay with me doing a couple of dives on you?"

To my surprise, he smiles and nods.

"Of course! Just let me know in the ring when you want to do the spots and we'll go from there."

I give him a thumbs up and he shakes my paw once more.

"Good luck out there!" he says before leaving the locker room.

I wave goodbye but speak up again before he leaves the room.

"Uh, Mr. Wrecking Ball, sir?"

He turns to look at me.

"Are you going to…you know…do your move?" I ask, feeling my face burn with embarrassment.

Indulge

He gives me a smug, almost knowing grin. "Obviously! Gotta give the crowd what they want!"

He turns and leaves, and I'm left standing there in silence. I'm so glad I'm wearing my mask right now, or else he would've seen the bright burning blush I can feel on my face. I ponder for a moment whether or not he was able to suss out the fact that I've wanted to be on the receiving end of that special move since the very first time I saw him do it on TV. The thought of having my snout wedged deep into the seat of Wrecking Ball's trunks has been the subject of my fantasies for many a moon. Obviously there was no way I would ever say that to him out loud, though. I try to shake the thought out of my head and focus on our upcoming scrap. I take a few deep breaths. The nerves are starting to settle in. One of the stagehands tells me that I need to be out in the ring in five minutes. I take a moment to look at myself in the mirror to make sure my gear is in order. As I study myself, I stare almost in awe at the gear that was designed for me. My long black tights were adorned with silver sparkle designs that glimmered in the light. They match well with my silver elbow pads and boots. However, the real triumph is my mask. It's a dark purple with a glittery silver trim around the eyes. The color palette compliments the dark orange shade of my fur really well. The entire entourage just screams, 'Diamond Dust.'

This is it. All of my training, all of the scraping by on the independent circuit, all of the non-televised dark matches, it was all going to pay off tonight. Tonight, I become a true wrestler!

I'm told to go to the ring before the cameras start rolling. Looks like I'm getting the jobber's entrance tonight. I'm a little disappointed, but at least I'm going to wrestle on TV! I walk through the curtain and start making my way to the ring, waving at the audience as I walk. I walk up the steps, wipe my boots off on the apron, and step through the ropes, taking my position in the corner.

I take a moment to look around the arena. Hundreds and hundreds of people buzzed excitedly in their seats. This is definitely a major step up from the bingo halls and community centers I was wrestling in just a year ago. I can feel the butterflies swirling around like crazy in my tummy, but now is not the time to be nervous. I need to focus on giving the best show I possibly can.

After a couple moments, the referee tells me the cameras are going to be rolling in a few seconds. I take a deep breath and try to get into character. The lights in the arena flash a couple times, signaling that we have gone on the air. The ring announcer steps up to the center of the ring.

"Ladies and gentlemen, it is now time for the main event, scheduled for one fall! Already in the ring, making his RUFF debut, Diamond Dust!"

I smile widely and raise both my arms in the air, receiving some moderate applause. At that moment, music begins to play loudly in the arena, and the audience starts raucously cheering. I look up at the entrance way, and there he is. The large, dashing Rottie is making his way down the ramp, eating up the adulation of the crowd. It's all I can do to stay in character and not join in on the massive crowd pop. Wrecking Ball arrives at the ring and lumbers onto the apron. He's so massive that he simply steps over the top rope to enter. He climbs up on the turnbuckle opposite me and raises his arms in the air, which signals an array of pyrotechnics to go off. He panders to the crowd with all of the swagger of a world champion wrestler. It's truly awe-inspiring to watch. I just hope that one day I can be half as popular with the crowd as he is.

Once the fireworks stop, Wrecking Ball hops down from the turnbuckle and we meet in the center of the ring. That's when the referee calls for the bell.

Ding! Ding! Ding!

As soon as that sound rings across the arena, my body freezes. My muscles all tense up and it suddenly becomes very difficult to breathe. The nerves have suddenly gotten to me all at once, and I can't make myself move. No, come on, not now! This is my big moment! I can't chicken out now!

Wrecking Ball saunters over to me, arms folded and with the most arrogant look I've ever seen someone wear. He has a sneer that clearly tells the crowd, "I'm about to flatten this runt!" His hulking frame towers over me, which makes me start to tremble. Yet, despite the cocky grin plastered on his muzzle, I hear him speak in a soft, gentle voice.

"You okay, kid?"

It's just barely audible to me, spoken softly enough to where the cameras won't pick it up. It throws me for a loop for a moment. The concerned question doesn't match the pompous aura he was giving off.

"I guess I'm nervous," I respond quietly so as to not ruin the illusion.

"You got this! Just follow my lead, okay? You'll be just fine."

I take a deep breath and nod subtly. He snickers and shifts his body, taking a combative stance.

"Okay, let's start with a lock up," he instructs me. "I'll push you down. Just take a bump and look surprised."

I lunge forward at him, and we lock arms. Almost immediately, he shoves me down to the mat with great force, causing me to roll backwards nearly the entire length of the ring. I look up at him, eyes bugging out in shock. The crowd erupts when I hit the mat. Wrecking Ball takes a moment to strut around in a circle, arms out wide with a gloating swagger. I slowly stand up from the mat. The fans are already eating this up! Maybe I can do this after all!

He turns to face me again, and I see him give me a small hand motion, signaling me to go for another lock up. I tentatively approach him and we lock arms again.

"One more shove," he mumbles to me.

I don't have much time to react before he thrusts my body roughly down to the mat again. I take my bump and add an extra backwards somersault to my landing, trying to sell his strength. The crowd cheers and he mockingly laughs at me. Alright, that's two bumps down and I'm still alive. That's something at least. He motions at me to lock up again and I do, however instead of shoving me to the mat, he pulls me in and wraps his arm around the back of my neck, securing me into a headlock. I pretend like I'm really struggling as he talks to me again.

"You're doing great, kid! Let's go ahead and do one of your spots. What do you have in mind?" he asks me while playing up to the enthusiastic crowd.

"Can you sell a hurricanrana?"

"Sure thing. I'll whip you against the ropes. You duck under me, and then I'll give you a boost."

I tap his arm discreetly, telling him I was ready to start the spot. He leans me against the ropes, grabs my arm and pulls me hard, sending me sprinting to the other side. I turn and rebound off the other ropes and start charging back towards him. He swings his arm at me, attempting to hit a clothesline. I duck under his massive arm and jump, springboarding off of the middle rope and sailing through the air towards him. I wrap my legs around his head and throw my body backwards. At the same time, he tucks and rolls his mountain of a body in one fluid motion, somersaulting across the ring.

As I pop back up to my feet, the crowd lets out a surprised cheer. I look over at Wrecking Ball who's scrambling back to his feet. He's giving me a faux surprised look, while I give him an actually surprised look. I can't believe we just pulled that off so smoothly! It's amazing to me that someone as bulky and large as him can move so effortlessly. We executed that move like it was a simple walk in the park! I'm so hyped that I almost feel like I'm floating. My confidence is at an all-time high.

He charges at me, and right before he's able to take me down, I hear him tell me to duck. I dip under him again, and as he turns back around to face me, I jump up, planting both of my feet into his chest to execute a run-of-the-mill dropkick. He stumbles backwards but doesn't fall. He instructs me to give him a flurry, so I start throwing whatever I can at him. A kick to the thigh, a chop to the chest, dodge his punch, kick, kick, chop, and then another dropkick. He starts swatting at me as if I was an annoying insect, but I just weave and strike. After a few seconds of that, he signals me to run the ropes again. I bolt to the opposite side of the ring, rebound off the ropes, and am suddenly met with a brick wall. Wrecking Ball body checks me almost immediately as I bounce off the ropes. I take a stiff bump to the mat, sending a resounding *crash!* throughout the arena. I lay there still, acting as if I was out cold. He leans down and grabs me behind my head, slowly lifting me up.

"You okay?" he asks, leaning in close.

"Yeah, I'm fine."

"Good. You're doing really well. Let's go ahead and do a rest hold for a bit. I'm going to put you in a Dragon Sleeper, okay?"

I give him a subtle verbal assent. He pulls me up so I'm in a sitting position. He holds my right arm with his and wraps his left arm around the front of my neck, trapping me in an odd kind of sleeper hold. He keeps me in that position for what was going to be a few moments. This is going to give us time for him to play up to the crowd some more and for both of us to take a breather.

There's just one little problem. The position he had me in was causing my entire snout to wedge snugly right into his armpit. Every time I take a breath, the pungent scent of his sweat completely fills my nostrils. I can feel my muzzle becoming slick with his perspiration. I try to adjust my position, but his grip is too firm. I'm at the mercy of this titan of a dog.

Indulge

My mind starts to go a little fuzzy the longer I breathe in his scent. I can't imagine that someone could work up such a powerful musk. The match hasn't even been going on for that long! When was the last time this guy showered?

Yet, despite the absolute potency of the smell, there's something...intoxicating about Wrecking Ball's strong musk. This rest hold is only supposed to last for a couple minutes at best, but I don't want it to end. Something about it is making me want to stay here, just basking in it all night long. I feel him give me a gentle squeeze, as if he's showing the crowd that he was tightening his grip. The increased pressure drives my snoot further into his swampy pit, and I let out a soft involuntary moan. Suddenly, I notice that my cock was stiffening quickly. Oh no, this can't be happening! Not on live TV! I reposition one of my paws in front of my crotch in a desperate attempt to hide any pitched tent that might be visible to the cameras.

After what seems like an eternity, he releases me from the hold and lets me slump to the ground. I take a few deep breaths, his pungent scent lingering on the tip of my nose. He picks me up to my feet and basically starts manhandling me. I spend the next couple minutes soaring through the air and crashing to the mat while Wrecking Ball executes just about every kind of slam in the wrestling handbook on me. Fortunately, focusing on selling the massive canine's moves was able to solve the precarious issue of my rigid shaft being on display. Before too long, he has me lifted on top of one of the turnbuckles. He starts climbing, planning to give me a suplex from the top. This was going to hurt...

"Kick me away and then jump at me," I hear him say.

I nod and start jabbing my foot towards him, striking him in the chest. He buckles and stumbles backward, giving me enough space for me to dive at him. I wait for him to face me, and then I leap at him. I fly through the air, arms outstretched, and brace for impact. He catches me in mid-air, stopping me dead in my tracks. The crowd whoops and hollers at his amazing display of strength. I pretend to struggle, as if I was trying to wriggle out of his arms.

"I'm gonna run you into the corner. Brace yourself!"

I feel him charge towards the turnbuckle. I quickly brace myself for impact. He slams me against the buckles, placing his paw against the small of my back to make sure I didn't get hurt. I sell the bump like it's the most painful thing I've ever experienced, yet I'm amazed at how safely he's been working the match with me. Despite me being thrown around six ways to Sunday, I have never felt like I was in danger.

"Alright, bud, time for the special move!" he mumbles into my ear.

Before I can process what he is saying, I feel him slide his foot behind my ankle and sweep me off my paws, sending me crashing to the mat in a seated position. The sudden motion leaves me slightly dazed, but I'm aware enough to hear the crowd noise growing absolutely cacophonous. I suddenly realize the position I'm in, and I know what's coming next...

The crowd knows it too, and they are going wild with anticipation. I sit there leaning against the bottom buckle, watching Wrecking Ball ham it up for the crowd. He puts his paw up to his ear, trying to get the audience to scream louder. Once the hype is at a fever pitch, he ambles slowly towards me. Before I know it, I'm staring up at his enormous rump. My maw falls open in awe. His cheeks are easily twice as big as my head. His sheer size and girth dwarfs me with no effort. I've spent years watching other people take this move. Despite my countless wet dreams, never once did I ever think that I would personally be on the business end of, well, his business end.

"Hold your breath, kid!"

That's the last thing I hear before his tail end descends upon me. My vision goes dark, and my muzzle sinks deep in between those meaty cheeks. Wrecking Ball's armpit scent was child's play compared to the rich tail musk that's assaulting my nose right now. I've never smelled anything so strong and pungent in all my days. Yet, despite how potent his scent is, it's driving me completely rowdy. Every breath I take fills my lungs with the strong odor of his musk and sweat. I can feel my shaft grow rock hard, pressing against the fabric of my jockstrap. I'm so lost in the world of his arousing smell that I don't even attempt to hide my very obvious erection. However, despite being unable to see anything beyond the mounds of buttocks engulfing my face, I can feel him subtly shift the position of his boot to obscure my groin. What a guy! He starts to grind his hips to and fro, making sure that my face is wedged as far as it can go. I'm in there so deep that I can just barely make out the crowd going crazy over my utter humiliation. After a few seconds of gyrating on my face, he stops moving and just sits there, increasing the pressure on my face. There is absolutely no way I'd be able to get him off of me, even if I wanted to. He's going to sit on me for as long as he pleases, and all I can do is lay here and huff his aroma.

My mind has now gone completely cloudy. I almost forget that I'm in the middle of a wrestling match being watched by hundreds in the audience and millions at home. None of that matters to me at the moment. All that matters is this ungodly intoxicating musk. This manly scent that is almost putting me into a subspace. No amount of money, or fans, or championship belts, or anything can satisfy me as much as breathing in this scent.

After what feels like an eternity, Wrecking Ball gets off of me and the bright stadium lights momentarily blind me. I immediately roll over onto my stomach to try to hide what had to be a very noticeable boner. I try to catch my breath, the strong musk lingering in my nose. The Rottie takes this time to play up to the crowd, giving me a couple moments to allow my stiffy to subside somewhat. After about half a minute, I feel him pull me to my feet and see him give me a cheeky little smile.

"Time to take it home, kid!"

He grabs me gently around my throat and prepares to lift me into the air. I jump to help him rocket me skyward. Once again, I come crashing to the mat, Wrecking Ball giving me a very convincing chokeslam. He grabs one of my arms and pulls me back over to the corner. I lay flat on my back, watching as Wrecking Ball climbs to the second rope. He's setting up for his patented finishing move, Demolition. I don't move a muscle as he jumps from the rope and comes crashing rump-first into my chest. He sits on my chest with his arms folded dominantly as the referee comes to count the pinfall.

1...2...3!

The bell rings to signal the end of the match. Even though the match is over, Wrecking Ball didn't get up right away. He continues to sit atop my chest, his large sweaty bulge nestled right against my snout. Once again, my nose is bombarded with a spicy, masculine musk. He lets me stew in it for a few moments as he plays to the crowd. Finally, he stands up and lets the referee raise his arm in victory. I slowly roll out of the ring and begin to walk to the back. As I slowly stumble up the ramp, I notice that people are clapping for me and reaching out for me to give them a high five. My heart grows warm and fuzzy, and I can feel myself tear up a bit. I walk up the aisle, shaking paws and taking pictures with the crowd, completely over the moon that I made an impact with the audience tonight.

I sit down in the locker room, replaying the last ten or so minutes in my head. I just had my very first televised match. Everything went off without a hitch, even though I spent a good chunk of the match with my face in the nethers of a big sweaty man. This is probably the greatest night of my life! I wouldn't be able to wipe the smile off my face if I tried.

As I sit and reminisce, the adrenaline starts to wear off, and all the aches and pains that come with being steamrolled by a massive dog start to set in. An inch of foam padding doesn't help much if you're being dropped from about seven feet in the air. I groan and try to stretch out my sore shoulders and back. I really feel like I was put through the wringer, and I loved every minute of it.

After a few moments, I hear someone else enter the locker room. I look over and see Wrecking Ball beaming at me.

"You really kicked ass out there, kid!"

I let out a sheepish laugh, "More like 'kissed ass' out there, eh?"

He gives me a playful little shove in response to my bad joke. "You took my move like a champ! It almost seems like you wanted it." He finishes his remark with a cheeky wink.

I feel my face go hot, and I turn away bashfully. He chuckles warmly and pats my back. "In all seriousness, you did an amazing job. I just got done talking with the boss and even he was super impressed."

I feel my chest swell with pride. Hearing my idol praise my in-ring work almost brings me to tears.

"Thank you so much! It was a real honor to work with you, sir!"

He smiles at me and shakes my paw. I can only imagine how brightly I'm blushing right now.

"I'm gonna head to the bar across the street here in a bit. Can I buy you a drink?" he asks.

Butterflies start throwing a rave in my tummy. I don't know what to say. All I can do is nod sheepishly.

"Great! See you there!"

He claps me on the back encouragingly and turns to leave. Right before he is about to walk out the door, he turns back to me with a smug, teasing grin.

"You should probably wash that mask."

Indulge

I feel my face flush and he lets out a chuckle and leaves the room. I slowly take my mask off and press it to my nose, taking a deep inhale. A wild concoction of Wrecking Ball's pit, ass, and crotch musk is still soaked deep into the fabric. The captivating scent dances around in my nose, making me salivate.

I quickly rush to the nearest bathroom and lock the door behind me.

In memory of Scott Henson. Keep burning bright, Big Cat. — Renard

Sliding In

Snepitome

As far as Max was concerned, there were three tiers of jobs.

The first were your dime-a-dozen, get-me-out-of-here, nightmares. The sort of job where you started counting down the days until you could quit the moment you got hired. The jaguar's first job had been one of those: a summer gig as a camp counselor that did little else but reaffirm that he didn't want kids.

Then there were the 'good' jobs. These were the ones you went to school for, that paid well and let you live out the two-point-five-kids-and-a-white-picked-fence suburban fantasy. Two problems: Max didn't want to spend his days answering emails, and he wanted kids even less.

That left the last tier: the ones where you spent your time off wishing you were back at work. Until he was nineteen, he would have sworn that these jobs were a myth, and that anyone who disagreed was lying to you, trying to sell something, or completely delusional.

The jaguar bit down harder on the thick roll of ruff in his muzzle. He wasn't too prideful to admit when he was wrong. The sound of his hips slamming against the raccoon's ass reverberated around the disused sauna, but Max wasn't worried: he knew just how thick the walls were, and this wasn't his first rodeo.

"Fuuuuuck meeee," the raccoon—Max hadn't caught his name—moaned.

Max turned his head to the side and sucked air through his teeth. The hot smells of sex, sweat, and energy, beat out the chlorine pouring in from the nearby pol. "Happy to," he growled.

Indulge

The raccoon had to be at least twice his size, and if he had to guess, at least twice his age. He slid a paw down the older man's back to squeeze his ass, grabbnig a thick pawful and extending his claws just enough to prick at his flesh. He got what he wanted: a hissing whine that interrupted the rhythmic panting that had been growing faster in time with the bucking of Max's hips. Not long left. While he still had him right where he wanted him, Max pressed his chest flat against the raccoon's back and hugged him from behind. Reaching for his dick was a non-starter thanks to all the gray flab in the way, but Max was more interested in a different kind of meat anyway. It rippled each time he slammed himself up into the raccoon's rear, soft and pliant in a way his muscles weren't. Each bounce drove him crazy, and that tiniest bit closer to the precipitous edge he was nearly ready to tumble off.

The raccoon came first, in a series of shudders that made Max's eyes roll back. Not wanting to be left behind, he picked up the pace and sprinted across the finish line just a second later.

Unlike some of his canine friends, Max was able to pull out immediately, and cleaned himself with one of the park-branded towels he'd brought. Covered in cum, the grinning face of Rising Tide's dolphin mascot finally had something to smile about.

"Damn," the raccoon swore, drawing Max's attention back to him. He was sitting on the wraparound bench, leaning back against the wall. "Been a while since anyone rode me that hard. I should've tried jaguar ages ago."

Max grinned. "Wouldn't have helped."

"No?"

"I'm one-of-a-kind," he winked.

That got a grin. As far as job perks went, a never-ending stream of fat DILFs was unbeatable. This was his fourth year working at Rising Tide, and what had started off as a summer lifeguard position after his freshman year of college had become an annual reward to himself for completing another year of school. Sure, there was the question of what he would do now that he'd graduated, but at least he had the rest of summer to avoid thinking about that.

"I can believe it," the raccoon smiled. "Say…" Max tried to keep his smile level, but he was already dreading what came next. It was easy, but never fun. "You wouldn't wanna do this again sometime, would you? Swap numbers? I'm from outta town, but I come here a fair bit. More if… y'know." If the slides weren't the only thing he could ride.

162

Three and a half years of practice made Max a pro at shooting guys down. "Sorry," he said, putting on his best approximation of an 'I-wish-I-could' frown, "but I'm not out." It was a lie, but the raccoon didn't need to know that.

"I can keep things secret," the raccoon shrugged, "not a problem with me." Max just smiled apologetically, and the raccoon sighed. "It's alright, I get it. Still, would've loved to go for seconds."

Max let them both out of the sauna and into the adjoining locker room as soon as the coast seemed more or less clear. Rising Tide had done their best to keep guests from fucking in the sauna, but had finally given up and resorted to locking it instead. Still, the damp environment meant it needed to be maintained, so the staff had keys, and in the years since many of them had taken a page out of the guests' book. He and the raccoon showered in separate corners of the room, though Max would've been lying if he said he didn't sneak a few looks. Sure, it could be fun to hit that again—he couldn't help but wonder what fucking the guy's gut would feel like—but commitment wasn't in the cards, and he didn't want to get attached.

Tail still twitchy from sex, Max didn't even notice the wolf waiting for him outside the shower building until he just about crashed into her. "Maxie! Finally, I was starting to think Bec was full of it."

"Bec?" Max asked, blinking the sun away. There wasn't a cloud in the sky, and the paved white paths of the park were particularly eye-searing.

"Yeah, she said Rick saw you head into the showers ages ago."

Max grinned, "I was checking out the sauna."

Kate barked out a sharp, canine, laugh. "Really? You know most people go home after their shift, right?"

"I wanted to de-stress. You know how the morning rush is."

"You're the worst." She looked behind him at the stream of guys coming out of the building. "So, who was it?"

"Ah ah ah," he chastised, "employee-guest confidentiality."

"Not how that works," she whined. "Come on, you never tell me who you hook up with." Max controlled his expression, but there was a good reason for that. Sure, everyone knew he was gay, but the exact details of his tastes were a carefully-kept secret. Kate sniffed, and Max thought she was just huffing until she said, "Raccoon?"

"What?"

"He was a raccoon. I can smell him on you."

Oh shit. Fuck her and her obnoxious sense of smell. "Shouldn't you be working?" he asked. "Where're you stationed today?"

"*Typhoon,*" she said, "but I don't start for another twenty minutes." She squinted at the people behind him, clearly watching for a raccoon. Before he could say anything else, a smile stretched along her muzzle and she tipped her head at him. "Max, really? With his family here?"

The jaguar's heart slammed into his stomach. He'd managed to keep this a secret for more than three years, and now it was going to come out with less than a month to go. "Kate, don't tell—"

The wolf just laughed. "Hey, I'm not gonna say anything. His dad doesn't need to know he was getting fucked by our one and only rosetted Romeo."

His dad? Max turned to look and saw the raccoon he had been fucking talking to a slim raccoon about his and Kate's age, presumably his son. His heart slowly started beating again. "What can I say? I always pity the guys dragged here with their families. Least I can do is show them a good time."

"Maybe he can put that in his review. You'll have twinks lining up outside the gates at dawn."

"There's only so much of me to go around," Max said, closing his eyes and holding one paw to his chest, "but I'll try my hardest."

"And you're so brave for that," Kate teased. "I'd better run, but text me later."

He shot her a thumbs up as she ran off, and let out a deep exhalation. Thank fuck, crisis averted. He stepped out from under the shade provided by the shower building, and let the afternoon sun dance across his golden fur. He'd had his fun for the day, and was ready to head home.

He only got a dozen steps toward the park gates. He might have made it all the way had he not happened to glance over at the outdoor showers, and stopped dead in his tracks. Standing there, one arm raised over his head as he scrubbed the chlorine out of his fur, was the fattest otter Max had ever seen. His belly, the first thing Max usually noticed about a guy, was massive. It surged out from his middle and sagged: while he was definitely round, beyond a certain point gravity would not be denied. Rolls of fat too thick and prominent to really be called love handles surged spilled forwards to join the lower expanse of his brown-furred belly. It dimpled in the middle, below his navel, itself a wide crease just begging to be filled to the brim with jaguar cock.

Max's gaze drifted down to the otter's thick legs. For just how wide his stance was, there was remarkably little space between them. He had a tail thick enough to put any body pillow to shame, and thighs just as juicy.

Up above, the otter scratched at his neck. In stark contrast to the rest of his fur, his head was clad in a creamy white that extended to just above his thickly-padded collarbones. The raccoon's ruff had nothing on this guy's: a thick spare tire of blubber just begging to be scritched.

The otter looked up and caught Max's gaze. The jaguar gave him a quick wink, something small enough to be overlooked if he wasn't interested. Instead, the otter grinned. Max held eye contact for a moment before very pointedly walking away and leaning against a pole nearby, not looking towards the showers. Tinny dance music with a vaguely-tropical bent played, and he couldn't help but sway his hips a little as he waited.

"Nice moves," said a rich voice nearly as heavy as the otter it came from.

Max looked over, and sure enough, there he was. Fuck him, he was even more attractive up close. If he wasn't six feet, then he was definitely close to it. Still shorter than Max, but not by much. "Yeah?"

The otter nodded. "Couldn't help but noticing you looking my way."

"Gotta make sure our guests are taken care of," Max replied easily, tugging at his bright blue shorts. 'STAFF' was written in blocky white letters just beneath the dolphin logo. "Especially our first-timers."

"And how do you know it's my first time?"

"Oh, I think I'd recognize you," Max smiled.

"Quarter-ton otters don't exactly blend into the crowd."

Five hundred pounds... and that's if he wasn't being modest. Max had to fight the urge to whistle. Instead, he waved a paw nonchalantly. "Blending in is overrated. Why do you think I paint my rosettes on every day?"

That got a laugh out of him. "Working with all this water? You'd spend all day reapplying them."

"And night."

The otter smiled and held out a paw to shake. "Name's Del."

Max took it. "Max."

"Well Max: how exactly do you take care of guests? Assuming you're not just getting paid to drool over whatever otter comes through your showers."

Hook, line, and sinker. "I know a couple places a bit more..." He gestured around at the milling crowds. "Private. Maybe we could sneak off for a bit, get out of the sun."

For the first time, Del didn't seem completely interested. "Tempting, but I don't like to fuck on an empty stomach. I was gonna grab a bite first, if y'wanted to come along?"

Max bit his lip. He usually made a point of minimizing time spent in the open with his hookups. Sure, if they were walking from place to place he could just

Indulge

tell his coworkers he was helping a guest out, but sitting down to eat? That looked like a date.

"Of course, if kitty needs to pounce on something right now, I'd get it." Del looked across the plaza to where a chunky lion in a floral shirt was heading into the shower building. "Plenty of meat on the menu."

As enticing as the side was, it couldn't stack up to the main course. He shook his head. "No, I'm good. Let's go."

Del smiled and said, "More than good." Max couldn't restrain a smile.

Of the restaurants clustered around the park's front gate, Del chose the buffet. While he waited in line, Max picked out a table for them, taking care to find one with the weakest sight lines to the windows. Del joined him shortly, carrying a tray piled with plates. "Oh, I meant it when I said I wasn't eating. I wasn't just trying to con a free meal."

Del raised a brow. "Who said any of this was for you?"

Max winced. "Sorry, I didn't mean—"

"—to call me a fatass?" Del asked. Max's tail curled tightly. It'd been a while since he'd fucked up with a guy before even getting him into bed. Usually if he fumbled, it came after they had both, well, come. Del waved a paw. "I've been called worse, in and out of the bedroom." Max tried to laugh, but his mouth was dry.

At least he didn't have to worry long: Max had expected to be bored, but he found himself sitting up straight and leaning forward, watching each bob of the otter's throat as he swallowed. His ears were perked, and he felt a strange excitement each time Del reached for another pulled-pork slider. This was the fuel that was going to pack more weight onto a body he was already going crazy for. Del was an efficient eater, and quickly moved onto a round of chicken quesadillas. "How long've you been working here?"

The question pulled Max abruptly back to reality. "Uh. About three years. Summers."

Del scratched his chest in what might have been an innocuous motion, were it not clear that he had Max's undivided attention. He was still only wearing a pair of tight black swim shorts that clung tightly to his hips and ass. Sitting down across from him, he might as well have been naked to Max. His breasts bounced, sending ripples sloshing down through his belly fat. "Distracted?" Del asked as he swallowed another mouthful.

Max squirmed in his seat: they'd only been sitting down for a few minutes, and he was already hard as a rock. "Sorry," he said. He was off his game: it was usually easy to lead the day's entertainment, but with Del he was floundering. Go figure that an otter would be the one to take him out of his depth.

"Not used to watching guys eat?"

Max felt like a dick. "I wasn't trying to stare."

Del snorted. "I'd be miffed if you weren't, and I was just putting on a show for nothing. I figured that with the way you were ogling my gut, you'd dig this. Not into the rest of it?"

"The rest of it?"

Del started in on his sweet and sour chicken balls and accompanying fed rice. "Everything *around* the sex. Sounds like you know you way around an ass well enough, but at least in my experience, most guys like you dig this part too."

Max didn't have to ask what Del meant by 'guys like him'. He shook his head. "I'm not used to it, but this"—he gestured between Del and the dwindling food on the tray—"is kinda doing it for me."

"Kinda, huh?" Del grinned and gripped the sides of his belly, scooping it up off his lap. The thick ball of fat rose like baking dough until he dropped it back down with a heavy slam. Max felt his cheek catch on fire, and had to look away.

"Maybe more than kinda. Is it that obvious?"

"Don't worry, it's cute. I like seeing you flustered."

Hot, sexy, handsome: Max knew how to deal with those. He was a jaguar, they were basically givens. Cute though, that was new. Before he could figure out how to respond, Del buried his muzzle in a fist and stifled a low, growly, belch. A shiver ran down Max's spine as his traitor of a cock stiffened and tented his shorts.

Del snorted. "If I'd known you were gonna react like that, I wouldn't have covered it up. Are you usually this much of a gut slut?"

Max found himself caught at the intersection of arousal and mortified embarrassment. "Maybe I'm learning some stuff about myself." Del smiled and went back to polishing up the last of the food. Desperate to steer the conversation away from his burgeoning tastes, he asked, "I've never heard the name Del before. Is it short for something?"

Del groaned, but there was a slight smile to his muzzle. "Way to cut right to something I hate. My full name's Delmar: it means 'of the sea'. I guess my parents were trying to be poetic."

"It's not that bad," Max said, rocking his paw back and forth in a so-so motion. "It could be worse."

"Sure," Del smiled, "but it could be a whole lot better. At least it makes sense, since we're sea otters."

"Yeah, speaking of: I thought otters had longer tails?" Del's wasn't exactly short, but it wasn't as long as Max had been expecting.

Del shook his head. "You're thinking of river otters."

"What's the difference?" Max asked.

Del scoffed. "Don't let my dad hear you say that, he'd cuff you around the ears. Sea otters are bigger overall, but we've got stumpier tails."

Despite getting flustered earlier, Max felt himself back on solid ground. For all that his hookups were on the chunkier side, he never really brought up their weight. It was what he liked, but talking about it directly seemed impolite somehow. Here though, Del had all but asked him to. Working to keep up a smile, Max said, "I'll say you're bigger. Now is that all sea otters, or are you just skewing the average?"

"Damn, kitty's got claws after all. I was starting to think you were just some nervous housecat." Max puffed his chest up at the compliment.

"Now guess mine," Max said. He couldn't pinpoint what made him say it: he typically hated his full name, and even his friends only knew it because one of them had seen his ID. Still, fair was fair.

Del chewed and looked up at the ceiling, as if he'd find the answer there. "Maxwell?" he asked.

"Keep going."

"Maximilian…?"

"Closer."

Delmar—scratch that, Del suited him better—hummed. "It's not Maximus, is it?"

"Ding ding ding."

"No way!" Del laughed. "Has weight to it, that's for sure."

Max cleared his throat and tipped his muzzle towards Del's gut.

"Yeah, laugh it up, Maxie."

"I didn't say anything."

"Maximus…" Del rolled the name over his tongue. "Can't say it doesn't suit you."

"Oh yeah?" Max asked, surprised. The only reason any of his friends had found out his full name was because they'd seen his ID: he'd never been a fan.

"Yeah. You're a big cat, of course your name would be full of itself."

"Hey! We just met."

"I'm not saying it's a bad thing, but I dated a snow leopard for a while. I know you cats like your egos stroked."

"I'm a jaguar, it's not the same at all."

Del's muzzle broke out into a wide, cheek-dimpling grin that told Max exactly what he was going to ask. "What's the difference?"

Max groaned. "Alright, alright, point taken. Snow leopard though, I've always wondered what that's like. That tail's gotta be pretty fun."

"Oh, it was. The cat it was attached to was a bit of a priss, though. Things probably wouldn't have worked out, even if it weren't for the closet."

"Ah, he wasn't out?"

Del shook his head. "Nah, I wasn't. Only came out a few years ago. Figured what the hell, I didn't want to spend the rest of my forties hiding." Del had finished eating and shuffled his tray out of the way. He looked Max up and down once before turning the topic of conversation back to him. "So, how's a cute little guy like you realize he's into flab more than abs?"

Max snorted, raised an arm, and flexed his bicep. "Little?" he asked.

Del raised an arm in kind, and gripped it with his opposite paw. His thumb and forefinger stood no chance of closing around all that otter meat. "Little," Del reaffirmed.

Max huffed, but thought back. "I would've been, fuck. Fourteen? Staying over at my best friend's house during the summer. His family had a pool, and his dad—"

"Figures."

"Shut up," Max laughed. "Anyway, I couldn't get him out of my mind. Wound up jacking off in the shower that night."

Del snorted. "Jagging off."

Max rolled his eyes, but smiled all the same. "Never heard that one before."

"Still though. At your friend's place?"

"I was fourteen!" It was his first time telling anyone about his sexual awakening. Usually he just lied and said it was an underwear model, or some athlete. Yet here he was, revealing hidden parts of himself to a total stranger. Something about Del just made him easy to talk to.

"So," Del said, dragging the word out, "I'm done here. You mentioned you had somewhere private we could sneak off to?"

"There's this boarded up sauna…" Max trailed off. If he hurried things along now, he wouldn't get to drool over the otter's fat ass for the rest of the afternoon. "But what's the rush? How much of the park have you seen?"

"I've really just been in the pool. You have something else in mind?"

As it happened, Max did. Minutes later he was eagerly leading Del to Typhoon, the tallest slide in the park. It was an absolute behemoth of white scaffolding surrounded by a serpentine mass of twisting blue tubes. As they walked, Max couldn't help but sneak looks over at Del: the pillowy roll of belly fat spilling over the waistband of his skin-tight shorts bounced with every wide-stanced step he took. The whole of him was in motion at once, five hundred pounds of squishy otter fat rippling like the water he so clearly belonged in.

"Easy," Del said.

"Hmm?" Max hummed, too busy studying the way Del's lovehandles bunched up with each step to fully listen.

"You might wanna adjust your shorts."

Max blinked: he was already at half-mast. Hurriedly stuffing his paws in his pockets to hide his erection he said, "Thanks for the heads up."

"Don't mention it," Del responded casually, "I was your age once. 'Sides, I like looking at you too." He gave the broad curve of his belly a slow rub, and Max took his meaning: he wasn't the only one getting hard, Del just had an easier time hiding it.

"I'm surprised I haven't seen you around before," Max said, turning the conversation away from his dick, "I thought otters liked water… I'm allowed to say that, right?"

Del laughed. "Don't worry, I'm not gonna drag you to sensitivity training. I'm new to the area. Figure I'll come by a lot more, if all the staff is as friendly as you are."

Max laughed, and after a moment of weighing whether he really wanted to go there, said, "They'd better not be: you're all mine." He wondered if it was too much. Judging by the otter's grin, it was just right.

Max and Del got into Typhoon's line. As the park's main attraction, it was anything but short. "You cool with waiting?" Max asked. "We could hit up another ride if you're not."

Del looked up at the structure. "You worried I can't do the stairs?"

All the blood drained out of Max's face. "What? No, it's not that—you're fucking with me, aren't you?"

"Ding ding ding," Del said, in the exact cadence Max had used earlier. "You don't carry this"—he picked his gut up in both arms and dropped it, a colossal motion that dilated Max's eyes faster than if he'd been on catnip—"around every day without putting on at least a bit of muscle. I'll be fine. Besides, I always stay at parks until close." He grabbed one of the two-person 8-shaped rafts from the collecting pool, and held it out for Max to grab the other end. He did.

As the line progressed and they hit the bottom of the stairs, Max found himself staring right at Del's ass. It was every bit as wide as the otter's gut, fat enough that its curves peeked out around his fat sausage of a tail. Every step up made first one cheek bounce, and then the other. They were only to the first turn in the staircase by the time Max was hard as a rock and wiping his muzzle free of drool. At least now, nobody could see.

"Y'know you're allowed to talk about my body, right?" Del asked, tearing Max out of his reverie.

"What do you mean?"

"Y'seem pretty shy about calling me fat," Del shrugged, making the raft they were holding bounce.

Max didn't quite know what to say to that. Sure, his hookups were fat, but that didn't mean he spent their time together rubbing it in just how big they were. The line was far from the most private space he could think of to get into this. "I just didn't want to be a dick," he said. "Seemed rude to call you... that."

"Sure, it would be if you meant it as an insult," Del said, without ever turning around. "But it sure doesn't sound like you think it is. I like myself the way I am, and it's pretty obvious that you do too, so why not own up to it? Trust me: I wouldn't be walking around shirtless like this if I wasn't happy with all this."

'All this' bumped back to smack Max straight in the face with tubby otter tail, right before climbing another few steps. The stop and go was the worst part. Over and over, Max was treated to the juiciest ass he'd seen in a long time, bouncing right in front of his face, with just enough time between each show for his heartbeat to go back to normal.

He sucked his teeth: he was going to go insane up here. It had only been a few minutes, but it felt like hours that he'd been forced to stare down a fat pair of cheeks he wanted nothing more than to fuck until they were both sore. He needed some kind of relief, but there were people on the stirs behind him: he couldn't just reach up, swing Del's massive tail to the side, and faceplant into his ass without anyone noticing. They took another step, and Max growled in desperation. Del's back rolls danced against one another as he moved, shifting from side to side with each step whose weight reverberated through the metal steps beneath their paws. Fuck, he needed to do something.

The next time he saw people ahead of them move, Max got a head start. He stepped up before Del was ready, crashing into his back and burying his muzzle into the otter's back fat. It was even squishier than he'd expected: pure, kneadable, chewable, blubber. Del jumped and gripped the railing, and for just a second Max swooned over what it would feel like to have the otter roll backwards onto him. He shook his head: his blood was too busy elsewhere to give his brain the time of day. "Sorry," he grinned guilelessly.

Del huffed, but didn't say anything… then, or the half-dozen other times Max managed to rub his face against the otter's back fat or tail on the way up. When they finally reached the top and Del turned around to face him, Max shot him a wink. "Guess I was just excited."

"Starting to think I wasn't the one who couldn't handle the stairs," Del said.

Max grinned and gently punched the otter's stomach. His fist sank right in, strength meeting squish in a dichotomy that didn't help calm his boner down. "Wouldn't have been an issue if you'd been walking faster."

Del opened his muzzle to reply, but someone else beat him to the punch. "Max! Who's this?"

Shit.

Kate was looking between him and Del, her tail wagging. Chatting with Del, he'd actually let his guard down for once, and had forgotten where Kate was working for the afternoon. The previous fear of being caught reared its ugly head, and he rushed to speak before either Kate or Del could say anything else. "This is Del," he said, successfully keeping his tone cool and confident, "Family friend. He and my dad worked together."

The wolf grinned, evidently sensing a way to put him on the spot. "Cool, cool. Say, if you were looking for another round with that racc from earlier, I saw him and his dad by the half-pipe." Del cocked a brow at Max, but the jaguar set the raft down at the top of the slide and gestured for Del to get in. Kate just barked out a laugh. "You're good to go." Max resisted giving her the middle finger, and sat down in the rear spot while Del lined himself up in front.

Max hadn't really thought things through: he'd just been desperate to get going, and hadn't braced himself for the realities of XL, double-wide, caked-up, otter ass staring him in the face. "You sure you want me in front?" Del asked, already halfway into a crouching position.

Max's sense of self-preservation was voted down by every part of his brain saying, "Yes."

"Your funeral." Del eased himself into position in the front hole of the raft… as much as he could, anyway. Max's eyes just about leapt out of their sockets as the otter's fat, squishy, cheeks contoured to the curves of the rubber floaty and spilled over. The jaguar's legs were forced wide out to the sides to accommodate all the otter-DILF crammed between them, and there was precious little room for Del's tail. After an awkward moment of shuffling, Max pulled it into his lap and around the right side of his waist, where it curled to wrap around behind his back. Del was holding him with his tail, he was holding Del between his legs: he'd been wanting to get intimate with the otter from the moment he'd laid eyes on him, but hadn't imagined he'd be doing it in front of a coworker.

"You two ready?" Kate asked, reminding Max that she, let alone anyone else on the planet, existed.

He tried to respond, but his tongue caught in his throat. Del's cheeks were trying their hardest to tear out of the skin-tight black fabric containing them, and every little shuffle he made as he fought to keep them from rushing down the slide prematurely only seemed to make the situation more dire. If they didn't get going, Max wasn't sure he'd be able to help himself. Already, his cock was stiffening in his shorts, and the warm heft of Del's fat tail in his lap didn't help.

Thankfully, Del had him covered. "All good."

"Have fun!" Max felt a rough shove at his back that pressed him even tighter up against Del's rear, and sent the two of them over the lip into the umbral depths of the slide. It yawned wide, swallowed them whole, and they were off.

Over his summers at Rising Tide, Max had grown used to the twists and turns of each of the slides, and that familiarity had stolen a lot of their excitement.

This wasn't familiar.

He'd never ridden with someone as heavy as Del, and the otter's bulk had them flying down the initial drop like a meteor; he was sure they were going to crash straight through the bottom of the slide and be sent hurtling to the ground. Instead, the sharp curve back upwards made his stomach lurch, and he was suddenly glad he'd skipped lunch. The slide's alternating bands of stygian black and vibrant blue blended together into a dizzying blur that made him close his eyes.

Each twist sent them sliding far up the outer wall, high enough that Max was sure they were going to flip before Del's weight dragged them back down and sped them up even further. Something halfway between a moan and a roar spilled from his muzzle, throaty and loud in the tight confines of the tunnel. It wasn't that he was trying to grind against Del, but every sudden movement forced the thick otter daddy further back into his lap until he was hot-dogging Del's cheeks through their swimsuits.

Indulge

Max had dry-humped before, but this was nothing like that. The water splashing between them made their suits slide easily over one another, so that he didn't even have to do any work. As Del slid back into his lap, Max pressed forwards under the otter's tail and leaned tighter against his back until his arms were wrapped around Del's chest. He squeezed tight, stealing a squeeze at Del's breasts: he couldn't help himself. They were finally alone together, and might as well have been naked. All he could feel around the swirling tumult of the slide was Del's warm heft, hot and heavy and crushing him backwards in his seat. Del's fat ass rubbed against his groin and he groaned, the sound lost amidst the otter's excited shouting and the rushing of the water all around them. His cock was rock solid, and every twist, turn, and dropped, ground it between Del's cheeks. Whether Del meant to or not, he was giving Max the world's most chaotic lap dance.

Max took a deep breath and tried to calm down, but there wasn't a chance in hell of that happening: not when he was rocketing down a slide at a billion miles an hour, not when he could feel Del's big, fat, ass, bouncing in his lap, not when he could feel the otter jiggling in his embrace and smell nothing but chlorine, the sweet cherry scent of his shampoo, and just the faintest hint of underlying otter musk.

Max just couldn't help himself. He gave himself over to the hot pleasure rising through his chest, and pounded up under Del's tail. "Oh, fuck," Del groaned, and Max had no idea whether it was because of the slide, or the jaguar meat sliding between his cheeks.

They dropped, and Max came as close as he could to entering Del with their suits in the way. So close, yet so far. Del grabbed one of Max's legs in a paw trembling with frantic energy, and that was all the encouragement Max needed. Instinct took over, he opened his mouth, and bit down around the thick collar of neck fat bunching up just in front of his face.

Del squirmed between his teeth, setting off every predatory urge buried deep in Max's feline brain. The otter's paws were vice grips around his legs, and it didn't matter that they were crashing recklessly down an enclosed water slide in the dark, Max managed to find a steady-enough rhythm that saw him desperately slamming his rock-solid cock up against Del's soft, plush, ass over, and over, and over.

It couldn't have been longer than two minutes—Max knew how long Typhoon usually ran—but time seemed to stretch and become elastic, measured not in seconds, but in the frantic, needy, crashes of his hips against

Del's rear. He snarled, throaty and feral, and Del let out an answering squeak that drove him nuts. The otter was his, and he was never letting go. "Fuck," Del groaned, "fuck, fuck! Max!" There was no doubt this time what he was shouting about as Max cupped the otter's hefty breasts and extended his claws just enough to prick.

Holding onto Del for dear life, Max could feel the otter's pulse dancing with his own. He had no plan, no thoughts about what would happen at the bottom of the slide: the world outside the confines of the slide might as well have ceased to exist. It was him, Del, and the incredibly-soft ass fat milking his dick for all it was worth. His thrusts grew quicker and more desperate. Del squirmed back against him, rolls bunching up with every rise and fall of the slide. His breathy panting was interrupted by deep moans and high squeaks. Max felt too big for his skin, as though every nerve was firing at once and all that energy was desperate for a place to go. He bit down, tightened his grip on Del, and slammed his hips up one last time. The lightning racing through his body had finally found an outlet: it dashed down through him, coursing through his stomach, his groin, and up through his dick. Downright feral now, he tossed his head back and let out an ear-splitting roar as daylight finally pierced the slide and he shot his load.

The raft crashed into the receiving pool and skidded hard, but Max was too far gone to care that they were tipping perilously to one side. He was hunched forwards, back arched as his eyes rolled back in his head: the only thing he could care about was riding out the waves of his pleasure, as hot spasms of tension roiled and melted away into soothing bliss.

Even Del tipping backwards and rolling the two of them out of the raft and underwater couldn't fully loosen the grip of Max's bright afterglow, at least not for a second. His eyes widened as he realized distantly that he and the otter were underwater, before Del was standing up and pulling them both out. Max had never let go, and so was left clinging to him in an accidental piggyback.

Neither spoke at first, both gulping down deep breaths. "Guess we should clear out," Max gasped finally, and Del nodded. Max jumped down, and together they clambered out of the pool. As far as public places to get off went, Max could definitely think of worse. He looked himself over, but the water soaking his swim trunks had hidden any evidence that he'd blown his load.

Looking up at Del, he almost wanted to apologize: they hadn't exactly agreed on fucking in the slide. Then again, Del had been game for going back to the sauna, they had just swapped the locale. "Holy shit," he settled on, the words escaping with a laugh. "I'm almost pissed at myself for not trying that sooner."

"Glad you had fun," Del grinned.

"Oh, sorry. We can still…" Max made a jacking-off motion with his paw. "Y'know, if you want me to return the favor. I wouldn't wanna have all the fun."

Del waved him off. "Trust me, you didn't. Definitely the quickest I've gone in… well, years at least." It took Max a second to pick up on his meaning, and then he grinned. Del took a look around at the crowds of the bottom of the slide. "Think we could sit down for a sec, though?" he asked, and nodded to a covered bench by the side of the path.

"Gotta catch your breath?"

"Something like that."

The two of them sat down together. Max figured they must have made an odd couple: clearly not related unless adoption was involved, but with an age gap that begged certain questions. That wasn't even getting into the fact that Del's gut alone probably weighed more than he did. Max watched it sidelong, as the light peeking through the circular gaps in the perforated metal awning dappled it. If they were somewhere more private, he'd love to rub his paws over all that flab, especially now that he knew just how pliant it was.

"So that was a friend of yours? At the top of the slide?"

It was enough of a non-sequitur that Max had to stop and think for a second. "Oh, Kate? Yeah, we've known each other a while. She really took me under her wing when I started working here, even though she'd only been here a couple years." Del nodded, but there was clearly something more on his mind. Max wanted to ask him if he was good, but something stopped him. Sure, he'd felt the man's cheeks around his stiff cock, but Del was hardly the only guy he'd fucked, and they'd only known one another for part of an afternoon.

"Mmm," Del hummed. "And she mentioned a raccoon?"

Max smiled, just a touch bashfully. He knew there was no expectation of exclusivity between the two of them, but it was still a little awkward to admit that someone was your second fling of the day. "What can I say? I saw you and just had to double-dip." He cleared his throat and quietly added, "Plus, cats have a quick refractory period."

Del wasn't looking straight at him, and instead seemed to be staring out into the middle distance. "I'd get it if you were closeted, or shy about your hookups, but it doesn't sound like that's the case," Del said. "So I'm just curious about why you told Kate I was a family friend."

Max furrowed his brow. He hadn't really thought much of it. "Oh, that. I mean, Kate knows I'm gay, sure, but she doesn't know what kind of guys I'm into. The whole thing with the raccoon was a misunderstanding anyway," he laughed. "Thankfully, the guy was with his son, and she guessed the wrong one."

No response came right away, but Del slowly nodded. "Look, Max, today's been fun, but I think I'm gonna spend the rest of it alone if y'don't mind."

The jaguar blinked. They'd only been off the slide for a couple minutes, and everything had seemed alright then. "Hold on, what?"

"You're young, I get that," Del said, "But that doesn't mean I'm gonna let you get away with being a dick." He stood up and looked down at Max, his disappointed expression contrasting darkly with the pop music playing over one of the omnipresent loudspeakers. "It's like I told you on the way up: I don't wanna be with someone who's more ashamed of my body than I am."

Max balled his paws into fists. "I'm not ashamed."

"Nah? Then what gives?" Max held Del's bright green gaze for several seconds, but couldn't come up with an answer. "The other guys you fuck might be happy with sneaking around in musty old saunas, but I've already spent too long in the closet, kid. Not keen on going back in."

That stung, and Max had to look away. By the time he tore his gaze away from the pavement, Del was walking through the crowds, paws clenched tight and tail twitching behind him. Desires warred within Max's chest: get up and yell at Del, say fuck it and head home, follow Del to apologize, bitch Kate out for teasing him about the raccoon in front of Del.

They all lost out, and Max stayed sitting, white-knuckling the edge of the bench. He had no idea what he would say if a coworker passed him by and asked what was wrong: how could he get into it with them, if he couldn't even bring himself to talk about his attraction in the first place?

And why should he? His tail lashed against painfully against the metal bench. So what if he wanted to keep parts of his life secret, wasn't that his right? And who was Del to get pissy with him about that? He'd said it himself, he'd stayed in the closet until his forties. Max huffed, roughly pushed himself off the bench, and walked briskly through the milling crowds. There were still a couple of hours until the park closed, but he didn't feel like heading home on a sour note.

He got into line for Precipice, the park's biggest drop slide. What better way to take his mind off of getting dumped—by a guy he wasn't even dating!—than by simulating a fatal free-fall? It seemed like a good idea all the way up until he was trapped in line with his own thoughts, no outlet, and no way to escape the line except for the coward's stairs: a route of egress that he would never hear the end of from his coworkers, if they found out. Grumpy, and tail flicking enough to earn him several complaints from the bear behind him, Max stuck out the line, stepped into the clear-fronted capsule at the top of the slide with little more than a nod to the coworker manning it, and waited impatiently for the floor to fall out from beneath him.

After a joyless minute, he hauled himself out of the receiving pool and shook himself off. Well, hey. If one heart-pounding act of exhilaration wasn't going to fix him, he had an idea about what might. Maybe it was true what they said, and there really was no better cure for a broken heart—again, not that his heart was broken, since Del had just been one hookup among a hundred—than fresh love.

The mostly-abandoned sauna may have been Max's go-to cruising spot, but he didn't particularly feel like returning there after the close call with the raccoon and striking out with Del. Better to hit up one of his backups, so he wouldn't be thrown off his game.

He headed for the back of the park, where there was a shady seating area surrounded by cabana-style booths. During weekends and peak hours, they sold drinks and packaged snacks, but otherwise they stood shuttered. As remote as the area was, there was little reason to sit there unless you were lost, wanted to get away from the crowds… or were looking for some less family-friendly entertainment. Rising Tide was surrounded on all sides by thick walls of trees that kept it insulated from the surrounding area, which made it easy to hit someone up at a table and steal off to a verdant hideaway, free from prying eyes.

As luck would have it, the seating area was practically abandoned by the time Max got there: go figure, seeing as it was almost four, and the park would be closing in a couple hours. A black bear family sat at one table, a pair of teenage rabbits were clearly playing pawsie under another, and… bingo. Max spotted a hefty fox in tight trunks, sitting by himself. The afternoon sunlight caught his fur and lit it up like a torch, making him look like a living flame. Definitely a bit lighter than Del, so he wouldn't be the heaviest Max had enjoyed that day, but that was fine. He liked his men bigger, but how much bigger didn't matter so much to him: he wasn't a size queen.

He pretended to look busy at one of the cabanas, inspecting it just enough to lend himself some plausible deniability, and giving him an excuse to repeatedly bend over, wiggle his butt a little, check to see if the fox had noticed…

It took a bit, but sure enough that vulpine gaze was eventually tempted his way. Max grinned to himself, stood up, and stretched his arms far above his head to show off his athletic physique as best he could. A familiar confidence danced in his chest, as the fox made no play of turning away, and he strolled over to sit down across from him. "Couldn't help but notice you looking," he said as he gave the fox a once-over. His muzzle was a lot broader than that of your typical fox, softened by chub that gave him a plush, squishy, appearance, and from what he had seen of the fox's hips, they were nice and wide: perfect for grinding against.

"Couldn't help but notice you showing off," the fox said.

Max leaned against the table with an elbow and propped his muzzle on the same arm's fist. "Can't help myself, when I have such an eager audience. My name's Max."

"Art," the fox offered, clearly looking him up and down. He had to like what he saw, because he grinned.

"Is that short for anything?"

The fox shrugged. "Maybe."

Maybe? Max resisted the urge to snort. Well, hey, it wasn't fair to expect him to open up without offering something first. "Mine's short for Maximus."

Art smiled. "That's cute. So, was there something I can help you with?"

That was quick, but hadn't Max typically been quicker? He and Del had only just started talking when he'd tried to invite the otter for a quick tryst in the sauna... then again, Del had also been chatty. Max shook his head: he wasn't going to get over him by thinking about him. "Couldn't help but noticing you sitting here all alone, and I thought you might like some company."

"You work here, right? Bet you know all sorts of places you could show a fox."

Max thought about it: of taking the fox behind the copse of trees, getting his paws all over that soft body, of finding out what it would feel like against his, and it was exciting: his cock stirred in his shorts like it always did.

But there was something missing, something he hadn't given a second thought before. Walking around the park together, sitting down for lunch, cracking jokes and teasing a guy he had just met as though they'd known each other for ages. When he thought about getting personal with the fox, it was hot, but it wasn't... interesting. It should have been: the fox was every bit his type, but suddenly that wasn't enough.

He shook his head. "Sorry," he said, "something came up."

Art squinted at him. "Something came up?" he asked. "Really?"

"Yup," Max replied dismissively, and got up. A moody huff sounded off behind him as he left.

Indulge

He'd fucked up, he knew that, but what was he going to do about it? It wasn't like he'd managed to get Del's number before putting his hindpaw in his mouth, and a single name and species wasn't enough to go off of to get his socials... plus he'd feel like a total creep messaging privately him out of the blue, after being ashamed of being seen together by his coworkers.

And that was just it, right? They already knew he was gay, so what was the problem with being seen with Del? So what if the otter didn't match up with their expectations of what gay guys were into? That was their problem: not his, and certainly not Del's.

He ground the heels of his forepaws into his eyes. He'd been crushing on fat guys since he was fourteen, and it had taken him this long to really come to terms with that? To stop caring that the image of gay men that other people had in their minds might be flawed in some way?

Max hurried through the park, hoping to catch a glimpse of Del before closing. He practically jogged along the pathways, taking peeks along all the little offshoots and branches that led to the rides, peering down from atop the bridge that looked over the lazy river, doing everything short of climbing each and every staircase to see if Del was there.

Max tracked the time by the slow closing of the less popular attractions. Even though it was getting close to the end of the day, he dismissed his worry that Del had already left: the otter had said he always stuck around until close, and even dealing with a fuckboy jaguar hadn't been enough to get him to leave early. Odds were, he was still around somewhere. The problem was where: there were just too many places to search, too many lines he could have been in at any one time. Tracking down a quarter-ton otter hotty might've seemed easy, but apparently not.

Max leaned against a tacky souvenir shop and groaned, knocking his head back against the building's brightly-painted side. The park wouldn't be open that much longer, and he was no closer to tracking the otter down. He just knew that if he went home alone, without at least apologizing, he'd be left agonizing over the day and wondering how he could have made it go differently. Three and a half years of hookups, and he'd had to catch feelings just half a summer from the finish line. He wanted to be mad at Del, but he knew that it was on him. If he'd just been more open, if he'd just considered that the men he got with had thoughts and feelings of their own, maybe he wouldn't be in this spot.

180

At the very least, he could thank Del for that. Down the line sometime, maybe he'd finally hit it off with another guy, and he'd have this experience to look back on to teach him not to fuck up in such an obvious way.

The thought was a thin silver lining, and provided the sort of distant, warmth-devoid comfort that you could only appreciate after the fact. Making matters worse, the nearby loudspeaker was playing the same shitty Top 40 pop song for what had to be the twentieth time that day, and the thousandth time he'd heard it at Rising Tide. He wished someone would interrupt it with an announcement already.

No sooner had the thought entered his head, than Max was sprinting towards the information hut at the front of the park. There was a steady exodus of guests heading for the front gates as they tried to beat the closing rush out of the parking lot, and he had to duck and weave through families and couples, all while keeping his eyes peeled for heavyset otters.

No such luck, but he did manage to make it to the kiosk with only a few near-crashes to his name. The little round building stood in the front plaza, and had just enough room inside for a trio of employees of employees at a squeeze. When he got there, Kate was sitting on the curved counter-slash-desk that separated employees from guests, and one of their managers was tidying up for the day.

"Demi," he asked the arctic fox behind the counter, "can I—hold on, Kate, aren't you supposed to be at Typhoon?"

The wolf shrugged. "Some kid threw up *bad*, so we closed up a few minutes early. You should've seen it, he was all like—"

While Kate mimed the act of projectile vomiting, Demi looked over at Max. "What's got you in such a rush?"

"Can I use the PA system? I need to make an announcement."

Demi raised an eyebrow at him. "I wasn't born yesterday. What do you need to say?"

"Just… just tell Del to come here."

"Del. Any last name?"

Max shrugged apologetically. "Please?"

Demi sighed, but picked up the phone. "This better not be a prank, Max." He gave her his most winning smile as she pushed the page button, and all the nearby loudspeakers finally, at long last, stopped playing music. "Del to the front information booth," Demi said, her voice echoed across the speakers not quite in sync, "Del to the front information booth." She set the phone down, leaving Max to wait.

Indulge

He couldn't even bring himself to speak to either of them: the conversation they had been having before his arrival, which they picked up once it was clear that he wasn't paying them any mind, was background noise to his intent monitoring of the crowds. Half a dozen times he saw an otter and perked up, but none were *his* otter... if he had an otter at all.

Finally, just when he was certain that Del had already left the park or was just ignoring the message, Max spotted him. He looked hesitant, a little closed off, and Max couldn't help but feel guilty about that. "This is a first," he said as he folded his arms across his chest. Given the circumstances, Max felt a little bad about just how fiercely the otter propping his tits up made his muzzle water. "Don't expect you're calling me over to tell me I forgot something somewhere."

"I'm not," Max said, "I called you over to apologize."

"It's fine—" Del started, dismissively, but Max wasn't going to let things end like this.

"It's not," he interrupted. "I thought... I thought that there was a right way to be gay. That if you just played by the rules, didn't act too queeny, were a jock who dated twinks, that then you'd be 'allowed'. Maybe that's why I wasn't so scared to come out." Max's muzzle ran dry: he could feel Kate and Demi right behind him, and knew that even if they were doing their best to pretend they weren't listening, they could hear everything he was saying. As soon as he spoke, there'd be no taking it back: right now, he could still turn around and claim plausible deniability.

He shook his head, feeling like a coward. Fuck that. "But I didn't really come out, did I? Sure, my friends and family know that I like guys, but that's all abstract. They've never seen me date anyone, and I was happy to let them think that hookups were all I cared about. Fuck, I even had myself convinced." Max's claws pricked at his pawpads as he curled his fingers painfully tight. "You deserve an apology, but really I want to thank you. Thanks for waking me up and reminding me that I can want more than..." He cleared his throat, "Musty old saunas."

He heard a scoff from behind him as Demi registered exactly what that meant he'd been up to, but mercifully she knew better than to interrupt. Max didn't care: he didn't even turn to see Kate's reaction, none of it mattered. All that he cared about was the otter in front of him, whose eyes had widened and whose tense stance had slowly softened as he'd spoken. "So you..." Del trailed off, head tipped slightly to one side.

Max took a deep breath: he supposed it didn't really come right out and say it. "I like fat guys," he said, "and I was dumb as hell to be ashamed of you."

Having got that off his chest, Max slumped. This was there the relief was supposed to set in, right? But instead he just felt drained. He stared down at the ground, and when he looked back up, Del had closed the distance between them. He took a deep breath, eyes fixed on Del's muzzle as he leaned in and—

The otter laughed. "Were you even alive in the nineties?"

Max blinked. "I. Uh. Yes?"

"Calling me over here, that confession, it was all straight out of a nineties rom-com, bud. This is your 'running to meet me at the airport' moment." Max's cheeks felt like they were on fire. Del must have seen that he was getting to him, because he smiled. "Don't get me wrong, I like it." He slugged the jaguar on the shoulder and grinned. "Thanks for the apology... Maximus."

That, at last, broke Kate's composure. "Maximus?" she snorted. "Seriously?"

That's what you latch onto?" Max asked, his voice high and crackly, his fingers twitching with nervous energy.

"Max," Del said, dragging the jaguar's attention back to him just in time for the otter to kiss him straight on the muzzle. A tremor ran down his spine and his legs threatened to give out, but Del's arm wrapped around his back to keep him upright. The otter was surprisingly insistent, pressing at Del's muzzle with his own like he had been waiting to do it all day. Max's tail curled up against his legs as their tongues met. Mirroring Del, he brought his arms around to hold as much of the otter as he could: he was supremely soft, and now he could appreciate it better than he could on the slide. Every squeeze made him roil like a waterbed, every breath made his heavy chest rise and fall against Max's own.

Del finally pulled away, cheeks dimpled in a playful grin. "Had to make sure you were serious when you said you weren't ashamed," he said, tipping his muzzle over Max's shoulder to Kate and Demi. Max gave them a quick glance: Demi was back to sorting out the booth, and Kate was shooting him an obnoxious thumbs-up. "You pass, in case you were wondering."

"Good to know," Max laughed, his voice still a little unsteady. Against all odds—or at least the ones he'd imagined—the world hadn't come crashing down. "That doesn't seem like the kind of kiss you give someone you're not planning on seeing again."

"It doesn't, does it," Del teased. "Y'know, I've got an apartment all to myself."

Max shook his head. "Actually, I was thinking we could go out for dinner."

Del squeezed Max's shoulder tight. "Careful Max, keep talking like that and you won't be able to get rid of me."

"Exactly what I'm hoping for."

Sliding In

About The Artist

Bravo Woof
(he/him)

Bravo Woof is a nerdy chubby pupper who has been drawing bespectacled cuddly anthros for several decades. He can currently be found in Dallas Texas, and is often hanging out in his discord chat.

FA: https://www.furaffinity.net/user/bravo

BS: https://bsky.app/profile/bravoart.nerdywoof.com

About the Editor

Buddy Goodboy, Esq
(he/him)

Buddy Goodboy, Esq. (he/him) is an author and multidisciplinary artist based in Chicago, IL. He plays online at being a Labrador retriever in glasses and a tie to remind himself to laugh more. His fiction explores identity, particularly LGBTQ+ and neurodiverse identities, taboo, kink, and taking life less seriously and more enjoyably. He shares his stories online at BuddyGoodboy.com and on platforms like FurAffinity (https://www.furaffinity.net/user/buddygoodboyesq) and SoFurry. (https://buddygoodboyesq.sofurry.com/)

He can be found on social media on:

Bluesky, (https://bsky.app/profile/buddygoodboy.com)
Mastodon (https://wobbl.xyz/@BuddyGoodboyEsq)
Tumblr. (https://www.tumblr.com/blog/buddygoodboyesq)

About The Authors

Ajax B. Coriander
(he/him)

Ajax is an editor, writer, and is the daily operations manger for FurPlanet. He lives in Dallas with his publishers/boyfriends/domestic wolves and is under the ever present danger of being crushed to death under 500 pounds of Kyell Gold books during 30% of his working hours. He can be found at https://bsky.app/profile/saintajax33.bsky.social and he can be found other places through:
https://allmylinks.com/saintajax33
Or
http://www.ajaxwriter.com/
(Ps: he also did the layout for this book. It took him 5 straight days).

Oswald Beese
(he/him)

Oswald Beese is a software developer from the east coast of the United States. He enjoys watching Real Housewives with his wife and playing with his great pyrenees. You can find him on Fur Affinity as "whatsonsecond" and Bluesky as "whatsonsecond.bsky.social".

Mackenzie Steele

Mackenzie Steele is an artist, writer, and aspiring game dev based in Treaty 1 territory of Canada. Whether working on urban fantasy and superheroes as Aximeck or friendly fat fellas as WideWobbles, you will likely find him with a slushie in his hand, an idea in his head, and a cat in his lap.

Frances Pauli

Frances Pauli writes about animals because she finds them infinitely more interesting than people. She's not terribly sorry about this, though she understands it might cause some of the latter distress. Still, when given the choice between a starship piloted by a human and one with a hippopotamus at the helm, she will inevitably favor the hippo.

Once upon a time she wrote about people, and you can still find those works milling about at large, but for the foreseeable future, expect pangolin pirates and savvy sword-swinging armadillos.

If that sounds appealing, you can find her work on her webpage at francespauli.com and at most retailers who sell that sort of thing. You can find Frances herself in the general Washington State area, often at writing, science fiction, or furry conventions. She is also, against her better judgement, present on most social media platforms.

But she'd rather be writing.

Indi

Indi has written expansion fiction for a decade, with works focused on a wide variety of kinks. He enjoys experimenting with long-form fiction that gives as much attention to plot as kinks. The bulk of his writing can be found on https://www.furaffinity.net/user/indigorho/.

Faux

Faux is an Atlanta-based author and attorney who has been crafting short fiction since 2015. He writes across genres, with a particular bent for lush, character-driven literotica. His work has appeared in several kink anthologies and 'zines as well as in FANG Vol. 7, PAW Vol. 1, and Clade: A Post-Self Anthology. His stories favor rich textures and generous detail—the kind that don't mind taking up space. Off the page, he's an avid coin collector and amateur jeweler, happiest while treasure-hunting at estate sales and antique markets. Read more at furaffinity.net/user/fauxhammer.

Ash Cinder

I'm a Texas coywolf, who has been writing fiction in the furry fandom since 2015. I primarily specialize in writing stories involving older dad types. You can find my stories on FA and SoFurry, though my output has slowed down, as I've started to focus my energy on more long term projects. But, I still plan to write furry stories when the inspiration calls me.

BlueSky: @beatlenumber9.bsky.social

FurAffinity: Beatle9

SoFurry: Ash Cinder Unable to link because SoFurry has been down for months now :(

Telegram: BeatleNumber9

Oswald Beese
(he/him)

Oswald Beese (he/him) is a software developer from the east coast of the United States. He enjoys watching Real Housewives with his wife and playing with his great pyrenees. You can find him on Fur Affinity as "whatsonsecond" and Bluesky as "whatsonsecond.bsky.social".

Pendoggo is a furry artist and writer that loves to write about characters, fantasy, and big guys. You can find his art on twitter and bluesky @pendoggo

Renard

Renard has enjoyed creative writing since he was young. He published his first novel, 'The Bones Behind the Glass' in August of 2025. He is thrilled to be included in 'Indulge!'

Jace Snepitome
(He/They)

Jace has loved furry fiction since before he knew what to call it. Within his debut year of submitting to furry anthologies, he received four acceptances—including the one in this book—and one, "No, sorry, but do you want your own anthology instead?". Like any good snow leopard, he loves skiing, making his habitation within Canada pretty convenient.

Snepitome @ FurAffinity and Bluesky